*Praise for C...*

"An enchanting tale of mystery, magical books, and endearing characters. Prepare to be charmed."
—Heather Blake, national bestselling
author of *Some Like It Witchy*

### Praise for the Amish Quilt Shop Mysteries by Amanda Flower Writing as Isabella Alan

"Alan writes the most captivating, fun mysteries!"
—Open Book Society

"A satisfyingly complex cozy."            —*Library Journal*

"Alan captures Holmes County and the Amish life in a mystery that is nothing close to plain and simple."
—Avery Aames, author of the Cheese Shop Mysteries

"In the Amish Quilt Shop Mysteries, Isabella Alan captures the spirit of the Amish perfectly. . . . Throw in the *Englischers* living in Rolling Brook and the tourists visiting, and you have a great host of colorful characters."
—Cozy Mystery Book Reviews

"A dead-certain hit."
—P. L. Gaus, author of the Amish-Country Mysteries

"This is a community you'd like to visit, a shop where you'd find welcome . . . and people you'd want for friends. . . . There's a lot of interesting information about Amish life, but it's interwoven into the story line so the reader learns details as Angie does."            —Kings River Life Magazine

"Cozy readers and Amish enthusiasts alike will be raving about this debut. It proves to be a great start for Isabella Alan."            —Debbie's Book Bag

*Titles by Amanda Flower*

**CRIME AND POETRY**
**PROSE AND CONS**

# CRIME AND POETRY

*A Magical Bookshop Mystery*

## AMANDA FLOWER

AN OBSIDIAN MYSTERY

OBSIDIAN

Published by New American Library,
an imprint of Penguin Random House LLC
375 Hudson Street, New York, New York 10014

This book is an original publication of New American Library.

First Printing, April 2016

For more information about Penguin Random House, visit penguin.com.

ISBN 978-0-451-47744-6

Printed in the United States of America
10  9  8  7  6  5  4

Designed by Kelly Lipovich

Penguin
Random
House

*for Laura Fazio,*
*for believing in the magic of books and me*

# Acknowledgments

I have always thought books were magical, so when I was given the chance to write a mystery series set in a magical bookshop, I took it. Thank you to my dream editor, Laura Fazio, for giving me this opportunity. We create some awesome cozy worlds together no matter the setting. Thanks also to my agent and dear friend, Nicole Resciniti, who is the best and kindest person in the book business.

Special thanks to my readers who have followed me to yet another series. Your love of my mysteries keeps me writing. I've taken you from the Amish world to a Civil War reenactment to a magical place, and still you read on. Thank you! I promise wherever we go, a funny mystery will be found.

Hugs to my dear friend Mariellyn Grace, who is my plotter in crime and has saved every book from destruction. Thanks to my beta reader, Molly Carroll, who reassured me that my ideas for this book made sense even before they did, and to Suzy Schroeder and Bobby Boos for helping me to craft the "rules" for my magical world.

Thanks also to Sarah Preston and Suzy for a girls' trip to Niagara Falls, so I could go on location.

Love to my family, Andy, Nicole, Isabella, and Andrew, for their unfailing support of my big dreams.

Finally to my Heavenly Father, thanksgiving for an incredibly unexpected year.

*Because I could not stop for Death,*
*He kindly stopped for me;*
*The carriage held but just ourselves*
*And Immortality.*

—EMILY DICKINSON

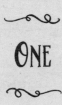

# ONE

"Grandma! Grandma Daisy!" I called as soon as I was inside Charming Books. There were books everywhere—on the crowded shelves, the end tables, the sales counter, and the floor. Everywhere. But there was no sign of my ailing grandmother.

Browsing customers in brightly colored T-shirts and shorts stared at me openmouthed. I knew I must have looked a fright. I had driven from Chicago to Cascade Springs, New York, a small village nestled on the banks of the Niagara River just minutes from the world-famous Niagara Falls. I'd made the drive in seven hours, stopping only twice for gas and potty breaks. My fingernails were bitten to the quick, dark circles hovered beneath my bloodshot blue eyes, and my wavy strawberry blond hair was in a knot on top of my head. Last time I caught sight of it in the rearview mirror, it had resembled a pom-pom that had been caught in a dryer's lint trap. I stopped looking in the rearview after that.

A crow gripping a perch in the shop's large bay window cawed.

I jumped, and my hands flew to my chest. I had thought the crow was stuffed.

The bird glared at me with his beady black eyes. He certainly wasn't stuffed. "Grandma Daisy!" he mimicked me. "Grandma!"

I sidestepped away from the black bird. I thought parrots were the only birds that could talk. The crow was the only one who spoke. None of the customers made a peep. A few slipped out the front door behind me. "Escape from the crazy lady" was written all over their faces. I couldn't say I blamed them.

A slim woman stepped out from between packed bookshelves. She wore jeans, a hot pink T-shirt with the bookshop's logo on it, and, despite the summer's heat, a long silken scarf. Silk scarves were Grandma Daisy's signature. I could count on one hand the number of times I had seen her without one intricately tied around her neck. Today's scarf was white with silver-dollar-sized ladybugs marching across it. Her straight silver hair was cut in a sleek bob that fell to her chin. Cat's-eye-shaped glasses perched on her nose. She was a woman in her seventies, but clearly someone who took care of herself. Clearly someone who was not dying.

My mouth fell open, and I knew I must look a lot like those tourists I'd frightened. "Grandma!" The word came out of my mouth somewhere between a curse and a prayer.

"Violet, my girl." She haphazardly dropped the pile of

books she had in her arms onto one of the two matching couches in the middle of the room at the base of the birch tree, which seemed to grow out of the floor. "You came!"

I stepped back. "Of course I came. You were *dying*."

More customers skirted for the door. They knew what was good for them. I wouldn't have hung around either. The only one who seemed to be enjoying the show was the crow. He was no longer in the front window, but on the end table to my right. Great. A crow was loose in my grandmother's bookshop. I wished I could say this surprised me, but it didn't.

Grandma Daisy chuckled. "Oh, that."

"'Oh, that'? That's all you can say?" I screeched. "Do you have any idea what you've put me through? I left school. I left my job. I left *everything* to be with you at your deathbed."

Grandma had the decency to wince.

"Look at you. You look like you are ready to run a marathon. When I spoke to you on the phone last night, you were coughing and gasping. You sounded like you were at death's door."

Grandma Daisy faked a cough. "Like this?" Her face morphed into pathetic. "Oh, Violet, I need you. Please come." Fake cough. Fake cough. "The doctor said I don't have much more time."

Heat surged up from the base of my neck to the top of my head. I couldn't remember the last time I had been this angry. Oh yeah, I did—it was the first time I'd left Cascade Springs, twelve years ago. I had promised myself that day I would never come back, and look where I was, back in Cascade Springs, tricked by my very own grandmother.

"You were dying," the crow said.

"Quiet, Faulkner," Grandma Daisy ordered.

The large black bird sidestepped across the tabletop. Seemed that the crow was a new addition to the shop. It'd been twelve years, but I would have remembered Faulkner. I wondered why Grandma Daisy had never mentioned the bird. I would have thought a talking pet crow would have made a great conversation piece.

Grandma Daisy searched my face. "I may have fibbed a bit. Can you forgive me?" she asked, giving me her elfish smile. It wasn't going to work, not this time.

I spun around, ignored Faulkner, who was spouting "You were dying!" over and over again, and stomped out of the shop.

Behind me the screen door smacked against the doorframe. I stumbled across the front porch and gripped the whitewashed wooden railing. Charming Books ("where the perfect book picks you") sat in the center of River Road in the middle of Old Town Cascade Springs, a historic part of the village that was on the National Historic Landmarks list. Every house and small business on the street was more adorable than the last, but none were as stunning as Charming Books, a periwinkle Queen Anne Victorian with gingerbread to spare and a wraparound porch that was twice the size of my studio apartment back in Chicago.

The tiny front yard was full to bursting with blooming roses and, of course, daisies—Grandma's personal favorite. On the brick road in front of me, gas lampposts lined the street on either side and prancing horses and white carriages waited at the curbs, ready to take tourists for a spin around the village and along the famous Riverwalk at a moment's notice. The horses' manes were elaborately braided with satiny ribbons, and their drivers wore red coats with tails and top hats.

It was charming. It was perfect. It was the last place on planet Earth I wanted to be.

I had half a mind to jump in my car and head west for Chicago, never looking back. I couldn't do that. My shoulders slumped. I was so incredibly tired. Coffee wouldn't be any help. Coffee had lost its ability to keep me alert my third year of grad school. And as much as she vexed me, I couldn't leave Grandma Daisy without saying good-bye. For better or worse, she was all the family I had left in the world. And then, there was the whole pom-pom hair situation, which could be tolerated for only so long. I'd need a hairbrush and maybe a blowtorch to get that under control.

The screen door to the Queen Anne creaked open. I didn't have to turn around to know it was my grandmother. The scent of lavender talcum powder that always surrounded her floated on the breeze. "Violet, I know it wasn't right for me to lie to you."

I folded my arms, refusing to look at her. I knew it was childish, but I was going on two hours of sleep and tons of betrayal. Being a grown-up wasn't on the top of my priority list.

She placed her hand on my shoulder. "It was wrong of me. Very wrong, but it was the only way I could convince you to come back here."

She was probably right in that assumption, but I wasn't going to make it easy for her. "So you pretended to be dying?"

She let out a breath. "What I said about needing you to come back was true. I do need you here. I want you to stay."

She had to be kidding. She knew what had happened to me in this town. She knew why I'd left the day after I graduated high school. She knew better than anyone. "Well, that's too bad," I said. "I'm not staying."

"Can't you stay a little while? For me?"

I felt a pang in my heart. I didn't want to leave Grandma Daisy, and despite the whole lying thing, it was wonderful to see her, but I couldn't stay. It was too hard. "I'll wait until tomorrow, but I'll leave in the morning."

Of course that last statement came to be known as "famous last words."

# TWO

"Well, then," Grandma Daisy said, her face breaking into a smile. "You should come inside, and I'll fetch you a cold drink."

My shoulders slumped in defeat. She got me, and she got me good. "Okay."

I followed Grandma Daisy back inside the shop. We were the only ones there besides Faulkner the crow.

I nodded at Faulkner. "What's up with the crow?"

She chuckled. "He showed up in the garden during the winter with a broken wing. He was a young bird then, barely more than a chick. I nursed him back to health, and he decided to stay. Every bookshop needs a mascot."

"What's wrong with a cat?"

"You know I'm not a traditionalist," she said with a smile.

I frowned as I looked around the shop. "I'm sorry I scared away all your customers."

She smoothed her silky bob. "It's no matter. If they needed something, it would have found them."

My eyes slid to her. "You mean they were just browsers?"

She gave a small smile. "You could call them that."

I wanted to ask her what that meant, but she scurried away, muttering about lemonade. As Charming Books was an old converted house, there was a full kitchen in the back. I almost followed her, but my surroundings stopped me. Charming Books was, well, charming. There was something about it that was beguiling. I had been to dozens of other bookstores in my life and never felt the same jolt of wonder as I did while in my grandmother's shop. It was a feeling of warmth and understanding I got as I looked around the room, like the books were alive and old friends. I knew that was ridiculous, and I would never say that aloud to anyone. The villagers of Cascade Springs thought I was a lot of things. I didn't need to add peculiar to an already lengthy list.

Now that I wasn't blinded by the fear I would find my grandmother dead, I was able to take in my surroundings. The bookshop looked exactly as I remembered it. A vaulted ceiling spanned half the room, stopping in the center of the shop at a metal spiral staircase that led to the second floor. The staircase wrapped itself around a live birch tree with three trunks, each as thick as a grown man. Once a year, grandmother had a tree service come in to prune the tree so that it didn't break through the historic building's slate roof. Currently, its branches stopped six inches from the ceiling.

Sunlight poured into the shop from the windows and the large skylight on the second floor and reflected off the birch tree's white, silver-flecked bark. The tree, just like the house, had belonged to my family for generations, since my ancestress Rosalee Waverly built the home at the beginning of the nineteenth century. Although the structure had shifted over the last two hundred years, the most notable change occurred at the turn of the twentieth century when one of Rosalee's descendants transformed the home into a Queen Anne Victorian, as was the fashion at that time.

At the top of the staircase, I could see through the black iron railing into the children's room, which was decorated as a wood sprite's palace that would have put Tinker Bell to shame. It had been the perfect place to hide during my mother's chemo treatments.

For the moment, I would have to wait to visit the fairy room. Faulkner the crow stared at me from one of the tree's branches as if daring me to climb the stairs. I wasn't up to facing him. I hadn't been the least bit surprised that my grandma had nursed Faulkner back to health. When I was a child, she had a revolving door of injured and sick animals going through her house. She was just kindhearted. I sighed. If she was that kindhearted, why would she lie to me, her own granddaughter, about being sick? What was so important that made her want me to move back to Cascade Springs? Part of me was afraid to ask, because Grandma Daisy could be very convincing when she wanted to be, and apparently, after the "I'm dying" speech over the phone, she could be quite an actress too.

It was beginning to ebb, but adrenaline still pulsed in my veins from fear that Grandma Daisy was ill. Even though I hadn't been back to Cascade Springs since I was seventeen, I saw my grandmother at least twice a year. She visited me in Chicago for Christmas, and every year we met somewhere in the world for our annual girls' trip. People might think it was odd I vacationed with my grandmother, but those people didn't have a grandmother like mine. I was the one ready to call it a day at eleven. Grandma could party the whole night through. Last year, she drank me under the table in São Paolo.

The front bell jangled, notifying the shop that someone had entered. Grandma Daisy rushed past me with a tray holding a lemonade pitcher and glasses. She shoved a sweaty glass of lemonade into my hand on her way to greet her customer.

As beautifully crafted and enchanting as the shop itself was, the books were the most eye-catching aspect. They were everywhere. Along the walls, bookshelves rose eleven feet high. In the middle of the room, much shorter shelves held even more volumes, and soft chairs were tucked in every corner for a quiet place to get lost in a book.

I walked around the shop, sliding my finger across the spines of all the lovely books. Charming Books had been the place where I had fallen in love with literature. When I was a child, I ran here every day after school, eager to see what new novels and plays my grandmother had in stock. Back then, I daydreamed of running the shop myself one day, and helping shoppers find the perfect book for themselves and their family or friends. That was before. Now I poured my love of the written word into my PhD program in American literature. After years of scholarship, I was one dissertation away from my culminating degree, and after that, who knew what would happen? I'd started submitting my vita to colleges and universities, but as of yet haven't yielded much more than a lukewarm reception to it. In the world of academe, a PhD in literature was easy to come by and the competition was fierce for the few open professor jobs in the country. I wasn't panicking. Or at least I wasn't panicking yet.

I heard muffled voices as Grandma Daisy chatted with the shopper about a book, and I smiled at the sound of her energetic voice. Nothing made my grandmother happier than talking about books. I stepped out from the bookshelves and found Grandma with a white-haired man in riding pants and a red jacket with tails. His riding boots were polished to a high sheen, and he tucked his black top hat under his arm. His and my grandmother's heads were suspiciously close together, much closer than in a typical bookseller-and-buyer transaction.

I cleared my throat.

Grandma Daisy jumped back from the man. "Oh, Violet, you gave me a start."

The man beamed at me. He had straight white teeth that sparkled against his tanned skin. "You're Violet. I've heard so much about you. I'm so glad to finally meet you. My, aren't you the spitting image of Daisy?"

I wasn't so sure about that. I still had the crazy pom-pom do on the top of my head. It couldn't have been more different from my grandmother's sleek and smooth bob. I frowned. "I haven't heard about you." Usually, I was a much friendlier person, but it was hard to be polite with a crow looming over you.

He laughed. "I see you get your spunk from Daisy too."

He held out his free hand. "I'm Benedict Raisin, the best carriage driver in Cascade Springs or on either side of the Niagara River. Don't let anyone else tell you different."

I shook his hand and smiled despite myself. "Nice to meet you." Self-consciously, I touched my hair. "I have to apologize for my appearance. I just arrived."

"Aww, what's to apologize for? I thought that's how all the young girls wear their hair nowadays," he said, releasing my hand.

I laughed.

"There, now, I see you have your grandmother's beautiful smile too."

I glanced at Grandma Daisy, and her cheeks pinkened. My suspicion returned. Who was this guy, and why was my grandma acting like a twelve-year-old girl with a crush around him?

"How do you two know each other?" I asked.

"He's a customer," Grandma Daisy said a little too quickly.

A customer? Just a customer? I wasn't buying it.

Benedict chuckled. "Seems to me you've been in the big city far too long. Everyone knows everyone in our little village." He dusted off the top of his hat. "I'm one of Daisy's *best* customers. I'm here to restock on my reading material. Being a carriage driver means that ninety percent of my time is spent waiting for the next tourist. It's good to have a book handy for the slow times of the day."

"What are you looking for?" I was always interested in what people were reading.

He cocked his head. "I'm not sure. I do like action. A

good thriller keeps the blood pumping in my old ticker." He rested a hand to his chest. "Poor old thing doesn't work quite as well as it used to, but I get by."

Grandma Daisy smiled. "Don't let Benedict fool you; he is the picture of health." She turned back to her friend. "Why don't you browse a bit? Would you like some lemonade?"

"I never turn down your lemonade, Daisy."

Again, I looked from Benedict to my grandmother and back again. There was definitely more to their relationship than my grandmother wanted me to know.

Grandma Daisy went to the tray on the counter and poured Benedict a generous serving of lemonade.

"Your grandmother tells me you're studying literature," he said.

I nodded. "At the University of Chicago. I'm working on my dissertation in Transcendentalist literature."

He frowned as if he wasn't sure what I was talking about. I got that look a lot when speaking about my dissertation. I supposed it wasn't a good time to share my interpretation of *Walden*.

"You must have gotten your love of books from Daisy," he said.

I smiled. "I did. In fact, if it weren't for Gran—"

A book flew off the shelf and nailed Benedict on the kneecap and fell open.

"Ouch," he cried.

"Where on earth did that come from?" I searched the room for Faulkner. I half expected the crow to be responsible for the projectile book. I was wrong. Faulkner sat silently in the tree, not moving a feather. He made eye contact with me, and I was the one who looked away.

Benedict leaned over to pick up the book. "Oh my. Emily Dickinson. You know I used to be a bit of a poetry buff as a young man. Here's my chance to brush up a little. I have always enjoyed Dickinson. 'The Carriage,'" he said, reading the poem that the book had fallen open to. "Doesn't that sound like the perfect poem for me?"

"I'm a fan of Dickinson myself," I said. "She was a contemporary with many of the Transcendentalist writers."

He cocked his head as if he considered that bit of information. "It will do me good to get some culture, then. It's been a long time since I read anything without an explosion in it. This seems to be a good place to start." He read from the book,

> *"Because I could not stop for Death,*
> *He kindly stopped for me;*
> *The carriage held but just ourselves*
> *And Immortality."*

He frowned. "It's not the most cheerful verse in the world."

"Emily wasn't all rainbows and sunshine," I said.

"Apparently not." He laughed.

Grandma Daisy abandoned the lemonade and hurried over to him. "This must be some kind of mistake."

Benedict and I both raised our eyebrows at her.

She cleared her throat and reached for the volume of poetry in Benedict's hands. "I mean, there are so many newer novels that you haven't read. Why don't we find something else for you? Dickinson is all right, but I'm sure I could find you something else that you would like even more."

Benedict stepped back from her. "But I want to read this one. Poetry is food for the soul."

Grandma Daisy took another step toward him. "What about some Tom Clancy? James Patterson? I'm sure James has published five books since you were last in the shop. He's so prolific. I know those are both your favorites."

I set my lemonade on an end table. "Grandma, why are you trying to talk someone out of reading a classic American poet?"

She turned to me, and there was a strange look in her eyes. Was it fear? Fear of what? A book?

My grandmother may have claimed to be the image of health, but maybe she wasn't. Maybe she wasn't right in the head if someone buying a collection of Emily Dickinson's poetry freaked her out. The thought made me shiver.

"Daisy, don't be silly. I have always wanted to read this. It will keep me company as I wait for my customers." He lifted the book in his hand. "Considering its size, it will keep me occupied for some time. I'll just take this one today."

Grandma Daisy chewed the pink lipstick off her lower lip. "If you're sure."

"I'm sure." He smiled good-naturedly. "Now, I must be returning to my post. Let's ring this up." He wagged his finger at Grandma Daisy. "And before you say it, I insist on paying for the book."

My grandmother and Benedict moved across the huge

Oriental rug that covered two-thirds of the shop floor. He had a bounce in his step, and Grandma Daisy dragged her feet.

After she'd rung him up, Grandma Daisy watched him stroll out of the store. She bit her lip, and I might have been mistaken, but I thought I saw tears in her eyes.

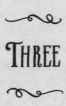

# THREE

I'd arrived in Cascade Springs in the early evening, but as we were just days from the summer solstice, the sun was still high in the sky.

"Why don't I close early tonight so we can catch up?" Grandma Daisy said. "I don't do much business on Monday evenings anyway, even in the summer."

She moved toward the front door, but before she could close it, a young woman bounced in. She wore a white sundress dotted with red and blue hearts, bright red lipstick, and saddle shoes, and her silky black hair was tied back into a high ponytail with a red ribbon. She clapped her hands. "Is she here?" She bounced—and I do mean bounced—with excitement.

Grandma Daisy grinned. "Sadie, I would like you to meet my granddaughter, Violet. Violet, this is Sadie Cunningham."

The small woman skipped over to me and gave me a surprisingly strong hug. "I can't believe I'm finally meeting you. Daisy talks of nothing else. She's always telling me how brilliant you are, but she never said how beautiful. Look at that hair and skin! I would kill for skin like yours. I guess you won't be needing the spa while you're here. And OMG, I love your T-shirt."

I looked down at myself. I was wearing flip-flops, yoga pants, and a Strawberry Shortcake T-shirt, all chosen for comfort for a cross-country drive. It wasn't my best look.

She put her small hands on her narrow hips. "Were you trying to achieve a beehive with your hair?" She squinted at me. "I can give you tips on how to make it a little straighter. It's all about the hair spray."

Grandma Daisy smiled as she picked up books customers had left lying around the shop. "Sadie knows everything about fashion."

Sadie beamed. "I own Midcentury Vintage across the street." She pointed at a small yellow cottage with lime green shutters on the opposite corner from Charming Books. Midcentury Vintage had a good view of the Niagara River and the Riverwalk, which was filling up with tourists out to dinner. My grandmother's shop sat on the curve on the L-shaped River Road where it turned west and started following the Niagara River out of the village and in the direction of the Falls. There was another house to the south of Charming Books, but to the north and east, it was surrounded by the village park. Over the generations, my family had owned the land on the edge of the park and many had tried to purchase it for access to the village's famous springs.

Remembering my manners, I turned to Sadie and said, "It's nice to meet you too."

She clapped her hands. "Well, I'd better be off and let the two of you visit. I just *had* to pop over and meet you!" She spun around and her ponytail flew out like a flag. Over her shoulder, she said, "Daisy, don't forget—Red Inkers meets tomorrow night! I can't wait. David is reading his next chapter. It will be *amazing.*" With that, she bounced out of the store.

After she left, I looked to Grandma Daisy. "Red Inkers?"

"It's a local writers' group. I let them meet here in the evenings once or twice a week. They're an interesting bunch. You should hang around the Springs to meet them."

I gave her a lopsided smile. "Nice try. I know you're trying to trick me into staying in Cascade Springs longer."

"Is it wrong for a grandmother to want her only grandchild close to her?"

I sighed. "No, it's not wrong, but it's not going to change anything either."

"It was so long—"

I shook my head. "Please, Grandma, I don't want to talk about it. I left because I didn't want to talk about it. That hasn't changed."

She didn't say another word about the incident, but I knew by the way her brow wrinkled above her cat's-eye glasses that this conversation wasn't over.

After we closed up the shop, I left my Mini Cooper parked on River Road, and Grandma Daisy and I walked to her row house one block over on another perfectly picturesque Cascade Springs street with iron lampposts dotted with hanging flower baskets.

"Before we go in the house, I have something to show you." She smiled brightly. "It's a surprise."

I narrowed my eyes. "Is this like an I'm-not-really-dying surprise? Because I don't need a repeat of that."

She chuckled. "No, you will like this one." Grandma Daisy ran into the garage through the back door and came out with a huge gift bag. "Open it."

I took the bag from her hand and riffled through the tissue paper until I came up with an aqua bike helmet with white and purple violets painted all over it. I blinked.

"One of the artists from the arts district painted it for me." She beamed. "What do you think?"

I swallowed. "It certainly stands out."

"Try it on," she said.

I placed the helmet on my head and adjusted the strap under my chin.

"Adorable."

I felt about as adorable as a thirteen-year-old with braces and headgear.

"Everyone will know it's yours." She smiled. "Do you like it?" She looked so hopeful.

I gave her a big smile. "I love it. It was so thoughtful." I paused. "But I don't understand. Why would you give me this? I don't own a bike."

"Sure you do." She winked at me. "You have your mother's bike."

I froze. "My mother's bike?"

Grandma Daisy grinned. "I had it tuned up for you,

so you could use it during your visit or if you decide to stay in the village."

"I'm not—"

She cut me off. "Do you want to see it?"

I did.

Grandma Daisy punched in the garage door code in the keypad on the side of the garage, and the door opened. Grandma's ancient compact car was parked inside, but behind it, just waiting to be ridden, was my mother's bicycle.

I touched the white seat. It was an aqua-colored cruiser bike and had a pink wire basket with a pink silk gerbera daisy on the front. It looked like new. Mom's bicycle had been the only way she'd gotten around. She'd hated to drive and said she could reach every corner on the village on her bike. If I closed my eyes, I could see her riding along the river, her strawberry blond hair flying behind her like a banner.

A tear leaked out of the corner of my right eye. It was such a thoughtful gesture by my grandmother, but I knew I still couldn't stay in the village. It just wasn't possible.

After our dinner, I made excuses and went to bed in my old bedroom at the top of the stairs. Grandma Daisy simply nodded as if distracted by something, but I was too tired to ask her what it was. As I stumbled up the stairs, I promised myself I would ask in the morning. I crashed into the bed fully dressed, completely exhausted from the day.

Because I had gone to bed so early, I woke up at three, four, and five in the morning. Each time I forgot where I was and I reached across the bed for my cat, Jane Eyre. When I remembered she was gone, it made my heart ache for my beloved tabby, who'd passed away from old age in the spring. Jane Eyre had been with me when I'd left Cascade Springs the first time. It was strange not to have her with me now. I knew it was time that I adopted a new kitten. I missed having someone greet me at my apartment door after a long night of studying in the university library, but a little part of me was worried that that would feel like replacing her.

I took a shower and dressed before padding barefoot downstairs. Grandma Daisy was still in bed, but she would be up soon. She rose every morning at six forty-five on the dot and had woken up at that time for as long as I could remember.

In the tiny kitchen, I started a pot of coffee. I found the mugs, spoons, and coffee filters. Everything was in the exact place it had been on the day I left Cascade Springs. Maybe I should have found that eerie, but instead, I found it comforting.

I drummed my fingers on the counter while the coffee brewed, and when there was just enough for one serving, I poured a mug of it from the pot while the coffeemaker was still percolating.

Cupping the mug in my hands, I peered through the window over my grandma's flower basket bursting with purple petunias. I blinked. Outside, a horse and carriage was parked in the middle of Grandma Daisy's driveway.

I stared at the ceiling. Did Grandma Daisy have a guest? I hadn't heard anyone else in the house last night, but I'd basically passed out before my head hit the pillow. I set my mug on the counter and started for the front door. I unlocked it and stepped outside.

I tiptoed through the thick grass, damp with dew. My toes curled from the cold. I came around the side of the house to the driveway toward the carriage. The horse turned his head to look back at me as much as his harness would allow. He stamped the driveway and blew mist from his nose. The back of the carriage where guests would sit was empty, but a white-haired man sat straight up in the driver's seat.

"Can I help you?" I called.

He didn't turn around.

"Sir?"

Still nothing.

I rushed to the front of the carriage and found it was Benedict Raisin. "Benedict?" I asked.

He didn't say a word. He didn't move a muscle. His eyes were closed, and his arms were over his chest, holding something.

"Benedict?" I reached up into the carriage and touched his arm, noticing that Grandma Daisy's ladybug scarf was wrapped tightly around his neck. He slumped over in the seat, falling onto his right side. I squealed. It was Benedict all right, and he was dead. In death, he clutched *The Selected Works of Emily Dickinson*, the book he'd purchased from Charming Books, to his chest.

When I stopped screaming, I ran back into the house to call 911 and wake up Grandma Daisy.

"Grandma! Grandma!"

Grandma Daisy was just coming down the stairs when I stormed into the house. "Violet, what in the devil has gotten into you?"

I stubbed my toe on an end table but ignored the pain

surging up my foot. "Benedict." I pointed to the open front door. "He's out there."

She stepped over to me. "He is? What's he doing here so early? Did you ask him?"

"I couldn't ask him." I took a deep breath. "Grandma, Benedict is dead."

She pressed a hand to her forehead. "Are you sure?"

"Yes." I bent over at the waist to catch my breath.

Tears filled her dark eyes. "I was afraid of this. This is exactly what I was afraid of."

I didn't have time to ask her what she meant because the sounds of sirens announced the police and ambulances' arrival. I went out to meet them.

An EMT, who looked like he was in middle school, approached me. "Who needs help, ma'am?"

I swallowed. "In the front seat of the carriage. H-he fell over."

The EMT and two others ran to the front of the carriage. I stared after them. I was frozen in place on the lawn. I no longer cared my bare feet were wet and getting colder by the second. How could this be happening to me again? I'd left Cascade Springs twelve years ago to escape something just like this. I was back less than twenty-four hours, and it had happened again. Was I cursed? One thing I knew, the universe was telling me to get the heck out of Cascade Springs, New York.

"Miss?" A man in a police uniform stood in front of me. "I'm Officer Wheaton of the village police."

I blinked at the scowling officer just a few years younger than me. His hair was buzz-cut and he wore mirrored sunglasses, making it impossible for me to see his eyes.

"Miss, would you like to tell me what happened?"

I wiped tears from my cheeks. "I—I don't know."

"You were the one who discovered the body." Officer Wheaton said this more than asked it.

I nodded.

"How did it happen?"

I ran my hands up and down my arms. "I was in the kitchen making coffee, and I saw Benedict's carriage, so I came out to say hello to him and see if he needed anything. And I found him." I swallowed. "Like that."

"So you know who the victim is, even though I've never seen you around Cascade Springs before." He said it as if he expected this.

I nodded. "Benedict Raisin. He was a sweet old man. I met him yesterday. He liked books." I don't know why I added that last part onto my summary of Benedict. Maybe I wanted the officer to know that he was more than just a dead body.

"And you were staying here with Daisy Waverly?"

I nodded. "Yes."

"And who might you be?"

"Oh, I'm sorry," I said. "I'm her granddaughter, Violet Waverly. I'm visiting my grandmother. I was supposed to leave today."

A flicker of recognition lit his eyes, but as quickly as it came, it disappeared. "My advice is that you stick around here for a while to be with your grandmother." He gave me a stern look as if he was deciding whether he could trust me. "I'm going to check on the scene, but I'm going to want to talk to you and your grandmother again. Okay?"

I nodded as he strode away. I looked back at the house. Grandma Daisy stood in the doorway, but she didn't cross the threshold. She'd draped a blanket over her body and had it wrapped around her like a cocoon.

I hurried up the porch steps to my grandmother. "Grandma, are you okay?" I knew it was a stupid question as soon as it popped out of my mouth. Of course, Grandma Daisy wasn't okay. I didn't know exactly what her relationship with Benedict had been, but I knew it was more than a friendship. And it wasn't the right time to ask her about it.

I wrapped my arms around her, and she buried her face in my shoulder. We had stood that way so many years ago when my mother had died. Back then, the roles had been reversed, and I had been the one crying in her arms.

"I knew this would happen," she mumbled. "I hoped that I was wrong. I hoped that the book was wrong, but I knew this would happen."

"The book?" I asked. "What are you talking about?"

Grandma Daisy didn't get the chance to answer, because a luxury car pulled up at the curb and a man in a gray summer suit jumped out. The morning sunlight reflected off his golden hair, which was perfectly styled. He moved through the police easily. They gave him plenty of space.

My heart constricted, and my mouth ran dry. I blinked a couple of times, hoping that I was just imagining the person talking to Officer Wheaton. No such luck. When my vision cleared, he was still there.

He nodded at something Officer Wheaton said and his head turned sharply to the porch, where Grandma Daisy and I huddled together. His dark, stony gaze focused on me. I stared back. I hadn't seen or spoken to my high school sweetheart, Nathan Morton, since the day I left the village twelve years ago.

"What's he doing here?" I hissed to Grandma Daisy.

"Violet," my grandmother whispered back, "he's the mayor of Cascade Springs."

The *mayor*?

Great. Just great.

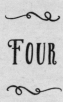

# FOUR

I tore my eyes away from Nathan. "Why would the mayor come to the scene of an accident?" I asked after finding my voice.

Grandma Daisy adjusted the blanket on her shoulders. "I'm sure he heard about it."

"But why is he here?" I hissed. "Do you think the mayor of Chicago shows up every time someone dies?"

Grandma Daisy's mouth shaped into an O. "No, I suppose that the mayor of Chicago doesn't, but things like this don't happen in Cascade Springs. Nothing like this has happened since—" She caught herself before finishing the sentence.

"Since I left," I finished it for her. With every mental faculty I had, I pushed the memories of twelve years ago back to the darkest, most hidden corner of my brain. I would not let my mind wander there, especially not with Nathan so close.

Nathan conferred with Officer Wheaton. The pair had their heads together, Nathan's golden blond, Officer Wheaton's buzzed to almost bald. It did not take a genius to know that they were talking about Grandma Daisy and me.

Grandma Daisy pulled away from me. "I want to see him."

"Nathan?" I asked.

She wiped a tear from her cheek. "Benedict."

I pulled my attention away from the two men talking on the tree lawn. "Wh-what?"

She removed the blanket from her shoulders and folded it. "I want to see him." She tossed the blanket on the white rocker beside the front door and marched down the porch steps and to the driveway.

I tripped down the steps after her, wishing I had taken time to put on my shoes.

"Wait!" Officer Wheaton called.

By the time the officer caught up to us, Grandma Daisy was already beside the carriage. Her hand covered her mouth as she saw Benedict for the first time. She lowered her hand. "I knew it was the book. The books never lie."

I glanced around, hoping that I was the only one who heard her say that.

"Ms. Waverly," Officer Wheaton said, slightly out of breath. "You can't come over here. This area is quartered off as a crime scene."

Grandma Daisy adjusted her glasses and wrinkled her

nose. Uh-oh. "Johnny Wheaton, my friend is dead. I have a right to see my friend's body on my own property."

"This is a crime scene, and—"

She pointed at him. "And nothing. Now, please give me a moment."

The two crime scene techs were frozen in place on the carriage and looked to Officer Wheaton for guidance.

"Just give her a couple of minutes, boys," a voice said only a few paces behind me.

Officer Wheaton's jaw twitched before he finally nodded. "Guys, you heard the mayor."

The two techs climbed out of the carriage and went over to their truck, which was sticking out of the end of the driveway.

To my grandmother, Officer Wheaton ordered, "Don't touch anything."

She nodded and stepped closer to the front of the carriage. She was still a good five feet away.

Against my better judgment, I turned around to face the mayor. He had his arms folded across his chest as he watched me. If anything, Nathan Morton was more handsome than he had been in high school. Age agreed with him. His signature golden hair was the same, but his features were sharper. Dark brown eyes sat behind heavy lashes with just the beginning of laugh lines splaying out from the corners. Long gone was any sign of boyhood, and I had known Nathan the boy. The man in front of me was a stranger. As I studied him, I came to the realization that he studied me right back. A blush crept onto my cheeks.

Nathan nodded to me. "Violet, I didn't expect to see you again."

I straightened and looked him in the eye. "It's nice to see you too, Nate."

"From what I've heard, you never visit Cascade Springs. Ever."

Had he been asking Grandma Daisy about me? That didn't matter. I didn't care, or that's what I told myself. "I'm here for a couple of days to see my grandma," I said.

He glanced over my shoulder at Grandma Daisy. I looked behind me to see that her head was bent and her lips moved as if she was whispering a prayer.

"You should visit her more often." His tone held a hint of criticism. "You're all she has."

I gritted my teeth. Of anyone in the entire world, Nathan Morton had no right to criticize me, not after what he'd done. I bit back the words before they escaped my mouth.

"What do you know about your grandmother's friend?" He nodded at the carriage.

"Very little. Like I told Officer Wheaton a few minutes ago, I met him yesterday."

"Your grandmother seems to care about him a lot." He raised his eyebrows.

I clenched my jaw a little harder. "He was her friend. Of course she's upset."

He opened his mouth as if to say something more, but then thought better of it. It seemed that both of us were holding back. There had been a time when we told each other everything. That time was long gone.

I folded my arms and matched his stance. "What are you doing here, Nathan?"

"I'm the mayor of Cascade Springs." He said this as if he were claiming to be the Dalai Lama, not the mayor of a Western New York village of just under five thousand souls.

"I heard, but that doesn't really answer the question, does it?" I was unable to keep the edge out of my voice. I had always wondered how I would feel if I ever saw Nathan Morton again. I finally had my answer as the old feelings of anger, betrayal, and hurt hit me like water crashing over the edge of Niagara Falls. I unclenched my hands. "What I'd like to know is why this has gotten the attention of the village mayor so quickly."

"It is a small village." He shrugged.

Nice try.

"Not small enough for the mayor to come to a crime scene." I tried not to think of Grandma Daisy's ladybug scarf wrapped around Benedict's throat.

He arched his brow. "A crime scene? So you think he was murdered?"

"I don't know," I snapped. "That's what Officer Wheaton called it a few minutes ago."

A hand touched my arm. "Violet, I'm finished," Grandma Daisy said. "I said a prayer for him. There is no more to be done." Her eyes were wet with tears, but behind them I saw the strength I'd depended on all my life. "The police want to question us. Officer Wheaton said we should wait inside for him." She nodded at Nathan. "It is nice to see you and Violet together again, Nathan. I wish it was under better circumstances."

I stiffened at my grandmother's comment, but Nathan smiled. "Thank you, Grandma Daisy. I'm so sorry for your loss."

My jaw twitched. *Grandma Daisy?* What gave Nathan the right to call my grandmother Grandma Daisy? I knew he'd called her that when we had been children, but that had been a lifetime ago. Things were different now, and that was his fault.

Grandma Daisy simply nodded. "Thank you." She hooked her arm through mine and pulled me away.

"I've been meaning to stop by the store to find a book for my mother's birthday," Nathan said as if he didn't want to see us go.

"Please do," Grandma Daisy said. "The right book will reveal itself."

A confused look crossed Nathan's face, and I winced, knowing he'd caught Grandma Daisy's odd turn of phrase.

I wrapped my arm around her shoulders and ushered her away without saying good-bye to Nathan. "Let's go in and let the police do their jobs."

"Ms. Waverly," Officer Wheaton said as he approached us, "our village police chief is caught away on another case, and he asked me to interview you."

"All right," I said, heading for the front door. "We can talk in the living room."

He shook his head. "I need to talk to your grandmother alone."

I glared at the officer. "I should be with her."

"Not going to happen." His voice was firm.

Grandma Daisy patted my arm. "Don't worry so,

Violet. I'll be fine. Why don't we go into the kitchen, Officer? I could use a mug of tea."

He frowned. "I would prefer you just answer my questions, ma'am."

My grandmother's shoulders slumped. "Very well."

Before I could protest again, they disappeared into the house. A knot grew in my stomach.

A new SUV with a state seal pulled up to the front of the house. It wasn't until I saw two officers pull the gurney with a black bag on top of it out of the back that I realized it must be from the medical examiner's office. A feeling of incredible sadness fell over me, and I had to turn away. I didn't know Benedict, but he had been my grandmother's friend or boyfriend or something and that made him special. It did not seem fair that Grandma Daisy would lose someone else. She had lost too many others.

"What are you really doing here in my village, Violet?" Nathan was back.

Why didn't he just leave me alone?

I turned to face him. "I told you, I'm here to visit my grandmother."

He frowned as if he didn't believe it. Could he possibly think I'd come back to Cascade Springs to hurt Benedict? The very idea was insane. I hadn't set foot in the village in twelve years.

"What I want to know is how you were elected mayor of Cascade Springs after what happened." I didn't have to tell him what I was speaking about. He knew. He knew better than anyone. "And I got run out of town."

He stepped closer to me, so close that I caught the

slight scent of aftershave, which was so adult, so unexpected. Adult was never a word I had associated with
Nathan before, but there he was just inches from me and
all grown up. "Vi, you weren't run out of the village, and
you know that. You fled." He walked away.

I let go of a breath I didn't know I had been holding,
wishing what he said wasn't the truth, but it was.

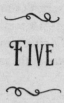

# FIVE

I was just recovering from Nathan's parting shot when Officer Wheaton flung open the front door to my grandmother's house, holding Grandma Daisy by the arm. He walked her down the porch steps and toward a police cruiser.

I forgot Nathan and raced after them. "What is going on?"

"I'm taking your grandmother in for questioning," the stone-faced officer said.

"What? Why? You said you would question her here."

"She's being unresponsive to my questions. I have no choice."

"He wants to know why Benedict bought that book from me," Grandma Daisy said. "And I calmly told him that I couldn't answer that."

I threw up my hands. "Because he wanted to read it. There's no mystery there. It's a book."

Grandma Daisy remained quiet, and Officer Wheaton studied her calm face. "There's something more to it, and I'm going to find out what. She's going downtown."

Downtown? What on earth was he talking about? Cascade Springs' *downtown* was a line of cafés and gift shops, not an NYPD precinct.

"You have no right." I tried to break his hold on my grandmother's arm. "I demand that you let her go."

"Do not touch me," the officer growled, "or you will be charged with assault of an officer."

I jumped back. I had every reason to believe that Officer Wheaton would follow through on that threat. I glanced around at the crime scene techs in search of a friendly face for help. No one would meet my gaze. "You can't take her. Wait until the police chief is here. It's his decision, isn't it?"

"He's not here, so the decision is mine." He stepped closer to me. "If you keep arguing with me, I'll take you too."

"Fine. Do it," I snapped. "I see nothing has changed. Cascade Springs police are still the same as always."

"No." Grandma Daisy spoke with more force than she had all morning. "No, Violet."

"Officer Wheaton!" one of the crime scene techs called from the driveway.

"What is it?" Wheaton snapped.

"You're going to want to look at this," was all the tech said.

Wheaton glared at him for a moment. "Fine." He turned back to Grandma Daisy. "Do. Not. Move." He stalked away.

"I can't believe this," I said. "It's just like last time. It's the same nightmare all over again."

"Violet." My grandmother's voice was tense. "Listen to me. You have to go to Benedict's house." She paused. "Now."

"What? What are you talking about?"

"You need to get the cat."

I blinked at her. "What cat?"

She watched Wheaton over my shoulder. "Benedict's. Oh, the poor creature is all alone in Benedict's house. You have to go over there and collect him. Who knows how long he's been alone, and he must be frightened wondering what's become of Benedict."

"Me? Why me?"

"I'd go myself"—her voice caught—"but as you can see, I can't. Even if I could, I wouldn't be able to. There are too many memories for me there."

Again, a part of me wanted to ask my grandmother to elaborate on those memories and define her relationship with Benedict, but I also didn't want to upset her more than she already was. "The police will be going to Benedict's house by now. Some could already be there."

She held my hand. "That's even worse. With them tramping in and out of the house, what if Benedict's cat runs away? Violet, I would never forgive myself if something happened to that creature. I'll have to take him in, of course." She glanced over my shoulder again. "Or maybe you'll want to adopt him. He is a dear, and you could use some company."

I held up my hands. Since losing Jane Eyre, in fleeting moments I'd thought that I might want to adopt a new kitten, but I wasn't sure I was ready to commit to that yet. The more sensible thing would be to see where I landed when I found a teaching job at a university and adopt a new cat then. That would be much more practical. I was nothing if not practical. "I can't adopt a cat right now. I don't know where I will be living in a few months when I'm completely finished with school." I sighed. "But I will fetch Benedict's cat for you if it's that important, even if I think I would be more help to you at the police station."

"This is more important. This is what I need you to do for me. Thank you." Tears glistened in her eyes.

"Don't thank me yet." I shook my head. "Chances are, the police are already there and won't let me bring him back here."

"If they have any compassion, they will. The address is 23 Puffin Lane. Benedict's house key is in the catchall bowl in the kitchen."

"You have a key to his house?" I asked.

"And he had one to mine." She buried her face in her hands. When she lifted her head again, she said, "Take the cat to the shop. Benedict's cat has been there before and will feel right at home. I want you to open the shop if I'm not there in time to do it."

"Grandma," I said, "I think it would be all right if you didn't open the shop today. I want to come to the police station and see you."

"No." Grandma Daisy shook her head. "I can't. The books won't wait, and I'm already an hour late."

I knit my brow. Didn't she mean "customers won't wait"?

"I left my car at Charming Books. I'll walk to the shop, so I can pick it up and drive to Benedict's for the cat," I said.

She shook her head. "There's no time for that. Take your mother's bike."

The bike. I had forgotten it in the chaos of the morning.

"Ms. Waverly, it's time to go." Officer Wheaton's voice carried across the yard.

I spun around. "I still think you are taking this too far."

He glared at me. "I don't care what you think."

I scowled in return.

He opened the cruiser's back door and told my grandmother to climb in the backseat.

"Is that really necessary?" I asked.

Grandma Daisy touched my arm. "Everything will be all right." She gave me a meaningful look, which I interpreted as "get the cat," before she climbed into the back of the police car.

Officer Wheaton shut the door after her and turned to me. "Your history is well-known at the police station, so don't make matters worse for yourself and your grandmother." With that, he ran around the side of the cruiser, jumped in the driver's side, and drove away.

I stared after the police car and concentrated on my breathing. This was no time for a panic attack. I had a cat to save.

I turned back toward the house. The crime scene techs were still at work on the carriage. One of them unhooked Benedict's horse from the carriage and walked him to the end of the driveway. The coroner seemed to be examining the scene before moving on to the body, and another police officer stood by answering his questions. No one was paying attention to me, which was just how I liked it.

I slipped into the house, grabbed Benedict's key from the bowl in the kitchen, and slid into my flip-flops. The plastic sandals weren't the most advisable footwear for a bike ride, but I didn't have time to run upstairs for more appropriate shoes. Somehow I had to get to my mom's bike in the garage and out of my grandmother's neighborhood without being noticed. Wheaton hadn't ordered me to stay home. I didn't know if the crime scene guys cared if I left, but I wasn't taking any chances.

I slipped out the French doors leading to the tiny backyard between the house and the garage. I peeked around the corner of the house. The techs, the coroner, and the officer were still engrossed in the scene. I dashed to the back of the garage. Inside, I squinted in the darkness and knocked my elbow on a metal shelf. I covered my mouth to stifle my cry of pain. I made it to the front of the garage, and clumsily maneuvered the bike to the back door. There was no fence between Grandma Daisy's yard and her back neighbor's. I saw my escape.

I strapped on my violet-painted helmet and pedaled out of there like my back tire was on fire. My grandmother's backyard neighbor was sipping coffee on his front porch when I peeled around the side of his house. He yelped and slipped coffee down the front of his robe.

Benedict Raisin lived a few blocks from Charming Books in the opposite direction of my grandmother's house. As I rode my bike through the village's wandering lanes and neighborhoods, tourists and locals waved and smiled at me. If I hadn't been on a mission, I would have waved back. The village was that kind of place. Colleen and I used to say that everyone who lived in the village drank the Cascade Springs happy juice, a nickname we had given the famous springwater from which the village got its name, in order to make them cheerful. I gripped the handlebars.

I had known that if I ever came back to the village, memories of Colleen Preston, my best friend, would follow. It was still hard to believe she had been gone for twelve years. Her family had moved away from the Springs shortly after I left, so at least there was no chance I'd have to face them again. Seeing Nathan was bad enough.

I took a deep breath and pushed memories—good, bad, everything—of Colleen away and focused on the bike ride.

By the time I arrived on Puffin Lane, I had regained control over myself for the most part. I could only guess what the tourists thought of a nearly thirty-year-old woman riding a bike with a violet helmet as if she were in a high-speed car chase. Good thing I wouldn't be in Cascade Springs for long.

Benedict lived in a narrow Victorian row house that had no front yard; the front stoop ended where the sidewalk began. A young maple tree, surrounded by curved iron bars, grew out of the middle of the sidewalk. The iron was twisted to resemble a kaleidoscope of butterflies taking flight.

His neighborhood was at the center of the thriving arts culture in the village and all the streets were named after birds. It was so well-known that it had been written up in a state magazine trying to bring tourists to Western New York. Although the bird neighborhood was a part of Cascade Springs, it had an identity all its own. It was like the austere village's beatnik cousin.

The houses on Puffin Lane were painted a host of colors that reflected the tastes of the artists who called them home. Benedict's home was the exception. His was painted white with clean navy shutters and front door. It stood out on the street due to its simplicity.

I had expected to find the police already there, and had even practiced my story as to why I showed up at Benedict's house unexpectedly. It wasn't so much a story as the truth. *I am here because of the cat,* I played over and over in my head. After all, it was hard for me to believe the police had already come and gone. Officer Wheaton had taken Grandma Daisy *downtown* less than an hour ago.

There weren't any police cars on the street. On the other side of the road, a woman with dreadlocks and patchwork pants walked a dog down the sidewalk. She didn't give my helmet or bike a second thought. Other than the woman and dog, Puffin Lane was absolutely still. The arts district was sleeping in the morning. Things would pick up in the late afternoon and evening. It was a good time to stage a cat rescue without being seen.

I parked my bike by the front door, removed my helmet, and hung it from the handlebars. I pulled Benedict's house key, which hung from a key chain with a glittery red heart, from my pocket. If I had any hopes that Benedict and Grandma Daisy had been just friends, that key chain squashed them. Benedict and my grandmother had definitely been an item. For how long still remained to be seen. I flipped the heart over in my hand. I wished that she had told me. I thought Grandma Daisy told me everything. If she kept her boyfriend secret from me, what other secrets might she have kept? Then I remembered she had never mentioned Faulkner the crow to me either. Did I know her at all? And did I have a right to be upset about it when I'd abandoned her after high school and gone out into the world on my own?

The key fit in the lock, and the door opened easily. "Hello? Hello?" I knocked loudly on the open door. If the police were inside, I wanted them to know I was there.

There was no answer. Afraid that the cat in question might escape, I closed the door behind me but left it unlocked. "Here, kitty, kitty!" I called.

With the door closed, the room was pitch-black. I couldn't see my hand in front of my face. I knew from the outside that Benedict's house had plenty of windows, but he must have covered them with industrial-strength blackout curtains.

I ran my hand along the wall, looking for a light switch. I didn't find one, so I inched forward into the room. I stubbed my toe on the leg of a table and yelped. The flip-flops had been a very bad idea. I fumbled for the lamp's switch, and it cast a dim yellow light in the room. It wasn't bright enough to illuminate the entire space, but I could make out the shape of a desk on the far wall. The drawers appeared to be opened.

There was still no sign of the cat. "Kitty, kitty?" I made a clicking sound with my tongue. It was something I used to do to get Jane Eyre's attention.

"Meow!" a small voice cooed, and a slim black-and-white tuxedo cat with a pink nose waltzed out from under the end table where I had stubbed my toe. "Meow!" he said confidently as if to reassure me that he was actually there.

I bent down and let the cat sniff my hand, and he turned his face toward me. "Oh, you are beautiful," I said. I bent to pick up the cat, and he let me hold him. The creature purred like a motorboat in reply.

"Aren't you precious?" I cooed, and my heart broke a little for the animal. He didn't know that Benedict wasn't coming home ever again. How long would the cat look for Benedict, waiting for his best friend to return? I understood that. I had felt the same about Jane Eyre. I had searched for her for weeks after she had gone. I petted his head. "I think you and I have a lot in common. What's your name?"

The cat shook his head and the collar around his throat jingled. There was a silver tag shaped in a cat's head on the collar, and EMERSON was engraved on one side.

I blinked. Could that really be his name? My dissertation was on the writings of Emerson and his Transcendentalist contemporaries: Thoreau, the Alcotts, and the others. I scratched him underneath the chin. "Emerson?"

"Meow," he repeated as if to say "That's right."

I felt myself relax. "I guess that really is your name." I flipped over the tag to see if there was writing on the other side. LOVE, D. My brow wrinkled.

"Police! Hands up!"

I dropped the cat on the couch, and he bounced on the cushion before streaking out of the room in a black-and-white blur.

"Hands up!" the angry male voice repeated.

I spun around to find a man standing in the doorway to Benedict's home with a gun in his hand, and that gun was pointed at me.

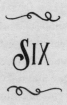

# SIX

The man with the gun was Native American and about my age. He wore his black hair cropped close to his head. The light caught his high cheekbones and the barrel of his revolver. "I said put your hands up. That is a direct order from the police."

I glared back at him. "How do I know you're really with the police?" Living alone in the big city of Chicago taught me not to trust strangers, and I didn't take anything on a stranger's say-so.

The man grunted and flicked back his sport coat, giving me a glimpse of a police badge clipped to his belt and of a small gun holster, holding a second gun. How many guns did a police officer in Cascade Springs need? I would have thought the biggest crime reported in the village was a string of jaywalking tourists.

I put my hands up. "I haven't done anything wrong. I had a key. I'm only here for the cat."

His dark eyes narrowed into black slits. "You were going to steal the cat?"

I shook my head. "N-no! I wouldn't do that. I'm here to make sure that the cat was all right and to take him back to my grandma. Someone will need to take care of him now that Benedict's gone."

He lowered the gun. "Your grandma? You're Daisy Waverly's granddaughter? Violet, right?"

"Guilty, but that's the only thing I'm guilty of." My hands were still in the air. "Can I put my hands down now?"

He holstered his gun. "Yes, but you shouldn't be in here. If you were concerned about the victim's cat, you should have told the officers at your grandmother's home."

I shook out my hands. "Sorry if I don't trust those officers since one of them took my grandmother to the station in the back of a police car."

"What?" he snapped as he stepped over to the wall and turned on the overhead light.

I blinked at the sudden brightness. When I could see again, his features came into focus. Amber-colored eyes, not that much different from Emerson's, studied me. Their color reminded me of warm maple syrup that I might drown in. He was possibly the most beautiful man I had seen in real life. I was ashamed to realize my mouth hung open. I snapped it shut. My cheeks felt hot. I hoped that he didn't notice.

"Who took your grandmother to the station?"

"Officer Wheaton," I said.

His maple syrup eyes narrowed into slits again as he removed his cell phone from his belt. "I have to make a call. Wait here." It was an order.

The officer marched out the front door with his phone to his ear. While he was gone, I called Emerson a few times, but the cat didn't appear. The poor thing must have been terrified by the officer busting into Benedict's house like that.

The officer stepped back into the house, and he frowned at something behind me. "Did you search the place while looking for the cat?" His tone was all business.

"No," I said defensively. "The cat came right to me. Now I don't know if he will again since you scared him so badly," I said a little more harshly than necessary.

He pointed behind me. "Someone tossed the desk."

I spun around and realized that he was right. The desk was a mess. All the drawers were pulled open, and papers and files were scattered over the top of it and onto the floor around it. The black desk chair stood a few feet away as if hastily pushed aside. The officer walked around me toward the desk. He peered at the papers. He looked over his shoulder. "Do you know anything about what happened here?"

"Nothing." I swallowed. "I told you I came for the cat. Why would I look in the desk for the cat?"

He didn't respond.

"Who's to say that Benedict didn't do this himself? Maybe Benedict was looking for something," I said. "You should see Grandma Daisy's desk in the back of Charming Books. It looks way worse than that."

A smile flashed across his face as he removed latex

gloves from the breast pocket of his jacket and put them on. "I've been here before and his desk is always neat."

"Why were you here?" I asked.

He didn't answer and instead sorted through the documents on the desk in silence.

I folded my arms. "You know who I am. It would be helpful if I knew your name."

He looked up at me over his shoulder. "I'm David Rainwater, Cascade Springs' chief of police."

I straightened my shoulders. "Well, Chief Rainwater, it was very nice to meet you, but now I will have to take Emerson and go. My grandmother is at the station being questioned by one of *your* officers."

Rainwater arched an eyebrow. "Emerson?"

"Yes." I nodded, trying not to squirm under his penetrating amber stare. "Emerson, the cat."

"Ahh, yes, the cat you came to steal from a crime scene." The corner of his mouth twitched.

I bristled. "I wasn't stealing him. Someone has to take care of him. You can't leave the poor creature here to starve or get lost, and this isn't a crime scene. Benedict didn't die here."

"It's true that the cat can't stay here." He paused as if to let the gravity of that sink in. "But this is a crime scene as of right this moment. It's been vandalized, and it's the home of a murder victim."

My knees began to wobble. "Murder? Is it really murder?"

He frowned. "Yes."

I sank onto the couch. "I guess I knew that. It wasn't like he could strangle himself."

He watched me with his maple eyes. "No, considering the angle of his injury, he could not."

I held my shaking hands in my lap. "I can't believe this is happening again."

"Again after Colleen Preston's death?" He stared down at me.

I lifted my chin to look at him. "How did you know?"

"Miss Waverly"—the police chief's voice softened—"for the last twelve years, Colleen Preston's suspicious death has been the biggest case Cascade Springs has ever had."

I felt sick to my stomach just as I had felt all those years ago after I found Colleen dead on the banks of the Niagara River. The last thoughtless words I had said to her still rang in my ears all these years later.

"You were a person of interest in Colleen's drowning," he stated as a fact. Clearly Chief Rainwater had done his homework on me. I wished I knew more about him to even the score.

"She was my friend, and I was one of the people who found her."

"And the mayor was the other." His face was blank and his friendly tone evaporated. Maybe I had imagined it.

I only nodded. "If I can just find Emerson again, I'll leave you to your police work." I jumped to my feet. I wasn't going to sit there and remember Colleen as the too-handsome-for-my-own-good police chief watched my every thought cross my face. "Here, kitty, kitty. Here, Emerson!" I called.

The police chief joined in. "Here, kitty. Come here, kitty!"

Emerson wriggled out from under the desk and meowed at the police chief. He scooped up the lithe cat and held him to his chest. From across the room, I could hear the cat purring. Rainwater carried the animal over to me, never breaking eye contact. When he settled Emerson into my arms, I found myself blushing. I dropped my gaze. "Thank you."

"I'll note in the report that you have the cat. You're right that someone has to care for him. My office will be in and out of here often as the case progresses. It's not a good place for a cat right now."

"Thank you," I repeated, holding Emerson under my chin. His short fur felt like silk.

As if on cue, the front door opened, and two men in uniform stepped inside. Officer Wheaton wasn't with them. "Chief," one of the two crime scene techs said, "we're here to search—" He stopped when he saw me standing in front of Benedict's sofa, holding Emerson.

"I'm only here for the cat," I said.

Chief Rainwater stepped forward. "It appears she's telling the truth. I told her it was all right to take the cat for now." He turned to me. "However, the cat will belong to Benedict's heir if he had one, and you will have to settle arrangements with that individual when the time arrives."

I nodded and carried Emerson to the door. When I reached the front door and saw the bike, I stopped. How was I supposed to transport the cat home on my mother's bike?

As if he could read my mind, Emerson jumped from my arms into the bicycle's pink basket and curled into a ball.

My mouth opened. "You have to be kidding me."

Rainwater stood in the doorway. "Looks like he's ready to go."

I picked up my helmet. "I hope he won't fall out."

"He looks pretty comfortable to me," Rainwater said. "Your grandmother should have left the police station by now."

"How?"

"I told Wheaton to release her from questioning. Your grandmother will be questioned, but I will be the one to do it." His mouth formed a hard line. "Not Officer Wheaton. She said to tell you she was going straight to the bookshop."

I frowned and put on the helmet. It seemed to me the police chief was going out of his way to help my grandmother. Wasn't that against protocol? Even I knew that as Benedict's significant other, Grandma Daisy had to be a suspect.

The police chief was grinning now. "I like the helmet, *Violet*. I really do."

I inwardly groaned. With flaming cheeks, I walked the bike with the cat in the basket to the street. As I straddled the bike, I looked back and saw Chief David Rainwater watching me. A shiver ran down my back. I told myself that it was because of his bringing up Colleen, and not due to the unusual color of his eyes. I pedaled down the street with my violet helmet held high.

# SEVEN

When I walked into Charming Books a few minutes later with Emerson in my arms, Faulkner squawked at me from the birch tree and puffed up his wings. "Go away!" he cawed.

I glared at him. Emerson shifted in my arms as if to get a better look at the crow. He stared at the black bird, and Faulkner hopped to a higher branch away from the cat. I scratched Emerson under the chin. He might not be a bad one to have around the shop. He could keep Faulkner in line.

A bang came from the seating area in front of the fireplace, but I didn't see anyone on either of the couches or armchairs. "Grandma Daisy?" I asked.

I found my grandmother sitting cross-legged in the middle of the Oriental rug with her back to the hearth between the two empty couches on either side of the fireplace.

I was relieved to see her. I'd only half believed Chief Rainwater when he said that my grandmother would be released from questioning. When I got a better look at her, my relief evaporated. Her characteristic silver bob was disheveled. Her glasses sat askew on her nose, and her blue T-shirt hung crookedly on her thin shoulders. Dozens of books were piled on the floor around her.

"Grandma," I whispered. "Are you all right? Was Officer Wheaton unkind to you?" I balled my fists at my sides. If that officer had hurt my grandmother in any way, he was going to have to answer to me.

She waved away my questions. "I'm not worried about Johnny Wheaton." She looked at me, and there was desperation in her eyes. "It's them I'm worried about. They aren't talking to me. They need to talk to me."

I clutched Emerson more closely to my chest. "Who's not talking to you?"

"The books," she said as she slammed a copy of *Pride and Prejudice* shut. "They haven't told me a thing I need to know about Benedict."

"Grandma, why would the books talk to you?" I kept my voice even to avoid startling her.

She frowned and offered me her hand to help her off the floor. I placed Emerson on one of the couches and pulled her to her feet. "What if someone came in and found you like this? You could scare customers away."

She shook her head. "Don't be silly. I'm a bookshop owner. People expect me to be eccentric, and besides, I wouldn't say anything to the customers about the books talking to me. They can't know. It's my job as the Care-taker to keep this secret."

"That a relief," I muttered.

"It's time." She smoothed her hand over her hair. "I had wanted to wait, but there isn't time now with Bene-dict's m-murder." She closed her eyes for a moment. "There are some things that I need to tell you now."

"That the books talk to you." I unwittingly arched my brow. I couldn't help it.

She shook her head. "That was a poor choice of words. They don't talk; they reveal things to me."

I blew out a breath. "That's what literature does. It reveals the human condition through prose and poetry."

She frowned. "No, that's not it."

"That's not it," Faulkner called from the safety of his tree.

I shot the bird a dirty look before I asked, "Then, what do you mean?"

I noticed now Emerson sat at the base of the birch tree watching the crow. His sleek black tail swished back and forth across the Oriental rug. Faulkner shuffled back and forth on his branch and cocked his head to point one black beady eye at the cat.

Grandma Daisy tossed the paperback haphazardly onto the couch and made kissy sounds at Benedict's cat. He trotted over to her, and she picked him up, cradling him in her arms like a baby. "Oh, you poor dear, I have some cat food in the kitchen for you." She turned and carried Emerson to the back of the shop.

"Are you going to tell me what you mean about the books talking?" I asked.

"This conversation needs a pot of tea," she said.

I didn't like the sound of that. All of Grandma Daisy's serious conversations had required a pot of tea.

After a beat, I followed her around the tree and under the archway that separated the front of the shop from the rest of the main floor. The first room in this part of the house was a small kitchen. There was no room for more than two people in the space at one time.

Behind the kitchen, there was a back staircase that led to the second floor. It was another way to reach the children's room and the apartment that my mother and I had shared when we lived in the shop. I was curious to see our old apartment, but I knew it wasn't a good time to leave my grandmother for a walk down memory lane. She needed me.

I'd spent countless hours on that stairway as a child. It was seldom used after my mother passed away, and it was the perfect place to hide from the world and read. That was something I'd done often. My mother died of ovarian cancer when I was thirteen in the spring before the end of my eighth grade year. Not that there is ever a "good" time for a girl to lose her mother, but I can say that thirteen was just about the worst. I retreated into my books. Grandma Daisy let me for some time. She seemed to know that's how I grieved. If it hadn't been for her encouragement, I would probably still live only in a world of books. Reading is what brought me back to the real world after my mother's death. The stories I read revealed life to me and showed me that it was worth living.

I suspected Grandma Daisy thought the books revealed things to her in a much more literal way. I couldn't shake the memory from my mind of that book of Dickinson's poems hitting Benedict in the kneecap and how upset Grandma Daisy had been when he insisted on buying it. It was as if she knew then he was going to die, but that didn't make a lick of sense, as my grandmother would have said.

I peeked in the room that neighbored the kitchen. It had once been a formal dining room, but now it served as a large stockroom for the bookshop. Like the main part of the shop, it was lined with bookshelves that ran floor to ceiling. But the books on these shelves either weren't for sale or had simply been returned since they hadn't sold. An old dining room table sat in the middle of the room, and more books sat on it in piles. Against the far wall was my grandmother's massive computer desk with her desktop computer and records. Half-unpacked boxes littered the floor. I had to stop myself from going in there and straightening up her desk. It was a wonder that she got any work done at all.

She noticed me staring at the desk in alarm. "I know you are dying to alphabetize something. The mess is my system, and it's worked for me for the last forty-some years just fine. I've never misplaced a bill or invoice in my life. I know exactly where each piece of paper I need is at all times."

"I could digitize everything for you and put it on the comput—"

She removed a bag of cat food from the cupboard and shook it at me. "Don't you dare! Nothing messes up finances more than a computer. I don't trust them. The only reason I have one is so I can e-mail."

I suppressed a smile, happy to see some of her usual spunk back. I hadn't realized how much finding my grandmother sitting on the floor surrounded by her silent books had frightened me.

And as much as her "system" drove me crazy, I knew better than to mess with it. My grandmother had managed Charming Books ever since her own mother died decades ago.

Like her mother and her grandmother before her, Grandma Daisy was the sole proprietor of Charming Books. Occasionally, she would hire a temp to help her with inventory or during the busy holiday season, but the majority of the work fell on her thin shoulders. I tried to tell her that she should hire some permanent help, but it was an argument that fell on deaf ears. She had always been reluctant for anyone other than my mother and then me to work in the shop. I wondered whether the so-called talking books had anything to do with that.

Grandma Daisy poured cat food from the bag into a cereal bowl on the counter. The dry cat food clinked against the sides of the bowl. She filled a second bowl with water and set both at Emerson's feet.

"Where's the cat food from?" I asked.

She straightened up. "I always keep a bag on hand in case a neighborhood cat comes by looking for a meal."

Emerson buried his pink nose in the bowl.

Grandma Daisy sighed. "It's just as I feared. The poor creature is absolutely starved. Benedict would have never stood for that. He adored Emerson. He treated him more like a child than a cat."

I sat on a three-legged stool in the corner of the kitchen. "How did he get the name Emerson?" The cat was a safer topic to start with than talking books and murder. It's best to work up to those, I thought.

Grandma Daisy filled a kettle with water and placed it on the stove. "I named him. The books helped me of course." She smiled.

I shifted uncomfortably in my seat. So much for avoiding the conversation about talking books. "And how did they do that?"

She removed two teacups from a high cupboard. "I can tell you don't believe me, and I understand that. I didn't believe it myself when my mother told me."

"Told you what?" I asked.

The kettle whistled, and she removed it from the burner, pouring the boiling water into a porcelain teapot with delicately painted strawberries all over it. "Let's start with how Emerson got his name."

"Okay," I said hesitantly.

"He showed up at the back door of the shop. He sat on the doorstep, waiting to come inside. It was wintertime, and I couldn't leave him out in the cold. I looked all over for the owner and never found one. I put up signs around the neighborhood about a found cat, and no one ever claimed him. I knew that Benedict could use a companion, so I convinced him to take the little cat. It took some arm-twisting to convince Benedict, but Emerson won him over with his sweet ways. They spent all their time together. Benedict even took Emerson out on the carriage. The cat would sit on the front seat like a footman waiting on his master." She looked away for a moment as if to collect herself.

"And the name?" I asked. "Why did you name him Emerson?"

"When the cat arrived, a copy of Ralph Waldo Emerson's essays appeared next to him on the floor. I knew that was the name. Now I know what it all means. Sometimes it takes time to decipher what the books are saying."

I narrowed my eyes. "What do you mean, *appeared*?"

"Emerson was meant for you in the end, not Benedict. That's why he's named after one of your favorite writers." She smiled.

My brow wrinkled. I wasn't making the mental leap with Grandma Daisy. "The books named him?"

"That's right." She beamed as if I'd just aced a test, but I was more confused than ever.

"How?" I asked.

"One second it was on the shelf with the rest of the classics; the next it was on the floor next to the cat," she said with a smile, handing me a cup of tea.

"You're saying someone moved the book, tossed it across the room, and it landed beside the cat? They could have hit the cat." I frowned and looked at Emerson. He still had his face buried in his food bowl.

"I was the only one in the store at the time. It was before I opened." She shook her head. "The essence of the shop moved the book."

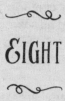

# EIGHT

I sputtered and nearly choked on my tea. I set the teacup on the island.

Grandma Daisy hurried around the island and pounded me on the back.

"Not"—cough, cough—"helping."

She gave me a final smack.

I always wondered who'd come up with the idea that the best way to help someone who was choking was to beat the person. I was pretty sure Grandma Daisy had given me a bruise between the shoulder blades. She was strong for her age.

"Did you say that the essence of the shop moved the book?" I gasped. "What essence?"

She stepped back and folded her arms. "I suppose I should start at the beginning."

"It might help."

"You know that Cascade Springs has always been famous for its natural springs. People come here from all over the world to drink and bathe in the healing waters. They have done so for centuries, long before the first French trader wandered into Western New York."

I sat back onto my stool. "I know the village has made a lot of money from gullible tourists over the natural springs."

"The water *is* special. It always has been. Our ancestress Rosalee realized that. After her husband, a ship's captain, was killed in the Battle of Lake Erie during the War of 1812, she brought her baby daughter here and settled in Cascade Springs. She knew it was the place where she and her child could build a new life and a place where she could use her gift."

"Her gift?" I asked.

"Rosalee had intuition. All of the Waverly woman do. Even you."

My brow went even higher. "Intuition?"

Grandma Daisy curled her hands around her teacup. "A way of knowing, an understanding. I guess you could say Rosalee was a mystic of sorts, or at least that was what they called her in her day."

"Because of her *intuition*."

Grandma Daisy nodded.

Her vague explanation didn't make it that much clearer to me. "What exactly does this have to do with the books?"

"Have you ever wondered why there is a birch tree in the middle of the house?"

"You told me because Rosalee was eccentric."

"Yes." Grandma Daisy nodded as if I were her star

pupil. "She knew the significance of the birch tree as a tree of protection in Native American folklore."

"Okay, I still don't—"

She held up her hand. "A normal birch tree lives one hundred years. That tree is over two hundred years old."

"Wh-what? How?"

She leaned across the island as if she was about to share a secret. "The water."

I shook my head as if to clear the cobwebs. I usually prided myself in catching on to things quickly. "Water?"

"Rosalee only used water from the springs to water the tree. The springwater has kept the tree alive these last two centuries, because the women in our family have been caring for it ever since Rosalee began her endeavor. By watering the tree with springwater, the water's essence manifested itself into the shop and the building became a mystical place. And when my grandmother decided to turn Rosalee's home into a bookshop, the books took on some interesting qualities." She sighed. "Or at least that's the best explanation I have for what has happened over these many years. The Caretaker interprets messages through the books."

I stared at her in a daze as my brain tried to make sense of what she'd just told me. Could it be true? It was impossible.

"Violet, stop," Grandma Daisy ordered.

I blinked at her. "What?"

"Stop thinking!" She poured tea into her cup and added milk and sugar.

"You're joking, right?" I gaped at her. "I'm an academic. That's like telling me to stop breathing."

She chuckled and refilled my teacup and handed it back to me. "All right, I won't ask you to stop thinking, but promise me you will keep an open mind, because everything includes you."

"Me?" I pointed at my chest. "What does this have to do with me?"

"You are the Caretaker now," she said as if I had just won a Pulitzer Prize.

It didn't sound like much of a prize to me. "What?" I squeaked. Maybe I had misheard her.

"You are the Caretaker. You are to care for the tree and the shop now. The books will speak to you now."

I hopped off the stool and set my teacup on the island. My hands were shaking. "What you're saying can't be possible."

She shrugged. "It's the truth."

"I can't believe it."

Emerson finished eating and walked over to me and mewed.

I leaned over and picked him up. He began to purr and I needed the comfort that he could give me at that moment. I took a deep breath and inhaled a whiff of his tuna-scented breath. I looked up from the cat. "This doesn't make any sense."

"Not everything in this world makes sense; you only need to believe it. You are the next Caretaker. I knew this time was coming. It was confirmed when that book hit Benedict when you were standing with him. Why do you think I tricked you to come back to Cascade Springs? I didn't want to. I know it was cruel, but it was the only way I thought I could make you return."

I buried my face in the cat's fur, and Emerson's purring ramped up.

She sighed. "You should have had this conversation with your mother after she had finished her duty as Caretaker and could in turn pass the responsibility on to you, but fate had other plans."

"You're telling me Mom knew about this and never said anything to me about it? I refuse to believe that. She told me everything." I choked on the last sentence because it had been true. My mother and I had been close. She'd had me when she was nineteen years old and raised me alone. My father had never been in the picture. It had been Mom and me against the world. We didn't need anyone else . . . until she got sick. When she was diagnosed with cancer, we moved in with my grandmother.

"Traditionally, the Caretaker doesn't tell the heiress until her eighteenth birthday. I had plans to tell you in your mother's place after high school graduation, but then Colleen was killed. Everything in your world was turned upside down. I couldn't burden you with your destiny."

"My destiny?" I yelped. "You couldn't burden me then, but you can burden me now?"

"You're older, and I won't live forever. You need to begin the transition while I'm here to help." She spoke calmly as if this made perfect sense.

I started to protest. "You're not sick, are you?"

She waved away what I was about to say with her hand. "Don't worry. What I told you yesterday is true—I'm not dying."

"Then drink some of the springwater. Maybe then you'll live longer," I said, and immediately regretted my smart retort.

She frowned. "Violet, you can make all the jokes you want

about the water, the tree, and even this shop. All I ask of you is that you open your mind to the possibility. You have the potential to be the most powerful Caretaker of us all."

I sat back down. All this Caretaker talk made my head spin. Mentally I recapped my day: I had found a dead body, run into my ex-boyfriend, been held at gunpoint by the village chief of police, and now I learned I was the Caretaker of some mystical heritage that has spoken to my family for generations through books. It wasn't even lunchtime yet.

Grandma Daisy set her teacup on the counter. "You look like you might be sick."

"It's a good possibility," I said with a shallow breath. "Say this Caretaker stuff is true. What makes you think I will be so good at it?"

"Because you've spent your life studying literature, and you will have a better understanding of what the books are trying to tell you. Who better to decipher their secrets than a scholar of literature?" Her eyes shone, but then she put her hands on her narrow hips. "I can tell by the way you're looking at me that you still don't believe it."

"It's a lot to take in."

Grandma Daisy watched me cradle Emerson in my arms. "What is it, dear?"

"Then why did my mother die so young? If what you said is true, and we have access to mystical water, why did she die? Why didn't she drink the water and get better?" I noticed my own voice go up an octave.

My grandmother looked stricken, but if I never asked, I would always wonder.

"The water can't heal completely. It only helps. It can't beat cancer," she said.

I set Emerson on the stool. "Then what is it good for?" I asked in a whisper.

She didn't have an answer for that.

I took a deep breath. "When I came into the shop with Emerson, you said the books wouldn't talk to you. You thought they should help you know what happened to Benedict."

"That's right," Grandma Daisy said.

"What do you mean?"

She licked her lips. "I wanted them to tell me who killed him, but I know now they will tell you, not me."

I blinked at her. "Oh."

"'Oh' is all you can say?" she asked as she watched me expectantly.

"I'm processing."

She gave me a small smile.

I started for the back door, which led into the back garden. "I think I need to go for a walk to clear my head."

She nodded and a sad smile played on her mouth. I wasn't sure whether it was over Benedict's death, my disbelief of my destiny, or both.

"Clear your head!" Faulkner cawed as the back door shut behind me.

# NINE

I walked through the back gate around the side of
Charming Books. A group of middle-aged ladies
smiled at me. They chattered among themselves as they
walked along the sidewalk and headed into the bookshop.
I heard my grandmother greet them with the usual cheer
in her voice. They would never have known that her boyfriend had been found dead in her driveway that morning
or that she'd been taken to the police station for questioning. I was in awe of my grandmother's strength.

I started walking in the direction of the river. The portion of the Niagara that flowed through the village was a
quarter of a mile across. There were four stone bridges in
the town, one of which I planned to avoid like the plague.
It was the bridge where I'd discovered Colleen's body
when I was seventeen.

To avoid that particular bridge, I headed west along the

river. A narrow park called the Riverwalk ran the length of the river on the north side of River Road. The only business on that side of the street was a luxury spa that boosted skin treatments with Cascade Springs' special waters.

The rest of the Riverwalk's businesses were on the other side of the street, including the village's formidable town hall, a large brick building with a domed clock tower at the top. It was the building where Mayor Nathan Morton now had his office.

A long white banner hung beneath the clock tower. "Cascade Springs Bicentennial: Celebrate two hundred years of the village. Bicentennial Gala on Friday!"

It was only Tuesday. I hoped I'd be back in the Windy City by the gala. Whether or not Grandma Daisy believed it, I was not the next Caretaker.

Next to the town hall, there was the main office of the Cascade Springs Water Company, the company that bottled and distributed that springwater from the natural springs. They had a factory just outside the village. The main office offered tourists a small museum, tours of the springs, and free water samples. Most of them visited the office for the samples, since one sixteen-ounce bottle of the precious water cost seven dollars.

When I was growing up in Cascade Springs, the springs were just part of life. Most of my friends during high school had one family member or another who worked for the water company. Everyone in Cascade Springs benefited from the natural springs. Without them, we would be just another Western New York town, but with the springs we were a destination, and with Niagara Falls a short drive away, there wasn't a day that went by that a tourist didn't wander into our little village, even in the deep depths of winter.

A teenage boy wearing an old-fashioned wooden placard stood on the sidewalk, shouting, "Take a tour and get a free bottle of healing water! You'll never drink tap water again!"

Across the street on the Riverwalk, there were three college-aged students holding placards too. Their message was much different from the boy's. One read, YOU CAN'T OWN WATER! WATER BELONGS TO ALL! They shook their signs at tourists entering the water company's building.

One of them, a young African-American girl, caught me staring. She handed her sign to one of her comrades and walked over to me with a clipboard. "Care to sign our petition?" She held the clipboard out to me.

The top of the petition read, "Stop Cascade Springs Water Company's monopoly of our springs!"

I frowned. "What is this about?"

"The water company has signed a deal with the village that they are the only ones with access to the springs. The springs have been part of this region for thousands of years, and they have always been part of a public park since the village's charter. They can't take that away now!" Her tight curls swung back and forth as she spoke.

"Isn't that the only company that sells bottled water from the springs?" I asked.

"They want more than that!" Her eyes blazed. "They want to be the only ones that have access to the springs at all. They asked the village council for all the rights to the water. Villagers won't be allowed access to the water."

I blinked in surprise, especially since I now knew

about my family's connection to the springs. Mystical or not, they had been the reason Rosalee settled here. "Why the change?"

"What do you think? Money. Everything comes down to money," she said with more bitterness than I would normally expect of someone her age.

"How much money?"

She shrugged. "It's an undisclosed amount, at least until the deal is final. After that, it will be part of public record. We have to stop that from happening!" Her voice grew louder with every sentence.

"I don't live in Cascade Springs. I don't think my signature will count for much."

"Sure, it will," she said. "We just want to show that the springs are more to the people who live and visit the village than a moneymaker. Will you sign our petition, then?"

Over her shoulder, her friends smiled eagerly at me. I took the pen she offered me. I had the pen poised over the piece of paper when a voice said, "You don't want to sign that."

I turned around and saw Grant Morton strolling up the Riverwalk. How many people from my past was I going to have to run into while in the village? Although seeing Grant was not as jarring as seeing his older brother, Nathan, had been.

Nathan's younger brother looked nothing like Nathan. He never had. He was a head shorter, was stockier, and had dark hair and brows, but he was just as handsome in his own way. He was a year younger than Nathan and I, and in high school he had no shortage of admiring girls following his every move. Today he wore a polo shirt with

CASCADE SPRINGS WATERING COMPANY embroidered onto it.

Grant took the clipboard from my hand. "This is a complete crock, Jade." He handed it back to the girl.

Jade glared at him. "The springs belong to all. You and your company care more about profits than the people living in the village."

He snorted. "Water is a commodity. Any commodity has to be managed. The water company is only making sure it's cared for to ensure its purity."

I raised my eyebrows. "Commodity" wasn't a word I had ever expected to hear from Grant's mouth. But then again, he'd been sixteen when I left the village.

"You say that because you're one of them," Jade spat.

"You work for the water company?" I asked. I had noticed the logo on his shirt, but I was still surprised by this news. I would have thought that Grant would work at his family's winery. In fact, I'd expected that both he and Nathan would end up there, but it appeared that neither of the brothers was following in their parents' footsteps.

Grant's eyes flicked in my direction. "I'm the VP of Strategic Development."

"Which means you are behind all of this." Jade's dark eyes flashed.

Grant wrapped his arm around my shoulders. "I think that's enough crusading for now, don't you? Now, let me have a moment with my long-lost friend. Go pester someone else."

Jade stepped back, clutching her clipboard to her chest. "I see." Her eyes narrowed as she delivered one more parting shot at Grant. "You know the water company only hired you because your brother is the mayor."

Grant's body stiffened, and I winced. Grant had grown up in his brother's perfect shadow. Jade couldn't have hit her mark harder than if she'd gone directly for the jugular.

Grant walked with his arm still around my shoulders, guiding me across the street toward the spa. "Those kids don't know what they are talking about," he muttered when he finally dropped his arm.

I cocked my head. "She seemed to know exactly what she was saying to me. I think it's good that she and her friends are concerned about the future of the village and the springs."

He frowned and stopped in front of the spa's main door. "You shouldn't sign that petition."

"Why not?" I challenged.

He frowned, and then his face broke into a smile. "See how easily we fall back into sibling squabbles. It's like you never left Cascade Springs."

I smiled back and relaxed just a little. "I'm glad some things in the village haven't changed."

He laughed. "Nothing in the Springs has changed a bit, but you have. How is it possible that you are even more beautiful than I remember?" A wicked grin slid across his face. "Did my brother swallow his tongue when he saw you?"

My anxiety was back up with his compliment. When we had been kids, Colleen had always suspected that Grant had a crush on me. I always claimed that couldn't be true, and even if it had been, the only reason that Grant would want me was that I was Nathan's girlfriend. The brothers had always been at each other's throats. But that old conversation with my late best friend made me wary. "Hardly." I inched back. "I think he was more preoccupied with the murder."

"Ahh." He nodded. "I'd heard about that. Benedict Raisin was a good guy. I'll miss seeing him around town in his carriage. He seemed to fit the part better than anyone else who worked for the carriage house. It was as if he was born to do the job."

"I'm glad the village's rumor mill is still in business," I said drily.

"You know the villagers of Cascade Springs like to talk, but no, I heard it before the rumormongers started wagging their tongues."

I raised my eyebrows. "From Nathan?"

"I heard about what happened on my police scanner. I recognized the address as Grandma Daisy's," he said, calling her Grandma Daisy just as he had when we were children. Nathan had done that too, but when Grant said it, it didn't bother me in the same way.

"You have a police scanner?" I asked.

"Sure, I do. I can't say much of anything exciting happens around here on it, except for this morning . . . " He trailed off.

I swallowed. "I know. I was the one who found Benedict." The image of Grandma Daisy's ladybug scarf flashed across my mind again. "It was my first shock of the day." First of many, I mentally added.

"Nate showing up being the second, I bet."

I nodded.

"If it's any consolation, the officers on the scene weren't happy he showed up either, from what I heard on the radio. John Wheaton sure had something to say about it."

"Officer Wheaton?" I asked. "He was the first officer at the scene this morning."

"I'm not surprised," Grant said. "He's probably been waiting for a case like this to hit Cascade Springs to avoid dying of boredom. From what I heard, he moved here from Cleveland. He was on the PD there."

"What brought him to Cascade Springs?"

"No idea, but it is a far cry from the big city."

"I think he believes my grandmother had something to do with Benedict's death."

"That's ridiculous. Grandma Daisy wouldn't hurt anyone." He paused as if considering what to say next. "I wouldn't tangle with him, Violet. The guy is bad news. If he thinks Grandma Daisy is somehow involved, he won't give up his theory easily. The guy is like a dog with a bone."

"What do you mean?"

He frowned. "Let's just say I've seen him in action."

I bit the inside of my lip. "Did you know Benedict? I mean other than seeing him ride around in his carriage?"

He shook his head. "Can't say I knew him better than anyone else. Sometimes he'd park his carriage outside the water company. It's a good place to pick up tourists for a ride, and we would let him. The carriage drivers in their red coats and top hats add to the charm of the village."

"Are there very many of them—carriage drivers, I mean?"

He was thoughtful. "About half a dozen, I think." He

pointed west along the river. "The carriage house is right down the river just beyond where the Riverwalk ends."

I looked down the Riverwalk. The direction Grant pointed was toward the last bridge. It was too far away to see, but I knew it was there and so were the memories of Colleen. "I'm kind of surprised you're working for the water company. I thought you would be in the family wine business by now."

He gave me a sideways grin. "Yes, I drank the Kool-Aid and work for the big bad uncle in the village, or at least that's what Jade and her pals would have you think."

I chuckled in spite of myself. "Does your family still own the winery?"

A strange look flashed across his face. "Yes. Rather than divide the business between Nate and me, my father thought it would be best for the family to put my brother in charge. Working for Nathan is not appealing."

My brow furrowed. "He's the mayor and running the winery?"

"Yep. Nathan can do it all," he said bitterly. After a half second his smile reappeared, but this time it seemed forced. "I should get back to work. It was good to see you, Vi. Stop by the water company while you're here. I'd love to take you over to the factory for a tour. Maybe that will prove to you that we aren't the big bad corporation that Jade claims we are."

He crossed the street, heading in the direction of the water company building. As I watched him go, a couple who were clearly tourists, given their matching board shorts and T-shirts, walked by me.

The man took a sip from a bottle of Cascade Springs

water. He handed the bottle to his wife. "I don't know what all the fuss is about," the man said. "It tastes like regular old tap water to me."

"George," his wife hissed. "You shouldn't say that so loud. You might offend someone."

"It's true," he argued, and the pair made their way bickering down the street.

I turned and continued along the Riverwalk. Jade and her friends glared at me accusatorially. Apparently conversing with the enemy made me one to them. The sooner I got out of the village, the better. The problem was, I couldn't leave until this mess with Benedict's murder was cleaned up. And I was beginning to wonder if that was something I would have to do myself, especially if what Grant said about Officer Wheaton was true. And I'd have to do it without any special books to help me.

# TEN

I crossed the street away from Jade and her judgmental pals. I knew I should head back to Charming Books and check on Grandma Daisy. But my empty stomach had other ideas. I realized I hadn't eaten a single bite all day. No wonder I was starving.

I slipped my tote bag over my shoulder and walked down the sidewalk past the town hall. I might have sped up a little when I walked by the building just in case Nathan was there. One door down from the hall there was a French café called La Crepe Jolie. When I had been a child, a post office had occupied that building. Trying someplace new and unfamiliar for lunch sounded good to me.

A bell on the door jangled when I stepped inside. Even after the lunch rush, the café was full. Ladies lunched, and young families looked out over River Road and the river on the other side of the street.

I wondered if I could place a to-go order and take my food to the Riverwalk. I might even check out the natural springs. Maybe being closer to the springs would help me understand Grandma Daisy's startling announcement better.

"Violet Waverly! What on earth are you doing back in the village? Why, it's been forever." A high-pitched voice broke through the rumble of table conversation.

I spun around and found a short, round woman bearing down at me. "Lacey?"

"Of course it's me." She grinned. "I might have put on a few pounds, but I'm the same Lacey Perkins—well, Dupont now." She flashed her wedding ring at me. "Married for five years. It's hard to believe it's been that long. I blame the weight gain on my husband. He is too good a chef. And I can't resist his heavy French cooking." She shook her head. "You look exactly the same."

I touched my long hair, which was still the same length as it had been in high school. Maybe it was time for a new, more sophisticated, adult look.

She put her hands on her hips. "It's been a lifetime since you left."

I forced a smile. "Not quite that long. Twelve years. This is your place?" I asked.

She nodded. "It's Adrien's and mine. Oh, let me get him. He'll want to meet you. I have told him so many stories of our growing-up years."

I was left at the hostess stand debating if I should bolt for the anonymity of the closest McDonald's.

A minute later, Lacey reappeared with a Greek god on her arm. The man was built. I could even see his thigh muscles through his black trousers, and his chef jacket looked as if it had been painted onto his chest.

I concentrated on keeping my eyes from bugging out my head.

"This is Adrien," Lacey said proudly, as she should. Adrien was someone to be proud of.

"It is so nice to meet you." Adrien had a thick French-Canadian accent.

"It's nice to meet you too. How did the two of you meet?" I squeaked.

She possessively patted Adrien's rock-solid chest. "We met on a blind date. Adrien had just moved here from Montreal to open the café."

Adrien stared at her adoringly. "I fell in love with her the moment I saw her."

She winked at me. "Isn't he perfect?" If Lacey smiled any more, she was going dislocate her jaw.

"Perfect," I agreed.

She beamed. "Where are my manners? You must have wandered in here because you were hungry. Would you like something to eat? Anything you want is on the house."

"You don't have to do that." I waved away her offer.

"I insist," Adrien said.

I smiled. "In that case, a sandwich to go would be nice and maybe one to take back to Grandma Daisy too."

"A sandwich," Adrien gasped. "Certainly not. A friend of *ma femme* must receive the royal treatment. Lacey, please find Mademoiselle Violet a seat, and I will make her a meal that will bring her to her knees."

Lacey clapped her hands and slipped her arm through mine. "I'm so glad to see you again, Violet." She led me to a small table by the window. "Adrien will make you a meal you will never forget. I know he will make you one of his crepes. They're delicious. Would you like something to drink?"

"Water would be fine," I said.

"Coming right up," she said, and headed back toward the kitchen.

I let out a breath of relief when she left.

She was back all too soon. She placed a water glass and pitcher on the table and took up the seat across from me. "It's so good to see you. I never thought you would come back after everything that happened with Colleen."

I took a big gulp of water.

She placed a hand on her cheek. "I shouldn't have brought her up. It must still be upsetting for you." She folded her hands on the white linen tablecloth. "What brings you to the village?"

"I'm visiting my grandmother."

"I heard about Benedict." Her face fell. "It's so sad. How is she holding up?"

I sighed. "How did you hear?"

She smiled. "A neighbor on your grandmother's street called the post office, and Mrs. Bumble, the postmistress, told General Renaldi, who stopped here for lunch. At least that was the course of how I heard it. I'm sure everyone in the village knows by now except maybe the tourists."

My fingers curled around my water glass. I thought that was the best way to control the shaking. This was too much like what had happened to me after Colleen died. My family had been at the center of village gossip back then. And now I was being hit with the worst kind of déjà vu.

Her face grew concerned. "This must be so upsetting to you. It must remind you of Colleen." She slapped her own cheek. "There I go again talking about sadder times. Adrien says I need to think before I speak sometimes." She chuckled.

"So you knew that Grandma Daisy and Benedict were . . ." I searched for the right word.

"A couple?"

I nodded.

"Oh, yes, they were such an adorable pair. They ate here at least once a week, usually on Saturday nights. Adrien and I always saved them a table if we could. Benedict was mad over Adrien's cooking. He said it reminded him of the best French restaurants in Toronto. I guess before moving to Cascade Springs, he went there often for business."

Again I wondered how much I really knew about my own grandmother. Ever since my mother's death, she had been the most important person to me in the entire world. I thought I knew everything about her, and here she was in Cascade Springs with a mystery boyfriend.

Adrien reappeared with a large folded crepe with cheese oozing out of the open end. Next to it was a serving of fresh fruit and a leafy salad drizzled with a light vinaigrette.

My mouth began to water. "This looks amazing."

Adrien beamed. "I could tell the moment you walked in you needed a savory crepe. I always know when someone needs a delicious crepe."

Lacey nodded. "It's true. Adrien is the king of crepes."

Adrien and Lacey watched me expectantly. "What are you waiting for? Try it," Lacey said.

I cut into the crepe and took a bite. I covered my mouth to unsuccessfully hide a moan.

Adrien clapped his hands. "I knew you would love it." He grinned from ear to ear. "Now, I must fly back to the kitchen. Enjoy!"

"Isn't that the best thing you ever tasted?" Lacey asked.

"It is," I said honestly. "It tastes like the ones that Grandma Daisy and I had in Paris years ago."

She clapped her hands. "People always say that, but I'll tell Adrien anyway. He'll be so tickled to hear the compliment again." She lowered her voice. "As a chef, he likes his ego stroked on a regular basis."

I sipped my water. "You said that my grandmother and Benedict were here a lot. Did he ever come in without her?"

She tapped her cheek with her index finger. "Now that you mention it, he was in here last week without Daisy."

"By himself?" I asked.

"At first, but then the mayor joined him. They ordered coffee and seemed to be having a serious conversation. You know Nathan Morton is the village mayor."

I gripped my fork. I knew there had to be a reason Nathan was at the crime scene that morning, and I was willing to bet all the crepes in Adrien's kitchen it didn't have a thing to do with my grandmother. I forced myself to relax. "I do. I saw him already this morning."

Her mouth made an O shape. "Where did you see him?"

I wasn't sure why, but I didn't want to tell Lacey that Nathan had come to the crime scene. "Ran into him. Cascade Springs is a small village."

She nodded. "It is that."

I finished off the rest of my crepe. "I had better go back to the bookshop and check on Grandma Daisy."

"Oh, yes, she needs your support right now. I'm so glad that you're here to be with her during this difficult time." She jumped out of her seat. "Let me have Adrien fix up a sandwich for Daisy before you go. The last thing on her mind right now will be food, and she has to eat to keep her strength up. You tell her I said that."

I promised that I would, and a few minutes later I walked out of La Crepe Jolie with a grocery bag full of food. Grandma Daisy wouldn't have to worry about what she was going to eat for at least a week.

# ELEVEN

After leaving the café, I saw Jade and her friends were gone, so I crossed River Road again and walked to the edge of the Niagara River. There was a riverside park there with picnic tables overlooking the turbulent water and a playground surrounded by a high iron fence. No one wanted children to fall into the river's swift current. Twelve miles northwest, the water pitched over the precipice of Niagara Falls on its way to Lake Ontario.

Beyond the park was a large forest green barn with golden barn doors and trim. Carriages with and without horses waited. "Cascade Springs Livery, est. 1850," was printed in calligraphy on the side of the building. Run by the Cascade Carriage Company, the livery was one of the longest-running businesses in the village. In the mid-eighteen hundreds when tourists started coming to Niagara

Falls in masses and exploring the surrounding area, the livery opened for business and had been in operation ever since.  •

I stared at the barn. This was Benedict's employer. Everyone who worked there, from the stable hands to the drivers, would have known him. They might also know who may have wanted him dead. With Grandma Daisy's food growing colder by the second, I walked to the carriage house.

The main barn door was wide open. The inside smelled like a heady mixture of hay, dirt, and leather.

A boy about Jade's age stood on a stool in the middle of the barn combing the braid out of one of the horses' manes. A chocolate brown Lab lay at his feet. The dog jumped up and came over to sniff my hand. Her tail wagged back and forth.

I scratched the dog between the ears. "Aren't you a pretty girl?" I said.

The teen stopped midbrush. "That's Java."

I looked up from the dog. "Named for her coffee-colored fur, I take it."

He jumped off the stool. "Everyone thinks that, but she's actually named after the computer language."

"Interesting," I said. "Do you like computer programming?"

"It's okay." He shrugged in a bored-teenager sort of way. "If you're looking for carriage driver reservations, those can be made with any driver outside. They would be happy to take you." He pointed with his horse brush to the door I had just come through.

I took a step farther into the barn. "I don't need a

reservation. I'd like to talk to someone who knew Benedict Raisin. He was a driver for your company, right?"

The boy flinched. "Benedict's not here."

"I know that." I bit my lip. Perhaps the boy didn't know what had happened to Benedict that morning.

"He died this morning," the boy said, squelching that fear.

"I know that too. Can I speak with someone about him? He and my grandmother were very close." An idea struck me. "My grandmother was wondering if the livery wanted to be involved in his funeral arrangements, since it was such a large part of his life."

The boy cocked his head and eyed me. "Who's your grandma?"

"Daisy Waverly. I'm Violet."

He picked up the stool and carried it to the horse's back end and began unbraiding its tail. The horse flicked her ears, but other than that, she remained perfectly still and let the teen do his job. "Daisy was good to Benedict. I've known him since I was a kid, and I have never seen him as happy as he's been with Daisy." The boy began to brush the tail. "You probably want to talk to my sister, Carly, about any arrangements. She runs this place."

"I sure do, and don't you forget it, little bro," a voice said from behind me.

I turned to find a tiny woman just shy of five feet tall wearing jeans, a blue work shirt, and cowboy boots. Her hair was styled with an asymmetrical cut that would make me look like I'd gone three rounds with hedge clippers, but it worked on the tiny woman. It gave her a pixielike quality that went with her small size.

"I couldn't help overhearing you talk to my brother, Trey, about Benedict. You're working on funeral arrangements?" She raised her brows.

I cleared my throat. "Nothing is for sure yet, but there will have to be a funeral, of course. I'm asking on the behalf of my grandmother, Daisy Waverly."

She relaxed. "Daisy is the dearest lady, and she made Benedict very happy. I'm not the least bit surprised that she's already thinking about his funeral. That's so like her." Tears sprang to her eyes. She wiped them away. "I'm sorry. It's been such a shock. The police were here earlier asking us all sorts of questions." She stepped forward and extended her hand. "I'm Carly Long. I'm the owner of the livery, and I was Benedict's boss. He was the best carriage driver I had. Always reported to work early and had more guests ride in his carriage than the rest of my crew combined."

"He was my grandmother's friend, but I only met him yesterday. He seemed like a very charming man. I'm sure that helped him with garnering rides."

She smiled. "It did. Why don't we talk in my office?"

Trey watched us over the back of the horse as I followed his sister through the barn. At the opposite end of the huge building, there was a room enclosed from the rest of the barn. A large window from the barn floor looked inside. I supposed that was so Carly could see everything that was happening while working in her office. Through the glass, I saw an enormous oak desk, and antique riding paraphernalia, including a saddle and some reins, hung from hooks on the walls.

She unlocked the office door and motioned for me to sit in one of the two paddle-back oak chairs in front of her desk.

She settled into the huge black captain's desk chair on the other side of the desk. The enormous chair seemed to swallow her. She leaned forward and placed her elbows on the desk. "What does Daisy have in mind for the funeral?"

"Oh, well, she's still very up in the air about it." That was an understatement, since she didn't even know she was organizing it. "But she wanted me to come by and find out if the livery wants to be involved."

She leaned back in the huge chair. "Of course, we do."

"Wonderful. I'll have her contact you about the details," I said. "Has Benedict worked for you very long?"

She frowned at my change of topic.

"I thought we might commemorate his years of service as a driver somehow during the funeral, since it was so important to him."

Her face cleared. "He's worked here over a decade. Before that, he was a driver in Niagara Falls, which is far busier. That's how Benedict learned how to hustle." She sighed. "My other drivers never caught on to that. He will be sorely missed by me if not the other drivers."

"Did he get along with the other drivers?"

She folded her hands on top of the desk. "Everyone loved Benedict. I can't think of anyone in the livery who didn't like him." She frowned. "But I suppose some of my other drivers were frustrated from time to time by how many guests he drove. They all work on commission. The more rides they give, the more money they make. Benedict was the best at his job. With a competitive job like this, there is a little bit of jealousy or sibling rivalry to be expected."

*Could one of Benedict's fellow drivers have taken his jealousy too far?*

Someone knocked on the office door.

Carly stood, and I did at the same.

A man in his midforties stood at the doorway. He was wearing the same riding uniform that I had seen Benedict wear the day before, but on this man, there was something a little bit off about it. The jacket was a tad too big and didn't sit right on his shoulders. Benedict's riding boots had been polished to a high sheen. This man's boots were scuffed and covered in dust. His dark brown goatee could have used a trim too.

Carly looked up. "What do you need, Shane?"

"A word," the man said.

I stood and moved toward the door. "I'm sorry to take up so much of your time. Thanks for chatting with me."

"Let me know what the funeral plans are," Carly said.

"I will," I promised, noting that I really needed to tell my grandmother that she might be planning a funeral.

Shane stepped out of the doorway just enough for me to squeeze by.

"Will you be in Cascade Springs long?" Carly asked when I was on the other side of the door and resisting wiping away any cooties I might have collected from brushing up against Shane.

I hesitated. "I—I don't know."

"If you are, maybe the two of us can meet for lunch. I spend my time with men all day. It would be nice to have some female conversation for a change." She smiled.

"I would like that," I said honestly. I told her good-bye and nodded to Shane.

He glared in return before turning to Carly. "I heard

the old man is dead. It's time we spoke about my position in the livery."

I gave a sharp intake of breath. He was talking about Benedict. I knew it.

Before I could say anything, he closed the door in my face, effectively excluding me from the conversation.

If I had come to the carriage house to find a suspect for Benedict's murder, it looked like I'd just found him.

# TWELVE

I returned to Charming Books with my grandma Daisy's lunch. The front room was empty except for Faulkner. The large crow fluffed his wings when I closed the door behind me, and squawked, "Where have you been?"

"I'm never going to get used to you talking," I said, but I supposed Faulkner's ability to mimic words wasn't the weirdest thing about Charming Books, not by a long shot.

"Settle down," Faulkner crowed.

I rolled my eyes at him. "Grandma!" I called. There was no answer.

A leather-bound book lay open and facedown in the middle of the floor in front of the birch tree. Emerson sat next to it and meowed. I hurried over to pick it up, afraid the expensive binding would be damaged. When I flipped it over, I found it was open to Emily Dickinson's carriage poem. The same poem that had fallen open at Benedict's feet the day before he died. I shivered.

My academic focus wasn't poetry, but Dickinson was a contemporary of Emerson, and I had read "The Carriage" countless times. I could quote the first stanza on command. The poem broke into five stanzas and was a contemplation of death. I couldn't stop myself from reading the words describing the grave.

> *We paused before a house that seemed*
> *A swelling of the ground;*
> *The roof was scarcely visible,*
> *The cornice but a mound.*

"That's cheerful," I muttered.

"Cheerful," Faulkner repeated, startling me.

I dropped the book back on the rug. It fell open to the same page.

"Butterfingers," Faulkner cawed, and Emerson meowed and pawed at the page.

"It's a coincidence," I told the crow and the cat. "That's all it is. Maybe a customer took this off the rare-books shelf and dropped it when he had to leave, or he left it on a table and Faulkner knocked it off." I gave the crow a beady look. That seemed the most likely scenario.

"Butterfingers," Faulkner repeated from his tree. Sunlight shone through the huge skylight above the tree and made his black feathers shimmer.

I carried the book back to the corner of the shop where the expensive leather-bound books were kept. Emerson was close at my heels. Immediately, I saw the space where the book belonged. I slid the book into the place, but every time I put it on the shelf, it popped back again into my hand. I removed it from the shelf and slid my hand into the place. My fingers searched for something the binding may have caught on. There was nothing there, just empty space.

I tried again to place the book in the spot, and again, it stopped.

Emerson, sitting at my feet, hissed at the bookshelf. I knew I liked that cat for a reason.

The front door of the bookshop opened.

"Daisy!" I recognized Sadie's voice.

"This is ridiculous," I said, trying to ignore the fact that I'd had to resort to talking to myself on more than one occasion since I had returned to the village. I'd worry about that later. Now I just wanted the blasted book to sit on the shelf where it belonged. I gave the book another shove, cursing it under my breath. I pushed as hard as I could. The book slid into the spot. I grinned. "Gotcha," I said under my breath.

The next thing I knew, the book came flying off the shelf and hit me in the chest. The impact sent me tumbling heels over head over the back of the couch behind me.

"Violet!" Sadie ran over to me.

I blinked from my spot on the couch. My back was on the seat, and my legs extended straight up in the air.

Sadie stared at me. "Are you okay? What happened?"

"I must have tripped while shelving a book." It was a lame excuse, but the best I could come up with. I couldn't tell her the truth, which was the book *pushed* me. *I must be losing my mind. Books can't push people. They're inanimate objects.*

Sadie gave me her hand and helped me up. "I didn't know book shelving was a full-contact sport."

I forced a laugh. If only it weren't.

She picked up the book of poetry that had flown at me like a missile, walked it over to the shelf, and slipped it into the empty space like it was the easiest thing to do in the world.

"Where's Daisy?" she asked, looking around. "I've been trying to find a spare minute to come over ever since I heard the news about Benedict, but I had one customer after another in my own shop." A tear rolled down her pink cheek, leaving a trail of black mascara behind it. "It's too terrible for words. Benedict was the sweetest man you would ever meet. I know it must be breaking Daisy's heart."

Emerson walked over to her and put his right forepaw on her saddle shoe.

She ran a finger under her eye, smearing her mascara even more in the process. "Isn't this his cat?"

"Grandma Daisy sent me to rescue him from Benedict's house earlier today."

She scooped the cat up and rubbed the top of his head under her chin. "Isn't that just like Daisy to take in a sweet animal like this when she's the one in the most pain?"

The cat gave me a look that said "Don't even think about trying this."

"It is," I agreed.

"It breaks my heart. Oh, is that lunch from La Crepe Jolie?" She pointed at the food bag on the side table. I had dropped it there when I picked up the book. "I'm starving.

I didn't have a chance for a lunch break today. One of the problems about being in business for yourself."

"Knock yourself out," I said. "Adrien sent home enough food for the entire village."

She lifted up the bag and underneath it was a book, a book that hadn't been there when I arrived. It was another volume of Dickinson's poetry. It was a slim paperback. The title was *Best of Emily Dickinson: Pocket Volume*.

Sweat beaded on my forehead, and I surreptitiously placed a hand to my head to see if I was running a fever. My forehead was cool to the touch. I didn't find that to be comforting. I was losing it. I was officially losing it. I always thought there was a chance I might crack under the pressure of defending my dissertation. Now it looked like I would fall apart even before I finished writing it.

I knew without a doubt that book hadn't been on the table when I'd come into the shop. At least I thought I knew that. Could I swear to it? I wasn't sure. Maybe it had been there. I had been distracted by the leather-bound book on the floor and Emerson's and Faulkner's running commentary. Maybe the paperback had been on the table.

Sadie stared at me with a piece of croissant hanging from her mouth. "Are you all right? You look like you might be sick."

I shook the litany of confused thoughts from my head. "I'm fine. Let me go find my grandmother for you." I picked up the book and slid the small volume into the back pocket of my jeans before walking through the shop, past the birch tree, and toward the kitchen.

In the kitchen, the tea Grandma Daisy and I had shared earlier sat in the middle of the island. Just on the other side of the back stairs, the door to the back garden was open. Grandma Daisy sat on a white iron bench underneath a weeping cherry tree. Silent tears slid down her face. I hated to disturb her.

Beyond her, a white picket fence surrounded the garden, and beyond the fence was the village park where the natural springs were. I wished now that I had taken the clipboard back from Grant and signed Jade's petition. I agreed with the college student. The springs belonged to everyone in the village, not some corporation. The village and the people who loved them could protect them better than any company ever could.

However, worries about the natural springs weren't as important to me as my grandmother, and she was hurting.

"Grandma?" I asked as I entered the garden.

She wiped at her face with the back of her hand.

"Sadie is here," I said quietly. "She came to check on you."

She took a deep breath and stood, patting her own cheeks and straightening her shoulders before walking toward the house. "She is such a dear girl. I knew she would come to see how I am."

"Have you been out here the whole time that I've been gone?" I asked.

She shook her head. "The police chief just left. He and another officer were here to question me. It was rather lengthy, but I was grateful that he spoke to me here instead of at the station. Chief Rainwater is a good man."

"Was Officer Wheaton with him?"

She wrinkled her nose as if she smelled something bad. "No, and I was grateful for that."

I frowned. Again, my grandmother had been questioned by the police, and hadn't been there. "I should have been here."

She gave me a sad smile. "No, this was a conversation that I needed to have with the police alone." She wouldn't meet my eyes.

Was she keeping something else from me?

"Grandma," I began.

She simply shook her head, and when she met my eyes, tears glistened in hers.

I stepped back. I could ask her later what the police chief had said. "I'm sorry, Grandma. I can't tell you how sorry I am about Benedict. Everyone I've spoken to only has kind things to say about him."

She smiled. "That comes as no surprise to me. He was the kindest of men and a good companion. I will miss him, but the best I can do is preserve his memory. He wouldn't want me to cry." She wrapped me in her warm lavender-scented hug as if I were the one that needed to be comforted, not the other way around. When she pulled away, she said, "I know this business with the books is hard for you. It was hard for me when my mother told me. You will see, and if you don't on your own, the books themselves will help you."

The volume of Dickinson's poetry felt like it was burning a hole into the back of my jeans.

As soon as my grandmother stepped into the shop, Sadie flew across the room and threw her arms around her. "Daisy, I'm so sorry. It's a terrible shock for the entire village."

Grandma Daisy hugged her back and patted her shoulder like she was comforting a small child. "There, there," she said.

Sadie stepped back. At this point her mascara was a complete disaster. She wiped at her cheek and ran a black streak to her right ear. "I texted all the Red Inkers and told them the meeting is off for tonight."

Grandma Daisy plucked a tissue from a box on an end table and handed it to Sadie. "Why would you do that? You can't cancel your meeting."

"But—"

"But nothing," my grandmother cut her off. "Benedict would have wanted life to go on as normal."

Sadie chewed some of the red lipstick off her bottom lip. "If you're sure. David won't be here, of course, because of, well, you know, but everyone else had planned to come."

I frowned. David? Where had I heard that name before? And then I remembered. The police chief I met in Benedict's house. He had said his name was David. It couldn't be the same person, could it?

"Who's David?" I asked.

Sadie wiped at her face with the tissue. It was black with mascara and so was eighty percent of her face. "David Rainwater. He's a member of Red Inkers, one of the original members actually. I think he and Richard started the group."

"You don't mean Chief Rainwater, do you?"

"Sure, I do." She twisted the tissue in her hands. "He writes the most amazing children's books. It's just a matter of time before he lands a dream agent." She lowered her voice. "Don't tell the others, especially Richard, because he would die, but David has the best shot of any of us of making it to the big time."

"Children's books?" I asked. I tried to file that in my

brain with what I knew about the police chief, which admittedly was very little. He was the chief of the village police, had pulled a gun on me, and liked my violet bike helmet. Oh, and Grandma Daisy claimed that he was a good man. That's all I had to go on. So why did I find this kernel of information so shocking and so appealing all at the same time?

"Yep, they're amazing. You should come to the next meeting when he's there and listen to him read. OMG, his voice makes me want to throw myself at his feet." She flashed her sparkling engagement ring. "Not that I would— I'm a taken woman. I'm engaged to an equally hot guy. He said the two of you went to high school together. Grant Morton."

"Congratulations," I squeaked. "I saw Grant in the village this afternoon. He offered me a tour of the water company." I looked down to hide my expression. Now Grant's flirtatious ways made me even more uncomfortable. How could he act like that when he was engaged to Sadie?

Sadie swayed happily. "He is so generous like that."

I glanced over at my grandmother. She only smiled. This information about the police chief would have been helpful. No wonder she was so comfortable with him on the case. He was in her shop at least once or twice a week. I, on the other hand, had a strong suspicion Chief Rainwater was a cop first and a budding author second.

# THIRTEEN

"Sadie," Grandma Daisy said, "can I ask you one favor about tonight's meeting? Can it be moved from seven to eight? I have an errand I want to run at seven right after the shop closes."

"No problem! I'm sure that will be fine with everyone. I'll go text them now." She bounced toward the door. "See you tonight!"

"What's your errand?" I asked after Sadie skipped back across the street to Midcentury Vintage.

"We need to collect water for the tree, and you're coming with me." She picked up the bag of food from the French café. "Adrien sent all my favorites. He's such a dear man." She removed a chocolate croissant from the bag.

I rubbed my temples. "Collect water for the tree?"

She held the croissant under her nose and savored the aroma of baked chocolate goodness. "That's right. I know you are still skeptical about all of this, but you need to at least see what it takes to be the Caretaker."

I rubbed my temples. "I think I might be getting a headache. I don't understand any of this."

She examined me over her baked treat. "Violet, sometimes you have to believe without understanding. That's called faith."

I held out my hand. "I'm going to need one of those croissants if I'm going to do this."

She handed the bag to me with a grin as if she had won the argument. I was afraid she just might have.

As I took a big bite out of one of the chocolate croissants, the shop door swung open with so much force it banged against the wall. "Daisy, love, I have come to comfort you in your time of need." A loud voice filled the bookshop.

Emerson arched his back and hissed.

Grandma Daisy made a strangled sound that was somewhere between a dog's whine and a mouse's squeak. "I'll be in the kitchen."

I grabbed her arm. I still had a mouthful of croissant, but I spoke anyway. "What's going on?"

"I can't face him right now. Tell him I'm not here."

"Who's him?" I chewed rapidly and swallowed the enormous bite.

"Daisy?" the booming voice called again.

I turned my attention back to the door. Grandma Daisy took that as her opportunity to dash into the kitchen.

I saw his cane before I saw the source of the booming voice. A wrinkled hand had a firm grip on the curved knob that made up the top of the cane.

The man was older—at least ten years older—than

Grandma Daisy. He leaned on his cane, but the way that he was able to stand ramrod straight made me believe that the cane was more for show than necessity. His gray bushy eyebrows drooped over his deep-set eyes. "You aren't Daisy."

"I'm her granddaughter, Violet. Who are you?" I asked.

"I'm Charles Hancock." He peered at me. "Granddaughter? In all the time that I have known her, Daisy has never told me that she had a granddaughter."

I frowned at this. According to everyone else I had met in Cascade Springs throughout the day, my grandmother spoke of me all the time.

"Where is Daisy?" he wanted to know.

Remembering my grandmother's instructions, I said, "She's not here right now."

His impressive eyebrows pointed down. "She's at home, then? Should I go to her there?"

"No," I said quickly. The last thing I wanted was this man staking out my grandmother's house waiting for her to return home. "It's not a good day for a visit."

He frowned. "I could wait for her to return."

"Oh no, Grandma Daisy isn't feeling well."

His face softened. "Was it because of what happened to that scoundrel Benedict?"

I stepped back. It was the first time that anyone had presented Benedict in less than a favorable light. "You didn't care for Benedict."

He gripped his cane a little more tightly. "He was a Casanova. He waltzed into town, and from that moment, my sweet Daisy never looked at me again."

"*Your* sweet Daisy?" I asked. "You dated my grandmother?"

In my peripheral vision, I noticed Emerson crouched around the corner of a bookshelf, poised to strike. Charles was his target. I hurried over to the cat and scooped him up in my arms.

Charles sniffed. "No, but she was about to agree to a pleasant evening in the village when that scoundrel stepped into the picture. I knew from the moment I saw him that he was trouble, and he would come to an end such as this."

"What do you mean?" I adjusted Emerson in my arms.

"In my opinion Benedict was never good enough for her. There was something dark about that man, mark my words. Whatever it was, it was the thing that got him killed."

I involuntarily shivered at his statement.

"Daisy deserves a decent man." He paused. "Like me, for example. Now that he's gone, we can be together." His eyes shone, and I wouldn't have said it was in a good way.

"Do you know anything about his death?"

"Me? Why would you think I know anything about it?"

I opened my mouth to answer, but he was faster. "Tell Daisy I was here."

"I'll make sure she knows," I said, fairly certain that my grandmother was listening to our conversation from behind the kitchen door.

He tapped his cane on the floor and turned to leave.

I watched him go. I could be wrong, but Charles Hancock might just have a motive for murder. The question was whether he'd been able to go through with it.

Grandma Daisy peeked around a bookshelf. "Is he gone?"

I put my hands on my hips. "Yes. Do you mind telling me what that was about?"

A large group of tourists came into the shop.

"Oh, look—tourists," Grandma Daisy said brightly. "I should go see if they need anything." She hurried to the front of the store.

I scowled after her.

From that moment until closing at seven, Grandma and I were kept busy with a revolving door of shopping customers, and Grandma Daisy's friends and neighbors dropping in to see how she was. Everyone seemed to know Emerson as Benedict's cat too, and he ate up their pats and condolences with his robust and magnanimous purr that seemed better suited for a feline twice his size.

After I locked the front door behind the last customer, a teenager clutching the latest YA blockbuster to her chest, I turned to Grandma Daisy, who was at the cash register counting the day's receipts. "That was a good business day."

"There's something about tragedy that makes people want to curl into a book and understand the human condition." She closed the cash drawer. "Are you ready to go?"

I sighed. "I was hoping you'd forgotten."

"Not a chance." She stepped around the counter. "Just let me go change."

"Change? Collecting water requires a special outfit?" I asked.

"Wait and see," Grandma Daisy said, and went to the back of the house.

"Wait and see," Faulkner repeated from his perch by the front window. Emerson, who lounged on the side table, and I shared a look. I thought the cat was as bewildered as I was.

While Grandma Daisy prepared for our expedition to the springs, I fell into one of the armchairs across from the fireplace. Emerson climbed onto my lap. When he moved, a hardback book lay in the place where he'd been. Emily Dickinson no less.

"I can't believe this." I rubbed my eyes. The book was open, but for the first time, it wasn't open to the carriage poem.

Against my better judgment, I lifted the book and propped it on the cat's back.

Emerson meowed as if to tell me he wasn't a book rest. I read the passage.

*Remorse is cureless,—the disease*
*Not even God can heal;*
*For't is His institution,—*
*The complement of hell.*

I looked up. "What does that mean?"

Emerson meowed. I interpreted that meow as "Got me."

"Violet! We'd better get going if we want to be back in time for the Red Inkers," Grandma Daisy called from the kitchen.

I threw the book across the sitting area onto the sofa like it had suddenly burst into flame.

I pointed to Emerson and Faulkner in turn. "No telling

anyone that I was talking to myself, not even Grandma Daisy."

"Don't tell," the crow said, and Emerson meowed as if in agreement.

I wove through the bookshelves toward the back of the house and into the kitchen.

Just inside the small kitchen, I pulled up short. Grandma Daisy stood by the back door dressed head to toe in black. She wore black leggings, a long-sleeved black T-shirt, and even a black headband in her silver hair. In her right hand she held an olive green watering can. In her left hand, she held out a black hoodie to me. "Put this on."

"Are we going to hold up a convenience store?" I asked.

"It's our disguise," she said in a muffled tone. "To avoid attention."

It was a little after seven, and this close to the summer solstice the sun didn't disappear until nine at night.

"Walking in broad daylight dressed as jewelry thieves won't raise suspicion?" I gaped at her.

"Hush, you, and put this on." She shook the hoodie at me.

I took the sweatshirt from her hand. Grandma Daisy seemed more like herself now that there was an undercover operation afoot. I hoped that it wouldn't include breaking and entering. It was hard to know, considering our outfits.

"Let's go out the back way," Grandma Daisy said.

Of course, because going out the front when dressed like an international spy would be ridiculous.

I followed Grandma Daisy into the back garden. My family owned at least an acre of the property behind the shop. It seemed that I was about to find out why every owner of Charming Books refused to sell the land behind it, no matter the price.

Beyond the picket fence, there was a line of trees that indicated the beginning of the woods. A well-worn path from the back garden led into the forest. I knew the path well. As a child, I had played in those woods for hours with Colleen. I had other memories from this forest too. It had been the place where Nathan and I would sneak off to be alone.

I caught up with my grandmother, knowing that I had to talk to her about Benedict's funeral. I didn't want the village's gossips to tell her before I got a chance. "Grandma?"

"Hmm?" she mused, looking at me.

"Are you going to tell me about Charles Hancock?"

She walked a little ahead of me and didn't say anything.

I caught up with her in two strides.

"Grandma? Why didn't you want to see him today? Are you afraid of him?"

To my surprise, she stopped in the middle of the path and burst out laughing. "Afraid?" she gasped. "Of Charles Hancock? Hardly. The man is annoying but harmless."

"Then why did you run away from him?"

She sighed. "I didn't want to see him so soon after Benedict's death. As you could probably tell, he didn't much care for Benedict. I'm afraid the feeling was mutual."

"Are you sure he is harmless?" I asked.

"Yes," she said firmly, leaving no room for argument, and increased her pace again.

I sighed and caught up with her a second time. "After eating at La Crepe Jolie, I decided to go for a walk and ended up at Benedict's old carriage house. The owner, Carly Long, was very nice and talked to me about Benedict. She's really broken up over his death."

"She would be. He was her best driver." She frowned. "That sounded callous. I do believe Carly would truly be upset over Benedict's death. He never had a bad word to say about her."

I stepped over a tree root. "I'm glad to hear it. I sort of gave her the impression you would be planning Benedict's funeral."

She raised an eyebrow. "I would be happy to do it if his daughter would let me. I don't know what she has in mind."

"Benedict has a daughter?" My heart constricted because I realized that Benedict did, in fact, have an heir, which meant she was the new owner of Emerson. In one day, I had already grown attached to the little tuxedo cat and didn't like the idea of being forced to let him go.

She nodded, and her silver hair swayed with the movement. "Her name is Audrey, and she's a piece of work. She and Benedict were estranged. She was always asking Benedict for money. They fought about it every time they spoke, which wasn't often because she avoided Benedict at every other occasion."

*So maybe Audrey killed Benedict to get her inheritance.* Another suspect for my list.

She stopped in the middle of the path and faced me. "But why were you talking to Carly about the funeral?"

I twisted my mouth. "I wanted to ask her about Benedict without raising suspicions."

She held her watering can to her chest. "Suspicions about what?"

"That I'm trying to figure out who killed Benedict. It's best that we keep that between us until we know more."

"David would never think I murdered anyone, if that's what you're afraid of." She dropped the watering can to her side. "Even if . . ." She trailed off.

"Even if what?" I asked.

She shook her head. "Even if Johnny Wheaton doesn't agree with him."

I frowned. Why did I think she'd been going to say something else?

"He's a cop," I said. "I know the police accuse innocent people of committing crimes all the time, or do you forget my firsthand experience?" I put my hands on my hips. "I'm not letting what happened to me happen to you."

She pursed her lips. "I suppose it wouldn't hurt to *help* the police with their investigation," she said, warming to the idea. "But I wouldn't try to prod Carly too much for information. She and Benedict had a father-daughter relationship. I'm sure she's heartbroken over his death. Poor child." She started walking again.

"I also met someone else at the livery. Do you know a man named Shane?"

She wrinkled her nose. "Shane Pitman. He'd be a good suspect if you're looking for one. Benedict didn't like him. He said Shane was trouble."

"Trouble how?" I skipped over a stick in the middle of the path to catch up with her.

She shook her head. "He didn't say."

My shoulders drooped, but I made a mental note to learn all I could about Shane Pitman. Maybe Carly could help me; she was his boss, after all. "Something else has been bothering me all day."

"What's that?" she asked.

"I can't figure out how Benedict got your scarf."

She wouldn't look at me. "I gave it to him."

"Why? And when?"

"After you went to sleep, Benedict came over. I didn't wake you because you were so exhausted from the drive." She paused. "A wee bit cranky too."

I threw up my hands. "You lied to me about being sick. I think that's a good reason to be cranky."

She waved that comment away. "Let's not get into that again."

I dropped my hands. "Fine. Tell me about Benedict and the scarf."

"We sat on the front porch drinking wine and talking. It turned chilly, and Benedict said he was cold. I gave him my scarf. Laughingly he wrapped it around his throat and said he was going to keep it as a memento. I let him have it. I have so many others." She frowned. "I don't know if I can wear any of them now. What if he used the scarf to . . . ?" She couldn't complete the thought.

I grabbed her free hand. "Grandma, he couldn't have killed himself with it, if that's what you think. It wouldn't have been possible. Chief Rainwater was very firm on that point."

"Good. Good. I know that he'd been anxious lately."

I perked up. "Anxious about what?"

"I don't know. He said that he didn't want to worry me. I wish that he had. I could have helped him." She shook her head. "I should have made him tell me."

I wished that he had told her too. It might have led to another suspect. At least Shane, the angry carriage driver, and Audrey, the money-grabbing daughter, were a good start.

The sound of water welcomed us as the trees thinned out, and we could see the springs for the first time. The springs were made up of a series of basins carved into the rock face of a steep hill. Rainwater coursed down the hill and mixed with the pure, clean groundwater bubbling up in the basins. Moss and lichen clung to the rock face in any little crevice they could. Dozens of stately birch trees circled the springs like a barrier from the rest of the forest and the park.

"The trees are birch. I never noticed that when I was a kid," I said in a hushed tone. There was something about the springs that made me want to whisper.

Grandma grinned. "I'm glad that you noticed that. I told you birch trees were special." She went to the edge of the closest basin and dipped her watering can into the crystal clear water.

I frowned. "I met some protesters in the village earlier. They said that the water company wants to restrict access to the springs. What will happen if they don't succeed? What if you can't collect water from the springs for the tree?"

"I don't want to think about it. Of course I signed that petition." She looked up at me from where she knelt on the rock. "Our family has been using this water for the birch tree for over two hundred years. Some rule set by the village won't stop me from continuing to take just enough to water the tree. The springs are on village land. The entire village should have access to it." She stood up and held the watering can to her chest like she was comforting a small child.

"Then what's with the secrecy now?" I asked, gesturing to her black outfit.

"It's the job of the Caretaker to keep the secret. Only the family knows of it." She climbed up the rocks. "Let's go home." She headed back up the trail.

I sighed and followed behind.

She stopped suddenly. "Did you hear that?" she hissed.

"Hear what?" I asked, looking around.

A twig snapped behind me, and I spun around to face the springs. Chief David Rainwater knelt by the water's edge, cupping a handful of springwater to his mouth. He was out of uniform and wearing running shorts and a loose T-shirt. I tried not to stare at the muscles of his bare legs as he stood.

"What are you doing back here?" he demanded.

When I spun around to see if Grandma Daisy was still ahead of me, she was gone.

# FOURTEEN

His amber-colored eyes were in tiny slits. "Violet?" he asked. "Are you lost?"

"I—I—" What was I going to say? That I was coming down to the springs to collect water for my mystical tree with my grandmother, who was one of his murder suspects? Not such a good idea.

He shook the springwater from his hands. "Are you all right?"

I straightened my shoulders. I took the same tone I did when trying to keep a drowsy undergraduate in line during an early-morning lecture. "I'm fine, Chief Rainwater. This is a public park. I'm allowed to go for a hike on public property."

He cocked his head. "A black hoodie seems like an odd clothing choice for a hike in the middle of summer."

I lifted my chin. "I get cold easily."

He frowned. The sweat on my forehead from the walk from Charming Books belied my statement.

He ran his hand through his short black hair, and by some miracle, each piece fell perfectly back into place. It was fascinating to watch. His shoulders relaxed. "I'm sorry. You have every right to visit the park. Did you get a drink of water while you were here? It tastes best straight from the source."

"How much longer will the water company allow you to do that?" I asked. "I heard about the deal they're trying to make with the village over rights to the water."

He frowned. "That won't happen if I can help it. The water belongs to the people, but I can't say I'm surprised that it's come to this. Honestly, I'm surprised that it hasn't happened sooner. It's how the village began."

"What do you mean?" My brows creased together.

He shrugged. "The Seneca tribe, my people, once lived all over this region. They used the land, the springs, the animals and plants, but they never thought they owned any of it. Land ownership is a white concept. When white fur traders moved across the country, a trader named James Cascade came upon the springs. There was a Native family bathing in the water. He offered them all his furs and a few pieces of gold for the springs and the land around it." He paused as if to gauge if I was listening. "They didn't have a complete understanding of what they were trading, but they took what that fur trader offered them. And that's how the village we have today began."

"I grew up in Cascade Springs and I've never heard that story before," I said quietly.

The corner of his mouth tilted up into a quarter of a smile. "They don't put that bit on the postcards."

"Maybe they should. At least it would be honest."

He smiled. "You sound like Jade."

I smiled back. "I met her at the Riverwalk today. She asked me to sign her petition."

"I'm not surprised. That girl will be president someday."

After a pause, I asked, "How is the case coming?"

His eyes narrowed again, and any goodwill I'd fostered while listening to his story seemed to have vanished. "It's still early in the investigation."

"I'm glad you see it that way because I think there are some other angles you could investigate."

His amber-colored eyes widened. "Is that so?"

I nodded. "I have it on good authority that Benedict didn't get along with Shane Pitman, a fellow carriage driver at the livery."

"I see," he said.

I took that as encouragement. "And then there's his daughter. I haven't met her yet, but according to my grandmother, she is a nasty piece of work. Grandma Daisy gives everyone the benefit of the doubt, so that is significant." I paused. "Don't forget Charles Hancock. He has a crush on my grandmother." I lowered my voice. "Maybe he strangled Benedict to get him out of the way."

"Anything else?"

"Not yet, but I'll keep digging." I smiled.

He grimaced. "That's what I was afraid you might say. Finding out who killed Benedict Raisin is not your job, Ms. Waverly. It's mine."

"Then let me ask you a question. Is my grandmother a suspect?"

He sighed. "I have to consider her a suspect. She and

Benedict had a romantic relationship. He was found in her driveway, and her scarf was the murder weapon." He ticked each point off on his fingers. With each point, I heard a key in a lock on a jail cell—with my grandmother on the other side of the bars—turn in my head.

"What's her motive?" I challenged him. "She didn't have one, that's what. She would never hurt anyone. My grandmother is one of the kindest people you'll ever meet."

"Murderers' families always believe that their family member could never possibly do anything wrong." His voice turned sad as if he spoke from experience.

"In my case, it's true." I raised my fists.

He raised his hands. "Calm down. You look like you are about to deck me. That's not a good idea. Gym shorts or not, I'm still a police officer."

I lowered my hands. "I wasn't going to hit you," I muttered. "And you're wrong about my grandmother. I'm telling you she doesn't have a motive."

"I think this is a conversation you need to have with Daisy."

I folded my arms. "What do you mean by that?"

He pulled his shirt away from his sweaty body as if to let cool air in. I averted my eyes.

"Have you asked her about a motive?"

A shiver ran down my back, and I looked back at him. He smiled. "I see."

I lifted my chin, and he stepped so close to me I could smell the coffee on his breath and the sweat on his clothes. I tried to ignore how his closeness made my skin tingle. "Violet, do everyone, including your grandmother, a favor and leave the police work to the police."

"Chief Rainwater." I refused to step back. "I will make this investigation my job as long as you consider my grandmother a suspect."

He sighed but didn't seem to be surprised that I stood my ground. I was Daisy Waverly's granddaughter, after all.

"I want you to keep an open mind that there are other suspects out there," I said.

"I always keep an open mind." He stepped back, and I resumed breathing.

I shuffled backward, lengthening the distance between us. "Good to hear. I'm glad we have an understanding. I'll just head back to Charming Books now."

"That's what I suggest you do. Concentrate on the books and leave the police work to my department."

I made no promises.

"I'm sure we'll meet again," he said before jogging down the path in the opposite direction.

After the sound of his footfalls faded, I whispered, "Grandma? Grandma Daisy, are you there?"

No response.

I groaned. She'd convinced me to go on her springwater-gathering expedition and then abandoned me when we were about to be caught. At least Chief Rainwater bought my story about the hike. It was much better than the truth, which he would never believe.

After my face-off with the police chief, I was boiling hot. I told myself that it was the high humidity in the thick woods that made me feel that way, not the handsome man on a jog. I removed the black hoodie, crushing it into a ball in my hand, and hurried back to Charming Books alone.

Before I reached the main path, I heard another twig snap. Could it possibly be the chief again?

A man's voice said, "Told you something like this would happen."

Was the chief talking to someone down the path? Strange, since he had gone in the opposite direction from where the voices came.

"Be quiet. Benedict's death has nothing to do with the project," a second, angrier voice said just on the other side of the trees.

I dove off the trail into the bushes.

# FIFTEEN

"All you care about is your precious idea," the nasal-sounding first man said. "You don't think about how it could destroy us both if it's discovered."

The men were on the other side of the trees. I couldn't see them from where I hid, and if I moved in order to see them, I risked showing myself. So I hunkered down and listened as hard as I could.

"I wish you would listen to reason," the second, lower voice said.

The other man snorted. "Reason? When was the last time you listened to reason?"

"Don't push me." The threat was so heavy in the air that I felt like I could reach out and touch it.

The nasal voice said something too low for me to hear, and then more loudly he added, "Benedict's dead. That's a problem."

"Benedict's not a problem any longer. Whoever killed him did us a favor."

"Not if Rainwater starts poking his nose in our business. You know where he stands on the issue, and he would do anything to stop it."

"Don't worry about it. I have everything under control." The second voice added something else that I couldn't make out. If I was a little bit closer, I would be able to hear every word, maybe even see their faces.

I stepped forward directly onto a twig and it snapped, sounding like a gunshot going off in the quiet forest.

"What was that?" the second voice asked. "Someone is here."

"No one is here," the other man said. "It was probably a squirrel."

"It must be a really fat squirrel," the second voice said.

I scowled in their direction. No one liked to be called a fat squirrel.

"It's nothing. Let's go." Their voices moved away, and after a beat, I climbed out of the bushes. Part of me wanted to chase after them, but Grandma Daisy would be back at Charming Books by now, wondering what had become of me.

I removed a twig from my wavy hair and threw it onto the path. What were those men talking about? It had to be something illegal if they worried about Rainwater finding out.

Should I call the police and tell them to come out to the woods and look for the men? These men might know something about Benedict's death. They might even be the killers. I yanked my phone from the back pocket of my jeans and stared at it. By the time the police reached me, the two men would be long gone. They could even be gone now. I slipped the phone back into my pocket.

With one more glance over my shoulder, I headed down the path toward Charming Books.

Grandma Daisy, out of her black SWAT-wear and back into her normal jeans and T-shirt, was in her garden tapping her foot. "What took you so long? We need to water the tree before the Red Inkers arrive."

I frowned. "You're the one who left me!"

She opened the gate for me. "I wouldn't want David asking any uncomfortable questions about my watering can full of springwater, would I?" She looked me up and down. "What happened to you? You have leaves in your hair. Did you take a tumble on the way back to the house?"

"Let's see. What happened to me after you bailed on me by the springs? I had a run-in with Chief Rainwater, but you already knew that. He wasn't too happy with my suggestions as to who might have killed Benedict, and then I heard two men I don't know talking about the murder."

She gasped. "About Benedict's murder?"

"Is there another one I should be worried about?"

"We shouldn't talk about this outside." Grandma Daisy latched the gate behind me. "Let's go in and water the tree, and then you can tell me everything that you overheard."

I followed Grandma Daisy through the garden and the back door into the kitchen. The green watering can on the middle of the island was filled to the brim with illicit springwater.

"There's not much to tell," I said. I repeated what I'd

overheard the two men say. "I wish that I had seen their faces. At the very least, we would know who they were and then we could find out how their conversation related to Benedict."

"You should consult the books."

I frowned. "I was thinking I'd do something a little more logical, like asking questions. When I was at the springs, I told Chief Rainwater about Shane and Benedict's daughter."

She sighed. "The books will tell you more, if you will let them."

I started to protest.

"We'll talk more about this later. The writers will be here at any moment." Grandma Daisy picked up the heavy watering can and headed to the main room of the shop.

Even though the sun wouldn't set for at least another hour, long shadows cast over the bookcases, illuminating some titles and leaving others in the dark. I didn't mention this observation to Grandma Daisy. She would say it was some kind of message from the bookshop.

Faulkner flew from the birch tree to his perch in the main shop window as Grandma Daisy moved toward the tree with the watering can in hand. She poured the clear water from the can into the ring of dirt surrounding the tree.

The can was half-empty when I asked, "Aren't you pouring water into the basement?"

"There is no basement on this side of the house. The basement begins under the kitchen."

Now that she mentioned that, I realized she was right. The basement, which was added a few generations ago, was about half the size of the huge Victorian. I had been down there only a handful of times as a child. I had never been one for dark creepy spaces. I'd much rather be outside on a sunny day than in a dark and dank basement. "Is that a good thing? Can't the roots hurt the house's foundation?" I asked.

She gave me a look.

I held up a hand. "Oh, right, I forgot. The water's essence. I guess that protects the foundation."

She sniffed. "The foundation protects the tree, which in turn protects the shop because the tree needs the shop to survive."

"Did one of your books tell you that?" I asked.

She shook the last of the water droplets out onto the dirt around the tree trunk. She didn't reward my sarcastic comment a response. "There," she said.

I waited, looking around the room. A tiny—very tiny—part of me expected something to happen. Maybe I was thinking of the wand scene in the first Harry Potter book. The shop was quiet. The only sound was Emerson's faint purring on the chair in front of the fireplace, and the shuffle of feathers as Faulkner shifted back and forth on his perch. Finally, I said, "That's it?"

She set the watering can on an end table beside the chair where Emerson slept. "That's it."

"But nothing happened." I realized that I sounded disappointed and changed my tone. "I mean I didn't expect anything would happen, but didn't you think something would happen?"

"The water is not instantaneous. You have to wait until its purpose is revealed," she said.

"Well, that's a letdown," I muttered. My gaze turned

to the front door. The copy of Dickinson's poetry that I had tossed on the couch across from Emerson was gone.

I frowned. "Did you pick up that book that was right here?" I pointed at the spot.

"I didn't move anything," she said, sounding extra casual. "What was the title?"

"I forget," I said nonchalantly.

Grandma Daisy smiled. She knew I was lying.

A knock at the front door stopped her from rubbing it in.

# SIXTEEN

Grandma Daisy opened the shop's door, and a tall, gangly man stumbled inside the bookshop. He wore wire-rimmed glasses and had elbow patches on his sport jacket. "Good evening, Daisy. It is so nice of you to allow us to meet here tonight after what has happened. I'm very sorry. Benedict was a kind man."

My grandmother gave him a kind smile in return. "Thank you, Richard. As I've already told Sadie, Benedict would have wanted my life to go on as normal, and that includes hosting your writing group."

He pulled his collar away from his throat. "Even so, his death is a real loss to the community. A real loss."

"Thank you." She turned to me. "I'd like to introduce you to my granddaughter, Violet."

Richard stepped forward and shook my hand vigorously. "It's so nice to finally meet you. Your grandmother talks of little else."

Grandma Daisy beamed. "Violet, Richard is an English professor at the Springside Community College in the village."

"Nice to meet you," I said. "Have you been at Springside long?"

"Fifteen years. We have a great student body and more than half go on to four-year colleges," he said enthusiastically.

"That's wonderful," I said.

He adjusted his glasses. "Daisy tells me you're a PhD candidate at the University of Chicago. Great school. What is your area of study?"

"Transcendentalist literature."

"Fascinating," he said. "My focus is American literature too. Postmodern mostly, but I teach the whole gamut. You have to in an institution of our size."

I found myself smiling. Richard was someone who understood the struggles of academia. Perhaps he would be a good one to bounce ideas off for my dissertation.

The door opened again and three more people stepped inside. Sadie, who had traded her dress and saddle shoes for bell-bottom jeans and a gauzy top, and two other women I didn't know. One was middle-aged, and the other must have been older than my grandmother.

Sadie bounced over to Daisy and examined my grandmother's face. "You've been crying," Sadie announced to the entire room. "I thought that you might have been, so I went over to the spa and picked you up a few things."

She reached into her expansive tote bag and rummaged around. She pulled out a paper clip and handed it to Grandma Daisy, followed by a lipstick, a tape dispenser, a thermometer, and finally a small glass tub of face cream. "Here it is. This is the spa's special recipe." She held her bag open with her other hand. "You can just drop all that other stuff into my bag."

Grandma Daisy did as she was told.

"Now, dab this under your eyes before you go to sleep tonight. It will take care of the puffiness and dark circles in one use," Sadie said. "I use it myself, and I never have dark circles."

The middle-aged woman snorted. "You are also twenty-five, Sadie. You could be out carousing all night and never have dark circles." The comment should have been delivered like a joke, but from the abrasive woman it came out like an insult, as if Sadie should be ashamed of her age.

Sadie frowned.

Grandma Daisy took the glass tub from Sadie's hand. "I promise to use it. Thank you," Grandma Daisy said with a small smile.

Sadie beamed. "It's the water from the springs that makes it work. At least, that's what the salesgirl at the spa claims."

The older woman patted the chair next to her. "Violet, come sit next to me, so I can have a look at you. I can't believe you're an adult!"

"Mrs. Conner." I blinked as I realized she was my first-grade teacher. I had thought that she was ancient when I was six. She had to be pushing one hundred now.

"Don't you think it's time you called me Trudy? So

much time has passed since I had you in my class. I always tell my former students that as soon as you are old enough to vote, you can call me by my given name."

"Okay, Trudy," I said, feeling out the name. "What do you write?"

Her eyes sparkled. "I like the spicy stuff. Sometimes I make the men uncomfortable when it's my turn to read. They can't handle my more"—she paused—"amorous scenes."

My eyes widened. For some reason, the image in my head of Chief David Rainwater listening to Trudy's romantic scenes made me blush.

She patted my knee. "Don't worry, dearie. It's not my turn to read tonight. It's Anastasia's night, since David's busy solving a murder." She lowered her voice. "She writes literary fiction, which means no one understands it. I think Richard pretends to, but David, Sadie, and I are all admittedly lost." She chuckled.

Trudy inclined her head at the fourth member of the group, who had criticized Sadie's face cream. She was a round, middle-aged woman with silky brown hair that stopped just below her shoulders. A plain black headband held the hair behind her ears. She had a huge stack of papers on her lap and sat up straight in her chair like she was pressed up against a wall. Maybe she was nervous about reading her piece. I had a freshman who looked like that once in one of the comp courses I taught, right before he threw up. I scooted closer to Trudy.

"Do you write, Violet?" Anastasia asked as she caught me looking at her.

"Only academically. I can't do what you all do. I'm

always amazed at the ideas that fiction writers come up with," I said.

"Some of us come up with worthwhile ideas that can further society." She touched her headband as if to assure herself that it was still on the top of her head. "Others of us indulge in the drivel that will appeal to the masses."

Next to me, Trudy snorted. "Don't be mad that a publisher won't pick up your work because no one knows what you are talking about."

"It is their loss," Anastasia said. "My goal is to elevate the world of fiction, not to make money."

Trudy shrugged. "My goal is to have fun." She leaned forward. "We'll just see who gets a book deal first."

Anastasia's blue eyes narrowed into navy slits.

Richard took his seat in the circle, breaking the tension between the two women. "Since David's not coming, I think we should begin."

Sadie bounced into the seat next to me. I was starting to realize bouncing was the way she made her way through the world. Her ponytail really added to her kangaroo-inspired form of motion.

I stood. "I should leave you to it."

"No." Trudy grabbed my hand. "You should stay and take David's seat in our group tonight."

"I don't want to intrude." I started to pull my hand away, but my first-grade teacher had it in a viselike grip.

"I suppose that would be all right with me," Richard said. "So long as Anastasia doesn't mind, since she'll be the one reading her latest chapter to us."

Anastasia appraised me. "I don't mind. It will be

interesting to hear what a literature scholar has to say about my work."

I cringed. Critiquing someone's writing, especially someone who wasn't ready to hear it, was one of the most uncomfortable situations in the world.

Grandma Daisy walked over to the circle. "Violet, would you mind if I head home? I'm feeling tired. This day has taken more out of me than I'd thought. Could you lock up the shop for the night after the Red Inkers leave?"

I jumped out of my seat. "I can walk you home and come back to lock up the shop."

"No, no." She shook her head. "Stay and get acquainted with the group."

"But—"

She placed a hand on my shoulder. "Please, dear. I think I need some time alone."

My shoulders drooped. "All right."

She patted my cheek. "Thank you."

After Grandma Daisy left, Sadie leaned forward in her chair. "How is she?"

I looked at the four members of the group. "She's holding up remarkably well, considering. . . ."

"Terrible thing that happened." Trudy clicked her tongue. "Do the police know what happened?"

"Chief Rainwater is on the case," I said.

Trudy nodded. "Good. Good. David could never believe Daisy was behind the murder. He's been a member of the Red Inkers for over five years. He knows Daisy as well as any of us do, and we all love her."

"He has to follow the evidence," Richard said.

Sadie leaned back in her chair and folded her arms. "But he can't suspect Daisy. She's practically a member of our writing group. That—that would be like suspecting family."

Anastasia straightened her stack of papers on her lap. "David has been a police officer for a long time. He's probably seen everything, including good people who are pushed to the brink and commit murder. I hope Daisy doesn't fall into that category, but he must entertain the possibility."

Sadie glared at her. "How can you even say that?"

"Actually, I'm more concerned that Officer Wheaton suspects Grandma Daisy," I said, thinking back to the young officer ushering my grandmother to his police car just that morning—had it really been the same day?

"David is the boss, not Wheaton. Don't worry about him." Trudy patted my hand and asked, "Do they have any other leads?"

I hesitated before answering. Grandma Daisy might trust the people in this group, but I didn't know them at all and I certainly didn't know what their connection might be with my prime suspects, Shane and Audrey. "Chief Rainwater is looking into all the possibilities."

"As he should," Richard said.

"How can we help?" Trudy asked.

I looked at each of their faces again. "Do you want to help?"

"Absolutely," Trudy said, holding up her pen as if it were a sword.

"What about Charles Hancock?" Sadie said. "He has

had a crush on Daisy for years. Maybe he killed his rival out of jealousy."

"He dropped by the shop today," I said. "He wanted to talk to Grandma Daisy, but she wasn't interested."

"See," Sadie said as if I had proved her point.

Anastasia sniffed. "Charles is on the other side of eighty. There is no way that he would have the strength to strangle a healthy man like Benedict."

My head snapped in her direction. "How do you know that Benedict was strangled?"

Her expression was neutral when she turned to me. "Doesn't everyone know that?"

"Anastasia," Trudy said, "you are an ageist. Charles Hancock is perfectly fit for his or any age." Trudy flexed her arm muscles. "I'm almost ninety, and I could do it in a pinch."

"I didn't know how he died either," Sadie said. "It's too horrible for words. Poor Benedict."

Anastasia didn't mention that Grandma Daisy's scarf was the murder weapon, and I had no plans to share that tidbit of information.

Anastasia cleared her throat. "We're not achieving anything here by speculating an octogenarian killed Benedict Raisin. This is a writing group, not a mystery club. I went to all the trouble to print out my chapter when it wasn't even my night to read. I believe I deserve to hear your thoughts."

Trudy rolled her eyes at me but made no further comment.

I cleared my throat to stop the laugh bubbling out. "I appreciate everyone's concern for my grandmother. She's lucky to have a group of friends like you, but Anastasia's right. You all didn't come here tonight to talk about the murder. You're here to share your work. Grandma Daisy would want you to do just that."

An hour later, Richard clapped his hands while Trudy and Anastasia argued over whether Anastasia's main character was likable. They both agreed that he wasn't, but Anastasia argued that that was necessary to tell a good story. Trudy begged to differ.

Trudy pointed her finger at the other woman. "No one wants to read about a cruel lout winning in the end. Where's the happily ever after?"

Richard clapped again before Anastasia could reply. "All right. All right. We can take this up next meeting. Hopefully, David will be able to join us then too. He always has a good comment or two to make."

"He can also break up a fight," Sadie whispered to me.

Richard stood, effectively ending the meeting. "I think we all have a lot to work on before we meet again."

While the other members of the group packed up their things, Richard came over to me. "I'm glad you stayed. You had some great insight on Anastasia's piece."

I gave him a lopsided smile. "Thank you, but I'm not sure she would agree with you on that."

"In any case, I have some revisions planned on my own work because of what you said."

I smiled. "Thanks. It was fun, and nice to think about something other than what happened to Benedict for a short while."

He nodded and cleared his throat. "What I didn't tell you before was that I'm the chair of the English department at Springside, and we're looking for a new adjunct professor of English for the fall semester. I think you should apply."

I blinked at him. "I have another year before I defend my dissertation."

"That doesn't matter to be an adjunct professor. All you need is a master's degree, which you have. The fact that you've almost completed your culminating degree makes you an even stronger candidate." Richard held his notebook and iPad to his chest. "I think you would have a very good chance if you decided to apply. The college is indebted to your grandmother. She lets our students hold meetings here and stocks many of our textbooks. And when we bring authors in for events, she always handles the book sales too. Hiring you would be a great way to repay her."

"I—I'll think about it," I said, even surprising myself with my answer.

"Excellent. Sometimes it's difficult to attract worthy candidates to our little community college. It would be quite a coup for us to have you join the department."

"Thank you," I said honestly. "I'm flattered."

He blushed. "Well, I should be going. There are always papers to grade."

I said good night to the group and locked the door after them. The job at the community college seemed a little too perfect. I gave the birch tree side eyes as if the water's essence was somehow responsible. Maybe it was? The fact that the thought crossed my mind worried me.

## SEVENTEEN

After the Red Inkers left the bookshop, I removed the thin volume of Dickinson's poems from my back pocket. I had been carrying it around ever since I'd spotted it on the table. I frowned at the book.

"Meow!" Emerson looked up at me.

"I think what I need is a good night's sleep," I told the cat. "Tomorrow, I'll be better suited to face murder and mystical messages via dead poets."

He wove in and out of my legs.

I collected my tote bag, and the cat followed me to the front door.

"Do you think that you are coming with me?" I asked.

He meowed, and I took that as a yes.

"Okay." I picked him up. "Ready for another bike ride?" He'd ridden in the bicycle once to the shop. There was no reason to believe that he couldn't do it again. "Night, Faulkner."

"Don't let the bedbugs bite," Faulkner said in return.
*My boring life just got weird.*

I locked the front door to Charming Books behind us.
My mother's bike leaned against the side of the building.
Emerson jumped from my arms into the pink basket. I
laughed and walked the bike out onto the street. It was
almost ten by the time I left the shop, and River Road was
quiet. I headed away from the river in the direction of my
grandmother's house. The neighborhoods in the old section
of the village were a maze of one-way brick streets and
dead-end roads, and I knew every last one of them. The
moon and the streetlamps provided me with more than
enough light to see my way to the house.

I was turning the corner onto Grandma Daisy's street
when I heard a car gun its engine from a cross street.
There was a screech of tires. I glanced over my shoulder
and saw a pair of headlights come straight at me. I turned
the bike sharply and hit the curb. I went over the handlebars just as I heard the car fly by.

I groaned. I was in the middle of the tree lawn. My
right palm stung. I must have scraped it across the sidewalk when I landed. I was lucky that most of me had
landed in the grass. I sat bolt upright when I remembered
the cat. "Emerson!" I cried.

There was a soft meow coming from the bushes in
front of the house where I'd fallen off my bike.

"Emerson," I whispered.

Crouching low to the ground, he crept out from under
one of the bushes.

The porch light of the house turned on. The front door
opened, and a man stepped out. The porch light shone on

his face. I inwardly groaned. It was Chief David Rainwater. Of course it was. Of all the tree lawns to crash into, it would be his.

I scooped up Emerson and stood.

The police chief blinked at me. "Violet? What are you doing out here?"

I gave him a weak smile. "I fell off my bike." I chuckled. "Clumsy."

He pursed his lips as he stepped into the yard. He looked me up and down. "Are you hurt?"

"Nothing but my pride, but that will heal. It has lots of practice healing, trust me."

He scanned the street. "I thought I heard a car gun its engine. That's what made me come to the door."

I stroked Emerson's back more to comfort myself than the cat. "There was a car. I don't think it saw me."

"The car made you fall off the bike." His jaw twitched.

I nodded. "I'm sure it was an accident. What else could it be?"

"You could have been killed." Anger laced his voice.

I knocked on my violet helmet. "I'm fine. I was wearing my trusty helmet. Nothing can get me with this thing on my head."

He didn't share in my laughter. "Can you tell me anything about the car that almost hit you? Did you get a look at it?"

I shook my head. "No. All I saw were the headlights bearing down on me."

His jaw twitched again. Apparently, that was the wrong thing to say to have him drop the issue. "I'm calling this in." He removed a cell phone from his jeans pocket.

I grabbed his hand holding his cell phone to stop him. "Don't, please. I really don't want to make a fuss. I want to go home and check on my grandmother."

We both stared down at my hand on his. Neither of us moved.

"David? Who is it?" a female voice called from inside the house.

I dropped my hand as if I had been burned and closed my eyes for the briefest of seconds. How could I have been so stupid? Of course the police chief was married or had a girlfriend. Guys like him weren't available, at least not to girls like me.

I stumbled backward. "I'm fine. I'll let you get back to your guest."

"Oh, she's—"

I ran back to my bike and lifted it from the ground with my hand that wasn't holding Emerson. "Grandma's house is up the street. I'll be fine." I hopped on the bike and was relieved to find it in working order. Emerson jumped into the basket. "Bye!" I called a little too cheerfully.

"Violet!" the police chief called after me, but I kept going without looking back. I pedaled with the same vigor as Miss Gulch did in *The Wizard of Oz* trying to outrun the tornado.

When Grandma Daisy's house came into view, I gave a sigh of relief.

I told myself the driver of the car was an inconsiderate jerk who had too much to drink at one of the many wineries in the area and had nothing to do with Benedict Raisin's death. I may have told myself that, but I can't say I actually believed it. I don't think Chief Rainwater believed it either.

The house was quiet when I went inside. Grandma Daisy must have already gone to bed, but she had left a light in the living room for me. That was good. She wouldn't see my grass-stained jeans or scraped palms. She had enough to worry about without adding me to her list. I turned off the lamp, and Emerson and I limped off to bed.

The next morning, more than my hand was sore. My entire right side felt like it had been used for batting practice. I took an extra-long hot shower, hoping to work the kinks out of my muscles. When I finally made it downstairs and staggered into the kitchen, Grandma Daisy studied me over her coffee mug.

"What happened to your hand?" Grandma Daisy asked, pointing at the large white bandage on my right hand.

I didn't want to scare my grandmother by telling her the truth: that I was run off the road by some crazy person. She would come to the same conclusion as I had during my restless night that it had something to do with Benedict's death. Instead, I settled on a half-truth. "I fell off my bike."

She set her coffee mug on the counter. "I suppose you're grateful for that helmet I gave you, then. It did its job and kept you safe."

"Oh, I love the helmet," I lied.

She laughed. "I bet. I saw your face when you put it on." She added more milk to her coffee. "I was wondering if you could open the shop for me this morning."

"Sure, but what's up?" I asked.

"I have a meeting with Benedict's lawyer."

"Why?" I asked.

She shook her head. "I have a few questions for him, and I want to know if he's been in contact with Benedict's daughter. I've tried to call her several times. Knowing Audrey, she doesn't want to be bothered with Benedict's funeral arrangements, but I want to be certain before I make any of my own. There is so much to do when someone dies." She stirred her coffee.

Her comment reminded me of a Dickinson poem that I'd had to memorize in high school.

*The bustle in a house*
*The morning after death*
*Is Solemnest of industries*
*Enacted upon earth,—*
*The sweeping up the heart,*
*And putting love away*
*We shall not want to use again*
*Until eternity*

Dickinson was certainly on my mind. I had dreamed about grim reapers making carriage pickups all night.

"Violet, are you all right? You look like you're a million miles away."

I blinked at her. "I'm fine. Do you want me to come with you? To the lawyer's, I mean?" I poured a mug of coffee and doubled up on the sugar. I could tell I was going to need it. Caffeine might no longer have any effect on me, but sugar still worked wonders.

She shook her head. "No, this is something I have to do on my own. Besides, I will feel better about going if I know the shop is taken care of."

Emerson walked into the kitchen and stretched. He didn't look any worse for wear from our encounter with the crazy driver last night.

"I see you brought him home with you. You two are certainly chummy." She smiled. "Are you sure you still want to leave him here when you go back to Chicago?"

As if he understood her question, he walked over to me and lay on my feet.

I tried to suppress a smile but failed miserably. "Oh, I don't know. I kind of like having him around."

Grandma Daisy grinned. "Good. One-third of my master plan is complete."

"What are the other two-thirds?" I asked.

"One-third is for you stay in Cascade Springs and run the shop for me."

"And the last third?"

She smiled. "That one is a surprise."

I knit my eyebrows together, but no matter how many ways I asked her, she never gave up that final third.

After Grandma Daisy left for the attorney's office, Emerson and I headed to Charming Books on my bike.

In the light of day, I checked the bike over for damages. It was fine except for the small scratch in the paint where it had hit the sidewalk the night before. I set Emerson in the basket and scanned the street for cars. "This is one of those situations where it's best to get back on the horse."

The cat meowed as if in agreement.

The ride from my grandmother's house to the bookshop was uneventful, even though I glanced over my shoulder every time I turned a corner.

When I unlocked the door, Faulkner squawked and flew

to the top of the tree. A stack of books was at the foot of the tree. They hadn't been there when I'd left the night before.

Emerson jumped out of my arms.

I put my hands on my hips. "Did you do this?" I asked the crow.

"Innocent!" was his reply.

My shoulders slumped, and I inched toward the pile of books. I could see only the cover of the volume on top. I wasn't the least bit surprised to see Emily Dickinson's portrait staring back at me. How many editions of her poems did Grandma Daisy have in the shop anyway?

"Okay," I said to the room. "I give up. I'll try it your way, but this is just between us. Got it?"

"Hello?" a voice asked.

I jumped, leaving the books where they were, and turned to the open front door.

Lacey stood in the doorway with a tray of beignets. "I hope that it's okay I dropped in on you like this. I know you aren't open yet, but the door was open. Adrien has sent over some beignets. They're some of Daisy's favorites. He thought he would raise her sprits. He would have brought them himself, but we're in the middle of the breakfast rush. It's our busy time. Everyone loves a good French breakfast."

I inhaled the scent of baked-dough and powdered-sugar goodness. "That was so kind. Grandma Daisy had an appointment this morning, but I know she will be excited to see these when she returns."

Her brow furrowed. "Were you talking to someone when I came in?"

I pointed a thumb at my chest. "Who, me?"

She nodded. "I could have sworn you were talking to the tree when I came in."

"The tree?" I yelped, and forced a laugh.

"It's so funny because sometimes when I would pop in on Daisy, she would be talking to the birch tree like that too." She set the tray on the sales counter.

My face grew hot. "I wasn't talking to the tree. I was having a chat with the cat. I guess I'm just one of those people who talks to animals." I chuckled.

Emerson slithered around a bookshelf and meowed. I appreciated his support.

"Oh, he's adorable. I didn't know what would become of Benedict's cat. Isn't that just like Daisy to take in a creature like that?" Lacey laughed. "Silly me for thinking anything else. That would be completely ridiculous if you were talking to a tree, wouldn't it?"

Yes. Yes, it would be. Completely ridiculous.

# EIGHTEEN

After Lacey left to deal with the breakfast rush at La Crepe Jolie, I grabbed one of the beignets and returned to the stack of Emily Dickinson collections at the base of the tree. The book on the top opened right in front of me. Its pages breezed by until they stopped abruptly and the book fell open as if with a sigh.

I nearly choked on my bite of beignet. The front door was closed, and so were all the windows. There was no breeze that would make the book do that. That would teach me to take small bites when dealing with talking books.

I looked down at Emerson, sitting at my feet, and his mouth hung open. At least I wasn't the only one in the shop that found this disturbing.

After I recovered from my near-death experience by pastry, I bent to pick up the book and walked over to the couch. Again, the book was opened to the poem about remorse.

*Remorse is cureless,—the disease*
*Not even God can heal;*
*For't is His institution,—*
*The complement of hell.*

I read the words under my breath aloud. "Cheery," I muttered.

"Cheery," Faulkner repeated from the tree.

Emerson jumped on the couch next to me and placed a paw on the word "remorse."

I scratched his head. "Are you trying to tell me something too? You know this would be way easier if all of you—the tree, the shop, Faulkner, and you—just spoke English. It would save us a whole heap of trouble."

He meowed in reply, and I sighed.

"Remorse" stood out to me on the page and not just because Emerson had put his white paw on it. Whoever had killed Benedict might be sorry. That would make sense, but it didn't tell me anything I didn't already know. There had to be more to it than that or it wouldn't be such an important message for me to receive.

I shook my head. If the springwater's essence could really send messages through the books, it would be helpful if they were a little less cryptic. For example, the name of the murderer would have been great. I didn't think that was asking too much. All it had to do was flip open to the right page in a baby-name book, and I was golden. I sighed again. I set the book aside. "Enough of this for now," I announced to my fur-, feather-, and bark-covered audience. "It's time to open the shop."

I was propping open the front door when a rail-thin woman, wearing heavy makeup and enormous hoop earrings that I could have fit my fist through, stomped up the walk and sailed through the doorway without slowing down. She would have knocked me over if I hadn't jumped out of the way.

"Can I help you?" I asked.

"Where is she? Where is that old crow?" the woman demanded.

On his perch in the tree, Faulkner cawed. "Crow?"

The woman's lip curled in disgust. "You have a crow in here. I should have expected something like this from a crazy lady," she added under her breath.

I set my hands on my hips. "Who are you looking for?"

Her eyelashes hit her cheekbones as she rapidly blinked her eyes. She had better be careful with those lashes. She might put out her own eye with them. "I'm looking for the harlot who runs this place and fleeced my father out of every last penny to his name."

"Excuse me?" I asked in the voice I typically reserved for undergraduates I had caught plagiarizing. I had no tolerance for plagiarism, and it was clear I was going to feel the same about this woman.

"Daisy Waverly. Where is she?" Her earrings shook with every word.

"Daisy Waverly is my grandmother, and she's not here right now. Maybe I can help you instead. Is there a book I can help you find?"

"I don't read," she said as if it were a disgusting hobby.

No wonder I didn't like her.

"This is a bookshop, so we do tend to cater to readers. Can I give you directions to a business more suitable to your tastes?" I asked, lifting my chin.

She pointed at me with a red talon. "What you can do for me is give that murderous grandmother of yours a message. I know she killed my father. She won't get away with it, and if she thinks that she will make off with *my* inheritance, she is sadly mistaken about that too."

"You're Benedict's daughter?" I blinked at her. She could have told me that she was a Martian, and I would have believed her more. I couldn't imagine neat and prim Benedict having such a train wreck for an offspring.

One of her false eyelashes came unglued from her right eye, and flapped back against her eyebrow, reminding me of a spider dangling from its web. It wasn't an image in the woman's favor. "You knew my father? I suppose you did, since your harlot grandmother dated him." She shook her finger at me. "I know her type, women who prey on unsuspecting older men to weasel them out of their money. She's scum as far as I'm concerned."

"I think it's time for you to leave." I stepped toward her.

"You don't know, do you? That your grandmother stole from my father."

"You don't know what you're saying."

"Don't I? I'm Audrey Fussy, and Benedict Raisin was my father, God rest his dishonest soul. I live in Rochester, and I came as soon as I could to settle my father's affairs." She waved her finger back and forth at me. "I had a meeting with my father's attorney last night as soon as I got in. His miserable lawyer informed me that I have no claim to my father's money, neither his life insurance policy nor his estate, none of it."

"Why not?" I heard myself ask, but a tiny warning bell went off in the back of my head.

"Because he left everything to your grandmother." She spat out the words.

"Wait, what?" I placed a hand on my forehead. "Are you sure? There must be some mistake."

"There's no mistake. My father's lawyer cleared that up for me very quickly when he showed me my father's will and the list of beneficiaries for his life insurance policy. There was only one name listed on both: Daisy Waverly." She glared at me through her eyelashes. "I'm his only child and have a right to his money, but no, not since your grandmother set her claws into him. Now he has only one heir and beneficiary, your grandmother. The lawyer said my dear old dad changed everything rather suddenly one month ago, and now he's dead. Your grandmother inherits the spoils. Where is the trollop who fleeced my father out of his money and me out of my rightful inheritance?"

I could feel myself begin to shake as what Audrey told me started to sink in. This was bad, very bad. Rainwater must have known about this when I stumbled upon him at the springs the day before. This was why Grandma Daisy remained a suspect more than anything else. Money was one of the oldest motives for murder in the books. I needed to talk to Grandma Daisy right away. I cleared my throat and spoke as calmly as I could manage. "I have to ask you to leave."

She walked over to the couch and sat, grabbing one of the throw pillows and holding it to her chest like a stubborn toddler. "I'm not going anywhere until I can give that trollop a piece of my mind."

I stomped over to her and glared. "If you call my grandmother one more name, I will forcibly throw you out into the street. Understand?"

"I'd like to see you try." Her loose eyelash flapped.

The front bell jangled, and I looked up.

"Violet, what's going on in here? I could hear yelling from the walk." Grandma Daisy set her tote bag beside Faulkner's perch. "Is everything all right?"

Audrey jumped up from her seat and pointed at my grandmother. "You!"

"Audrey?" Grandma Daisy asked in surprise. "What brings you here?"

"You know exactly what brings me here," Benedict's daughter spat.

Grandma Daisy took a step toward her. "Oh, I do. You dear child." She walked toward the other woman with her arms wide for a hug. "I can't tell you how sorry I am over you losing your father. He was such a kind and good man."

Bad idea.

"Grandma," I started.

Audrey backed away. "Don't touch me with your filthy hands."

Grandma Daisy's arms dropped uselessly to her sides. "What's going on here?"

"You stole from my father," Audrey blurted out.

Grandma Daisy reeled back as if Audrey had physically slapped her across the face. "What?"

Benedict's daughter twisted the corner of the pillow in a stranglehold. I could easily imagine her wrapping a scarf around her father's neck and twisting it tight. "Don't play innocent with me. You got just what you wanted. Did you kill him to have your money sooner—is that it? Or did you kill him because he wanted to change his will back, so that I would get what I deserved?"

"Now, wait just a minute," I said.

Grandma Daisy pulled up short. "What are you talking about?"

Audrey repeated what she had just told me moments ago, using a bit more colorful language this time around.

Emerson stepped between Grandma Daisy and Audrey and arched his back. He was ready to defend my grandmother from Audrey and her wild eyelashes.

She pointed a sharp fingernail at Emerson. "You have my father's cat too! Is there nothing you won't take from me?" She stepped forward. "That cat, just like everything else my father owns, belongs to me. The cat is coming with me."

I stepped in front of her. She was taking Emerson over my dead body. "I can't let you take him. Chief of Police Rainwater let me look after him until things could be sorted out with Benedict's affairs."

"The police had no right to do that. They can't give you my father's cat without asking me." She pushed me to the side and reached for the cat.

Emerson lashed out and scratched her before running into the maze of bookshelves.

Audrey stuck her finger in her mouth. "I'm bleeding. That beast scratched me. I could have rabies."

"It's time for you to go," I said.

She glared at me. "You put that mongrel up to this. Fine, you can have the cat for now, but I will be back to take him." She glared at Grandma Daisy. "You will never see one cent of my father's money, even if it takes everything that I have to stop you."

"Caw! Caw!" Faulkner jumped from his favorite limb in the middle of the tree and dive-bombed Audrey.

Audrey screamed and ran around the couch. "Ahh!" A colorful string of curse words trailed after her. "You'll be hearing from my lawyer." She yanked her cell phone from her oversized purse. "Art!" she yelled into the phone. "You need to drop everything and drive to Cascade Springs immediately!" She flung the door to Charming Books open. "I don't care what you have on your agenda. I need you—"

The rest of the conversation was cut off as the front door slammed behind her. I felt sorry for Art.

# NINETEEN

After Audrey stormed out of the shop, I nodded to Faulkner. If not friends, at least we were allies in the common goal of keeping Audrey Fussy out of Charming Books.

"I think I need to sit down." Grandma Daisy lowered herself onto an armchair, holding its arms tightly as she sat.

Emerson reappeared and jumped on my grandmother's lap. As soon as he was settled to his liking, he began to purr.

I perched on the arm of the couch. "Did you know about Benedict's will and life insurance policy?" I asked.

She shook her head. "No, I knew nothing about it until yesterday."

"Yesterday! And you said nothing about it to me."

Grandma Daisy sighed. "David asked me about it when he questioned me yesterday while you were on your walk. That was the first that I had heard of it."

"Why didn't you tell me?" I asked, failing to keep the hurt out of my voice. Didn't my grandmother trust me with this kind of information?

"I wanted to know why Benedict did it before I told you. I never wanted him to cut his daughter out of his will and put me in her place. Even if the two of them were estranged, I would have never wanted that."

"This is what you talked to his attorney about this morning?"

She nodded miserably. "Yes."

"What did the attorney say? Why did Benedict change his will and life insurance? Because his daughter is so . . ." I trailed off.

She gave me a small smile. "She's a piece of work. Benedict didn't talk about her often, but whenever he did, it was with a pained expression on his face. He and I were"—she paused as if searching for the right word—"good friends for these last few years, and I only met Audrey a few times. Whenever she came to the village, it was to ask her father for money."

"Grandma, it's all right. I'm not a child. You can say that Benedict was your boyfriend. I would never want you to be lonely." I lowered my voice. "You could have told me before too."

She dug her fingers into Emerson's white ruff. "I know. I should have, but after being alone so long, I wasn't sure how to behave. You've been so stressed and busy over your schoolwork, I didn't want to give you something else to worry about. You have dealt with enough in your young life."

I knew she was trying to make me feel better, but

Grandma Daisy's words only made me incredibly sad. She hadn't told me about Benedict because she wanted to protect me, and now I would never really have the chance to know the man my grandmother loved.

"Well, if he didn't like his own daughter and chose to leave the money to you instead, that's not your fault."

Her shoulders drooped. "I don't know the reason. It's likely I will never know. The attorney said Benedict never told him why he changed his will."

I stood up and started to pace. "But we have to be sensible and realize this isn't good for you in the eyes of the police."

"What do you mean?"

"It gives you a motive to murder Benedict." I saw no reason to sugarcoat it.

"But I would never——"

I stopped moving and faced her. "I know you had nothing to do with Benedict's death, but the police would be stupid not to give you a good hard look."

"But David——"

"But David nothing," I interrupted her again. "He's still a cop, and don't forget Officer Wheaton."

Grandma Daisy shook her head. "It gets worse and worse."

"There has to be a reason Benedict changed his will and life insurance policy so suddenly. That's a lot of trouble to go through without a good reason."

"He never said a word about it," my grandmother said.

"Did he believe that he was in danger?" I asked.

She touched her forehead. "I don't think so. He had been preoccupied lately. I told you that before. He said he was worried about someone, but he didn't say who. I didn't press when it was clear he didn't want to talk about it." She paused. "But now that I think about it, the night before he died," she said, "when he came to the house after you had fallen asleep, he was much happier."

"Why?"

"He said the friend he was worried about was going to do the right thing."

"Who?" I stopped midstride.

"He only said he was happy that he was righting a wrong from his past."

"What wrong?"

She shook her head. "I don't know." She scratched Emerson between the ears. "It seems that Benedict and I both kept secrets from each other. He didn't know anything about me being the Caretaker either." She looked up from the cat. "There's a reason why the women in our family tend to end up alone. That's a big secret to keep from the one you love."

I resumed pacing. "Are you trying to convince me to be the Caretaker with talk like that? It's not a great argument."

"I don't need to convince you. You already are the Caretaker. You only need to accept it." She pointed at the stack of books at the foot of the birch tree.

I frowned. "Tell me more about Benedict. What do you know about him before he moved to the village? Carly at the livery mentioned that he was a carriage driver in Niagara Falls prior to his job here. What brought him to the village?"

Grandma Daisy nodded. "Benedict was a good man. He told me he made mistakes in his past, and he came to

Cascade Springs to escape them. He was very clear about that, but he had learned from those mistakes. He changed." She paused. "But I felt like at times he still worried about things he had done. Whatever happened the day before he died made him feel like he had made up for his past, or at least that's what he said. He said, 'I finally righted a wrong.'"

"Then we have to find out what that wrong was," I said.

Dickinson's poem of remorse came to mind. Maybe the remorse wasn't from the person who killed Benedict, but was Benedict's own remorse about his past. I picked up the book from the side table where I had left it and reread the poem.

"You are going to use the books?" she asked.

I kept my eyes on the page. "At this point, I'm willing to try anything."

"I'd be happier about the decision," she said, "under different circumstances."

I looked up from the poem. "This still doesn't mean I'm staying here permanently." Before she could argue with me over that point, I said, "Can you tell me anything you might know about Benedict's past? Do you know the name of his old carriage house?" I asked.

She shook her head.

"But it's in Niagara Falls, right?"

She nodded. "On the American side. I'm sure of that much."

"Then I need to go to Niagara Falls," I said.

How many carriage houses could there be in the Falls area? I had to find the right one.

"I could go with you," she said eagerly.

"No," I said. "You should stay here and mind the shop.

You need to act as normal as possible. We can't raise any suspicions. If you close the shop for a day, the police will start to wonder why, especially when you were open the day Benedict died. I want to check out this lead before the police find out about it."

Grandma Daisy frowned. "Violet, I don't know about this."

I perched on the arm of her chair and gave her a squeeze. "Don't worry, Grandma. I'll be fine."

At the time, I really thought that was true.

# TWENTY

There wasn't a moment to waste, so I said good-bye to my grandmother, Emerson, and even Faulkner as I left Charming Books. Before I left, I stuck the thin volume of Dickinson's poems into my tote bag.

I marched to my car, happy to have a plan about how to help Grandma Daisy. I wasn't sure how I was going to find Benedict's old carriage house when I arrived in Niagara Falls, but I would track it down somehow. Even if I had to visit every last one.

I froze with the door to my car open as an idea struck me. Carly Long from the Cascade Springs Livery might know the name of Benedict's old carriage house. It must be in his personnel file. Would she tell me? She did say for me to look her up so we could get to know each other. It sounded like a better plan than wandering around the crowded Falls on a hot summer day, bumping shoulders with thousands of sweaty tourists.

I slammed my car door closed and decided to ride my bike to the livery. The Riverwalk would be crowded with tourists and cars by now; I would make better time on the bike than I would in my car.

As I rode along the Riverwalk, sunlight sparkled on the surface of the river. A large white tent was being set up on the lawn beside the town hall. I assumed it must be for the bicentennial gala. I had hoped that I would be back in Chicago by the night of the gala, but at present, it wasn't looking good.

It was close to noon when I reached the carriage house, and I hoped that Carly hadn't gone out to lunch. I couldn't waste any time. I needed to drive to Niagara Falls as soon as possible.

Pedestrians waved to me as I rode down the street as they went in and out of the boutiques and shops along River Road. I waved back, and it was hard to believe there was a killer among them. I knew there was.

I turned the bike onto the winding gravel driveway that led to the livery's main barn. Several outbuildings surrounded the green-and-white building. As I put down the kickstand of my bike by the barn door, a carriage clomped down the driveway on its way to the village. The driver scowled and flicked his reins. The messy goatee told me right away that it was Shane, even though I caught only a glimpse of his profile as he went by. If he recognized me from the day before, he gave no sign of it. He was definitely someone I wanted to talk to, but that would have to wait until after my excursion to the Falls.

"Violet?" Carly stood in the doorway of the main barn. She wore tight jeans and a polo shirt that showed off her athletic build. "I didn't expect to see you back here so soon."

I smiled and walked up the ramp into the barn. "I didn't expect to *be* back so soon."

She raised her eyebrows.

I cleared my throat. "I was wondering if you can help me."

Her eyebrows went higher. I thought Carly seemed to be a no-nonsense person, so I decided to be straight with her. "The thing is, the police suspect my grandmother killed Benedict."

She placed a hand over her mouth. "How could they think that? Benedict and Daisy were a beautiful couple and so much in love. She would never hurt him."

My shoulders relaxed. This was the reaction I needed. "I agree, so I need to find who is really behind Benedict's murder, and I thought you might be able to help me."

She became guarded. "I can tell you no one in our carriage house would hurt someone like that. I would never hire someone who was prone to violence."

*Not even Shane?*

"Actually, I was just wondering if you could tell me where Benedict worked before coming to Cascade Springs."

"Why would you need to know that?" She sounded suspicious.

I paused, wondering how much I should tell her. "I think something from his past might be related to his death."

"I suppose I could look in his file," she said slowly,

"and see where he worked before coming here. I'm not sure I have it. Benedict worked here for over ten years, and I wasn't the owner when he started."

"If you could check, that would be great, and would save me from talking to every carriage house in Niagara Falls."

"Wait right here," she said.

As she disappeared into the barn, I waited outside. Through the open door, all but one of the horse stalls were empty. It was the middle of the day during the height of tourist season, so it made sense that all the carriages—except for Benedict's—were on the road.

The smell of horse and barn filled my nostrils, reminding me of lazy summer days from my childhood. The lone horse remaining in the barn was in the third pen on the right side of the barn. He hung his black head over the stall door, drawing my attention to the pristine white star on his forehead. I recognized him immediately as Benedict's horse.

Even though Carly had asked me to stay outside while she looked for Benedict's file, I stepped into the barn. The horse blew air out of his mouth, and I caught a strong whiff of horsey breath.

"I'm glad you're okay." I scratched the star in the middle of his face. "You must miss Benedict."

There was a loud bang, and the next thing I knew, Trey appeared in the horse stall next to Benedict's horse. I placed a hand on my chest. "Where did you come from?"

The teen gasped as if he had run down the Riverwalk at a full sprint. "What are you doing here?" he asked while trying to catch his breath.

"I dropped in to visit your sister." I leaned over the door of Trey's stall. "How did you get in there?"

Trey's dog, Java, lay in the back of the stall and bounced to her feet. Had I missed both Trey and the dog when I walked by the stall? It seemed odd. Trey hadn't said anything to me when I walked by.

"I was here all the time." He sounded breathless. "You didn't notice me. I—I was working on something." He held up a stout crowbar. "Just mending the floorboards." He swallowed. "I'm handy, so I do most of the fixing around this place for my sister. To save money on a professional."

I didn't believe him. "Why do you need a crowbar for the floor? Where are your other tools?"

"Trey?" His sister's voice ended our conversation. "What are you doing?"

The teen's eyes widened. "Fixing the floor." He gave his sister one last furtive look and left the barn with his crowbar. Java bounded after him.

She scowled in her brother's wake. "Sorry about that."

I watched him go. "Is he all right? He seems to be a little jumpy."

She waved my comment away. "Trey has always been high-strung, even as a kid."

"I think—"

"He's fine," she said, cutting me off. "I think I have what you need." She handed me a small piece of paper torn from a memo pad. "Benedict put Falling Waters Livery on his application as his previous place of employment. He was there for nearly twenty years. I couldn't tell you if the company is still in operation or if there is anyone there who might know him. He left there so long ago."

I took the piece of paper from her hand. "This gives me something to start with. I really appreciate it."

"I included the address from his application. Like I said, I don't know if it's still there." She shoved her hands into her jeans pockets and rocked back on the heels of her cowboy boots.

"Thank you," I said, folding the piece of paper and slipping it into my jeans pocket. "You don't know how much help this is to me."

She gave me a half smile. "I hope it is a help. I think everyone in my carriage house would like to know what happened to Benedict. Some of the drivers are anxious about picking up customers just in case the murderer was some crazy person with a vendetta against carriage drivers. One even threatened to quit over it. I know it's a ridiculous notion, but I'm already down my best driver. I can't afford to lose anyone else at the height of tourist season."

"Chief Rainwater doesn't believe it was random, and strangling someone, at least to me, seems like a very personal way to kill someone."

She nodded. "I imagine it would be. Can you let me know what you find out?" She paused. "It might put my guys at ease."

I nodded. It only seemed right to share what I learned from Benedict's old carriage house with Carly, since she had been so helpful. I gave Benedict's horse one more scratch on the head. "Maybe I can visit Benedict's horse then too. I love horses, but don't get much time to spend with them in Chicago."

She brightened. "Sure, come by anytime, and I was serious about what I said yesterday about going out to lunch while you are in town."

"I would like that," I said sincerely.

## TWENTY-ONE

With the address to Benedict's old livery, I pedaled back to Charming Books as fast as my legs would go. Niagara Falls was only twenty minutes away, and I could be talking to someone at Falling Waters Livery within a half hour.

I took the turn off River Road onto the sidewalk in front of Charming Books at a coast. I parked my bike on the side of the shop but didn't go inside. I was eager to hit the road.

"Violet," Grant Morton called from the front steps of Charming Books. "I was dropping in to see you."

I fished the keys to my car out of my tote bag. "You were?"

His face broke into a grin as he skipped down the steps and onto the lawn. "You seemed to be down yesterday on the Riverwalk, and I wanted to make sure you were all right."

I cocked my head. "I'd just found a dead body in my grandmother's driveway."

He nodded. "Good point."

"I appreciate your concern, but I'm fine." I started walking to my Mini Cooper, parked in front of a house turned salon two doors down.

He fell into step beside me. "Where are you off to in such a hurry?"

"I have an errand to run." I removed my phone from my bag and punched the name "Falling Waters Livery" into the browser. Bingo. It came right up and the address matched the one Carly had given me. I was in business.

"You seem to be distracted," Grant said.

I looked up from my phone. "I'm sorry, Grant, but I really have to go. It was nice of you to check on me." I unlocked the Mini with my fob.

"Mind if I tag along? It will give us time to catch up."

I frowned. "I don't think—"

Grant ran around the side and opened the passenger-side door. "I insist."

I frowned. "What about your job?"

He laughed. "I'm a vice-president. I can come and go as I please."

My frown deepened. "Then go hang out with Sadie, *your fiancée*. I'm sure she'd love it if you dropped by her shop."

"That's not a good idea." He waggled his eyebrows. "I distract her too much from her work." He slipped into the passenger seat.

I groaned and climbed into the driver's side. "You seriously want to come along?"

He buckled his seat belt. "Yep."

I rubbed my forehead. "You're as annoying as you were when you were a kid."

"I take that as a compliment. It means I haven't grown up yet."

"Okay, Peter Pan," I groused.

He shifted in his seat and played with the levers that moved it up and down and forward and backward. "Could you have bought a smaller car?"

"It works fine for me and is perfect for living in a big city. I can park it just about anywhere, even on the sidewalk in a pinch."

"I bet." He grinned, settling back into the seat. "So where are we going?"

"Niagara Falls." I started the car.

"Interested in a little sightseeing?" he asked.

"Something like that," I grumbled. I wasn't happy that Grant had invited himself along, but I couldn't think how I could get him out of my car without wasting a huge amount of time or causing a scene in front of Charming Books. Heaven knew, the bookshop didn't need any more negative attention.

"This wouldn't have anything to do with Benedict Raisin's death, now, would it?" he asked.

I pulled away from the curb and said nothing.

"I see. The silent treatment." He snuggled back into his seat and knocked his knees on the dashboard. "That's all right. I can keep us entertained. Do you want to know what Nathan has been up to since you left?"

"Nope," I lied.

He laughed. "Thought so. He's dated all sorts of women but never married, although he was engaged once. He was the one who called it off."

"I don't really care." I gripped the steering wheel a little bit harder.

"Nate has lived up to every expectation my parents set out for him, just like everyone thought he would. He went off to college, earned a degree in political science, and came back to Cascade Springs to take his place on the throne as the leader of the evil empire."

"The evil empire?" I asked.

"The village council," he said with a shrug. "The same difference."

"I would think you would be happy that your brother was the mayor. Doesn't that make it easier for you to achieve your goal and have exclusive rights to the springs for the water company?"

He snorted. "If anything, it makes it harder. Nate scrutinizes everything I say. He doesn't believe this is the best way to protect the water. Personally, I think he's doing it out of spite."

I liked Nathan a little bit better after hearing that. The rumor was the village council was going to let the water company take over because Nathan and Grant were brothers. I was happy to hear the opposite was true.

"I see your smile. You don't agree with my plan?"

"No, I don't."

He frowned.

"In any case, your parents have to be happy with your success." The elder Mortons owned a winery in the country a few miles from the village. They were perfectionists and expected perfection from both of their sons. I'd had countless conversations with them about their unrealistic expectations of Nathan when we were teenagers. It appeared that both Morton boys had lived up to those impossible hopes and dreams set for them by their parents. Nathan was the mayor of Cascade Springs, and Grant was vice-president for the most powerful company in the village.

I realized after we had driven a few miles that Grant had not responded to my comment. I glanced over at him. He held the strap of his seat belt in a vise grip. Apparently, the Morton boys' parents were still a touchy subject.

I turned my eyes back to the road. "I guess I should tell you where we are going."

He visibly relaxed. "About time."

I handed him the scrap of paper Carly had given me.

"A livery? Are you interested in buying a horse?"

"That's not a livery where you buy a horse. It's another carriage house like the one in Cascade Springs."

"O-kay," he said, exaggerating the word. "I'm sure if you'd wanted a carriage ride so badly, Carly would have one of her guys take you on a spin."

I sighed again. "It's the one where Benedict worked before moving to Cascade Springs. I thought I would check it out and see if anyone remembers him."

"He's lived in Cascade Springs for years. What makes you think anything this far back is significant to his death?"

When I didn't answer, he said, "This address is really

close to the park beside the Falls. We should park there and walk. It's the best chance for a parking space. The Falls on a summer afternoon like this, even in the middle of the week, is bedlam."

"Sounds like a plan," I agreed, happy that he didn't question me more about my motivation to visit Benedict's old employer.

As we drove closer to the Falls, the traffic picked up, and all conversation stopped as I concentrated on the road. By some miracle we found a parking place near the park as Grant suggested. The spot was tiny but gave me a chance to show Grant what the Mini he'd mocked could do.

"Okay, the tuna can car is good for something," he admitted.

As soon as I put the car in park, he was out of it and following the masses to the Falls. The sound of the crashing water was deafening. I yelled at him to be heard over the din. "Where are you going?"

He spun on his heels. "To the Falls."

I tapped my foot. "We should go straight to the carriage house."

He shook his head. "You can't come all the way to Niagara Falls and not visit the Falls. It's against the laws of nature."

I folded my arms. "Says who?"

He grinned. "Me and probably the thousand or so other people here today heading in that direction." He started walking with the crowd.

I groaned and jogged to catch up with him.

He didn't say anything when I was at his side, only

smiled as we followed the throng of tourists toward the crashing water.

The metal bars at every view of the Falls were bursting with tourists jostling one another for a position with their cell phones and cameras in hand. Walking down the paved path from the visitor center to the Falls, I heard at least three different languages. Japanese and German tourists snapped countless selfies of themselves and the Falls.

Finally, there was enough space for Grant and me to reach the railing.

Water poured over the American Falls and crashed to the rocks below. I had been there countless times, but the sight of the Niagara dumping tons of water over its side still took my breath away. When I was a child, my mother and I had visited the Falls almost every weekend, and she would tell me all about the history and folklore of the Falls from prehistoric times to the present day. She was a bit of a local-history buff and had been drawn to the history books at Charming Books, while I was always attracted to fiction and literature.

But if what Grandma Daisy said was true and the springwater in Cascade Springs had some kind of mystical properties, why hadn't my mother ever told me the stories about that? It was local folklore and would have been right up her alley.

"You could stare at it all day," Grant said, shaking me from my memories.

I cleared my throat. "You certainly could. I was thinking about the times my mother and I came here."

He nodded.

I wasn't sure why I felt compelled to tell him that. Maybe because he'd known my mother. As time went on, fewer and fewer people in my life had. However, that didn't dispel the nagging question as to why he was standing next to me overlooking the American Falls. The Grant Morton I remembered did everything with an endgame in mind.

~~❧~~

# TWENTY-TWO

~~❧~~

G rant and I made our way away from the Falls and toward the street on the other side of the park, dodging clusters of international tourists as we went. He put his arm around my shoulders and steered me away from the tourists to the other side of the street.

When we made it to the sidewalk, he said, "I'm glad we made it out of there alive."

I wasn't really listening. I was looking at my phone's map app to point me in the right direction of the Falling Waters Livery.

When we had crossed the street, I'd wriggled out from under his arm. He didn't seem to mind. He pointed in front of us. "It should be right up this street here."

Since my phone agreed, I followed him. Near the end of the street, there was a long driveway. A sign sat on a post announcing FALLING WATERS LIVERY. As we were about to walk up the long gravel drive, a horse and carriage driver clomped down it, turned onto the street, and headed straight in the direction that we'd just come from, the tourists.

"This must be the place," I said, relieved. I'd half believed I wouldn't be able to find it.

In the front of the property there was a small office building built to look like an old barn. The actual stables were three times the size of the stables in Cascade Springs and were set farther back. I started toward the office.

Grant grabbed my arm. "The office staff will be no help. They probably have rules in place about not talking about old employees. Everyone is afraid of getting sued nowadays. Let's go to the stables and see if someone back there knew Benedict and is willing to talk to us."

"Good idea," I agreed.

He smiled, and I tried to shrug off my misgivings about him coming along on this trip.

A teenage girl sat on a white resin chair by the barn door, polishing a saddle. "Can I help you?" She had a large wad of gum in her mouth.

I stepped forward. "We're looking for someone who might know our friend Benedict Raisin. He worked here about ten years ago."

"I've only been working here since this summer. I don't know him. Did you try the office?" She chomped on her gum.

"Is there anyone here that might have known him?" Grant asked.

The young girl jerked her thumb at a gray-haired African-American man at the edge of the barn, buttoning up his riding jacket. "Old Les might know him. He's worked here since before I was born. The guy is close to a hundred."

The old man turned our way. "I might be old, but my hearing is just fine."

They shared a laugh, and it made me think that it was a common joke between them.

Grant and I ambled over to the older man.

He concentrated on his buttons. "So you want to know about Benedict Raisin. I haven't heard of or thought of that old coot in half a decade. He doesn't work here anymore, hasn't for ages. Took the easy life in snooty Cascade Springs."

"We're from Cascade Springs," Grant said.

"That makes you snooty Cascade Springs people, then, doesn't it?" He secured the last button.

"Hardly," I said. "I live in Chicago."

He sucked on his front teeth. "Can't say that's much better. Do you have one of the natural wonders of the world in your backyard, like we do here?"

"No," I said.

"Didn't think so." He removed a tiny lint brush from the inside pocket of his driving jacket and began to brush down his sleeves. "How is old Benedict doing?"

"He's dead," Grant said without preamble. "Someone murdered him yesterday."

The old man dropped the lint brush. "Don't that beat all? I always knew Benedict would come to a bad end. My wife, God rest her soul, said I had a gift for knowing what's going to happen to people. I knew when she got the cancer, she wouldn't make it through. Had one of those—what-do-you-call-them"—he tapped his index finger to his temple—"premonitions."

I bent to pick up the lint brush. Before I handed it to him, I dusted off the dirt that clung to it the best that I could. I gave Les the brush. "I'm sorry about your wife."

He took the brush and stuck it back into his inside pocket. "I appreciate it. It was over thirty years ago now that I lost her, but I can't say the missing her gets any easier."

The same was true for me when it came to my mother.

"What can you tell us about Benedict? You said you always thought he would come to a bad end. What do you mean by that?" Grant jumped in, getting us back on track.

Les grabbed his top hat from the front seat of the carriage and punched it lightly on the inside as if to stamp out any creases. "It will cost you a ride. I don't have time to chew the fat for free."

"If we go on a ride with you, you will tell us what you know about Benedict?" Grant asked.

"Sure will." When Les grinned, I saw he was missing some of his teeth, but the teeth he did have were sparkling white.

"How much?" Grant asked.

"A hundred dollars for an hour ride," Les said.

"A hundred. That can't be the going rate," I said.

He shook his head. "Suit yourself. I can always pick me up some nice Norwegian couple. They don't mind paying my price."

"Fine," I said as I opened my purse. "I only have forty."

"Well, I guess the Norwegians it will have to be." He smoothed down the front of his pristine coat.

"Wait!" Grant removed his wallet from the back pocket of his trousers and pulled out a stack of crisp twenties.

"Grant," I said, "you don't have to do that."

"You want information, and I want to go on a carriage ride with you. Everyone wins." He grinned.

"He's a romantic, sweetie," the old man said. "You should keep him around." He accepted the bills, folded them, and tucked them into the inside pocket of his jacket.

I shook my head. "No, it's not like that at all."

Grant and Les shared a laugh.

Scowling, I climbed into the carriage without further comment. Grant slid his hand under my elbow to help me up. I jerked it away, and he chuckled. All I could think of was bouncy Sadie back in Cascade Springs, completely unaware as to where her fiancé was at the moment.

"Giddyup, Maisie!" the man called, and the horse backed out of her place, turning out of the small space as if she did it every day, which I suspect she did.

We clomped down the driveway. Les waved to the teen with the gum as he went by. I leaned forward, grabbing onto the back of the driver's seat. "How long have you known Benedict?"

"Settle down, little miss. At least let me make it to the road before you start your questions."

I fell back in my seat.

Grant patted my knee.

"Knock it off," I whispered.

"He might be more willing to talk if he thinks we are a couple," Grant whispered back.

"That's the most ridiculous—"

The carriage turned onto the main road. Les peeked

over his shoulder. "Before I start, maybe you two love-birds should introduce yourselves."

"We're not—"

Grant cut me off. "I'm Grant, and this is Violet."

"Maybe I can regale you with some history of the Falls."

"I'd really like to hear about Benedict," I said, scooting forward in my seat and away from Grant.

"If that's what you would like," Les said, warming to the subject. "I've been a carriage driver around the old Niagara for close to forty years, and I learn something new about the waters every single day. Thousands of people come here every year from all over the world, but they don't really know it. They can't know it like I do. You have to be here for a while to know what the water is saying."

I felt my body tense. This sounded too much like my grandmother and her books.

"What do you mean?" Grant asked.

"The waters are special. The water in the Niagara region has always been special. The six Iroquois nations have claimed that it has healing powers for hundreds of years. The Native American tribes had many rituals associated with the water to show their respect. They claimed it could choose to heal or kill. Respect is what it wanted."

A chill ran down my back, and I thought about the story Chief Rainwater had told me about his people at the springs back at the village.

"Of course, you two would know all about healing waters if you are from Cascade Springs. That little village has made a fortune off the springs' water. They have been tricking people out of their money for two centuries to visit them."

Beside me, Grant stiffened. It was the first time that I sensed he was uncomfortable since we'd arrived in Niagara Falls. Maybe he didn't like to hear criticism of the village.

"You don't believe the springs in the village have healing properties?" I asked.

"I didn't say that," he said. "I believe like the Native Americans did that you can't force the waters to do anything. They may heal; they may not. It is up to them to choose."

"Sounds a little unreliable," Grant said.

"Magic is unreliable." He shrugged. "That's the only reliable thing about it. If it were reliable, everyone would believe it and know about it."

Magic. There was the word that I had been avoiding the last few days. It rolled off Les's tongue casually, as if he were talking about the weather.

I cleared my throat. "What about Benedict?"

He sighed at my change of subject. "Oh, I suppose that's what you really want to know."

"It is," I said firmly, pushing thoughts of magic and healing waters out of my head.

"Since I've worked here forty-some years, I knew Benedict, of course. He started driving just six or so years after me. He and I got along fine, but I knew he was attracted to trouble."

"Why's that?" I asked.

Les pulled on the reins as an elderly couple jaywalked across the road in front of the horse. The old driver took the near pedestrian-carriage accident in stride. I suspect he dealt with jaywalkers all day long. "He wasn't happy with his station in life. He was always trying to make a quick dollar. Being a carriage driver, you meet all sorts of people. Good people, but unsavory folks too. Benedict didn't mind taking the unsavory folks for a ride. I tried to avoid them if I could. I have enough troubles in my life as it is without tempting fate."

"What kind of unsavory people?" I asked.

"Rich folks that needed a lackey type to do things for them. Benedict was happy to oblige." He shook his head.

My brow wrinkled. "Benedict worked for them?"

"Can you be more specific?" Grant asked.

Les sucked on his teeth. "Don't know the details. After a while, I think Benedict saw the light and wanted to get out from under those folks' thumbs."

"How was he going to do that?"

"I don't know the particulars, but I heard through the grapevine he struck some sort of deal with the FBI. The next day, he was gone. It wasn't until two years later than we learned that he had only gone as far as Cascade Springs. By then, the man he had been working for was in prison."

"Who was the man? Do you have a name?" Grant asked.

Les whispered something.

I inched closer to him. "What?"

He turned and looked at me over his shoulder. "Wolcott. The man's name was Wolcott."

"Who is he? Where can I find him?" I wanted to know.

"You don't want to find him, if you know what's good

for you." The elderly carriage driver spoke so fiercely, I slid back into my seat next to Grant.

"That's all I have to say about him," Les said. "Anything else you will have to find out on your own. Nothing good happens to anyone who speaks of Wolcott in Niagara Falls."

"Would anyone else at the livery know more?" I asked. "Or be willing to talk about this Wolcott person?"

He shook his head. "Don't think so—the business has changed hands twice since Benedict left, and I'm the only one still working at Falling Waters who knew him." He pointed in front of us. "Here's another good view of the American Falls," Les said over his shoulder as if we had been talking about the scenery all the time. "'Course everyone likes the Horseshoe better, but the American Falls are mighty impressive. They only look small in comparison to the ones on the Canadian side. In any other place in the world, they would be a wonder all their own."

I had to agree both of the falls were beautiful, and I would have enjoyed seeing them even more if I weren't so preoccupied with the information Les had told us.

"I'll take you down this way. You get a good view of the Horseshoe Falls on the Canadian side from here." He flicked the reins. "Are you two planning to stay to see the Falls all lit up at night? It is an amazing sight."

"No," I said. "We have to return to Cascade Springs." I was eager to return to the Springs and research who this Wolcott person was. There had to be something about him online if he was so notorious in the area.

"That's a real shame," Les said as if he meant it. "You

make sure you see it before you go home to Chicago or wherever you said you were from."

"I'll try," I said.

Grant smiled. "We can make a date of it."

*I don't think so.*

"I hope you two lovebirds don't care if I drop you off back at the livery. I have to make a pit stop. I drank too much coffee today." He grinned, showing off white teeth again.

"We aren't lovebirds," I said.

At the same time, Grant said, "No problem!"

The carriage clattered down the side street where the livery was.

Grant touched my shoulder. "I wish you'd relax. Everything will work out—you'll see."

"How can I relax?" I asked. "My grandmother is a murder suspect. It's so much like . . ." I didn't finish the thought.

I didn't have to finish it; Grant knew. He had been there during the foolhardy search for Colleen's supposed killer. He'd witnessed his brother turn away from me to save himself.

"We have company," Grant murmured.

I lifted my gaze from my folded hands in my lap and saw Chief David Rainwater staring at me through the windshield of his departmental SUV. Not good.

# TWENTY-THREE

The late-afternoon sunlight reflected off the police chief's blue-black hair as he stepped out of his car. He was out of his running clothes and back in uniform, and I couldn't help noting he looked just as handsome in both.

Rainwater held up his hand to stop the carriage's forward motion.

"Can I help you, Officer?" Les asked.

"I'm not sure," Rainwater said, "but I think your two passengers can." He leveled me with a look. "Violet, I didn't expect to see you again so soon, and in such an unusual place. You certainly have a knack for popping up."

"I'm full of surprises," I said, trying to force the nervousness from my voice.

"We'll end the ride here, Les." Grant stood up and

jumped out of the carriage, and then he gave me his hand to help me out.

I didn't need his help, but I took his hand to avoid embarrassing him. He didn't let go of my palm when I hit the ground. I thought yanking it away would be too obvious with Rainwater watching us so closely.

The police chief's eyes narrowed on our clasped hands as if it told him some new information he didn't care for.

He nodded at Grant. "Grant."

"David," the other man said back with a scowl.

Rainwater didn't take his amber-colored stare off my face. "Mind telling me what you're doing here?"

Grant released my hand. "I was just taking Violet for a tour of the Falls, like old times."

Like old times? Grant and I had never visited the Falls together.

Rainwater's jaw twitched. "I see. And your impromptu trip to the Falls has nothing to do with Benedict Raisin's murder, I presume."

"Not a thing," Grant said.

I stepped away from Grant. "It does have to do with Benedict. Les knew him and knows the reason he left Niagara Falls."

Rainwater studied the older man with interest. "Is that so?"

Les licked his lips. "I never knew the details, just knew that Benedict got tangled up with the wrong crowd, is all. I couldn't tell them much more."

Chief Rainwater flashed his badge. "I'd like to hear your story too, if you don't mind."

Les swallowed. "Sure thing, Officer."

"We'll leave you to it," Grant said, and grabbed my hand, yanking me down the long driveway. But we didn't get out of earshot before I heard Chief Rainwater call after us, "I'll be seeing you, Violet."

Back in the car, I tried to shake off a sense of foreboding. There was something about Rainwater's threat that frightened me. As much as I was relieved to see the police chief was following up on other leads, I knew he wouldn't let my grandmother off the hook until he had someone else in custody. What could I do to change his mind, other than to find the killer myself?

"We can't go home until you start the car," Grant teased.

"Sorry." I turned over the engine and backed out of the space.

Grant was quiet on the ride home. I was grateful for the silence. It gave me time to mull over everything we had learned from Les before I saw Grandma Daisy in Charming Books.

As I pulled into the spot in front of the store, I saw a man on the front porch of the shop in the same spot Grant had been a few hours ago. This time it was his brother. Nathan Morton ran down Charming Books' front steps to meet us on the sidewalk. Apparently, I had no hope of escaping either one of the Morton boys that day.

Nathan glared at Grant as his brother got out of the car. "What are you doing with her?"

Grant held up his hands. "Hey, calm down. Why are you so upset? Vi and I went for a drive."

"Don't call her Vi," he ordered.

Like he was the only person with the right to call me Vi. He'd lost that privilege when he let me take the blame for Colleen's death.

I ignored Nathan. "Thanks for going with me, Grant."

He grinned from ear to ear. "Anytime, *Vi*."

Nathan positively growled. What was it with the men of Cascade Springs? I certainly didn't get this much attention back in Chicago.

Nathan stepped toward his brother.

I slid between them. "I don't know what problem you two have with each other, but leave me out of it."

"Back off, bro," Grant agreed. "I don't know why you're upset over two old friends spending some time together."

"Does Sadie know?" Nathan asked. "I don't know why that poor girl puts up with you."

I glanced across the street to Midcentury Vintage and was happy to see the front door closed. Sadie didn't need to see her fiancé and her future brother-in-law fighting, although I bet she had seen it many times before. These two had been at each other's throats since birth.

"Grant accompanied me on an errand. That was it," I said.

Now it was Grant's turn to scowl.

"Is there something I can help you with, Nate?" I adjusted my tote bag on my shoulder.

He cleared his throat. "I came to see how you were. I felt bad about how we left things yesterday."

He felt bad how we left things yesterday? How about how we left things twelve years ago?

When I didn't say anything, he added, "And I came

here to find that birthday present. The one I'd told your grandmother I planned to get."

"I suppose I should return to the office." Grant curled his lip as if in disgust. "And leave the perfect son to his shopping."

Nathan's shoulders drooped. "Grant . . ."

Grant ignored him. "It's been a pleasure, lovely Violet." Before I could stop him, he kissed me on the cheek. "I'll see you later." He winked.

I resisted the urge to wipe my cheek. I knew Grant only did it to infuriate his brother, but it felt to me like a betrayal of Sadie all the same. From across the sidewalk, I could practically hear Nathan grinding his teeth.

Nathan watched him go. "What are you doing with him?"

I glared at Nathan. "What do you care?"

"He's engaged."

"I know that," I snapped. "And Sadie is a great girl. She doesn't have anything to worry about from me."

"She may not have to worry about you, but there are others she should worry about."

I didn't like the sound of that. I hated what Nathan was implying, that Grant was cheating on bouncy Sadie. I didn't know if the cheerful girl could stand having her heart broken. I had barely survived it, and I was made of sterner stuff. Remembering that time, I scowled at the man who had broken my heart all those years ago.

"He's trouble and no good for you. Stay away from him," Nathan ordered.

"Nathan, what makes you think you can tell me who to see and not see? I haven't spoken to you in twelve years, and you act like no time has passed."

"For me, no time has. Violet . . ."

I headed for the shop. I wasn't going to listen to this.

Nathan caught up with me. "I still need a gift for my mom."

I didn't want Grandma Daisy to miss out on a sale, so I said, "All right. We have the best selection of books anywhere. I'm sure we can find something your mother will love."

He followed me across the front yard and up the steps into Charming Books.

When I strode into the shop, the only indication that Grandma Daisy saw us was the slight tilt of her head as she listened to a middle-aged couple who were in the market for some new mystery novels.

"What about this for Mom?" Nathan held up a copy of *Selected Works of Emily Dickinson*.

"Very funny," I said to the room.

Nathan's brow wrinkled. "I wasn't joking."

My face turned hot as I took the book from his hand. I laughed it off. "I just don't think that is the right fit for your mom. I don't remember her being interested in poetry."

He relaxed. "You're right. I don't know if my mother's ever read a poem."

I walked to the front of the store where our adult genre fiction was shelved. "I remember your mom liked science fiction. Does she still?"

"You remember that?" He sounded so pleased.

"Sure. I remember what people like to read. Occupational hazard, I guess. Like I remember that you used to love spy thrillers and have an entire collection of Spider-Man comic books."

He stared at me.

I swallowed and turned to the shelf, reaching for a popular sci-fi novel I thought his mother would like. "What about this one? I've heard great things about it. It's been on my to-be-read pile for months."

"I thought you said no to that one."

I looked at the book in my hand and found a volume of Dickinson's poems. My face flamed red. "I didn't mean that one." I pulled another book from the shelf. "This—" Again I had a copy of Dickinson's poems in my hand. I hid it behind my back.

"What about this one?" Nathan asked. He reached around me, brushing my arm with his in the process. "I think she'd like this."

I willed my cheeks to stop flaming. "Great!"

He studied me as if he thought he might be missing something but wasn't sure what. He was missing something, all right. He was missing the fact the bookshop was trying to make a fool out of me.

Nathan studied the hardback-covered novel with the spaceship, the novel I had wanted to give him. "I'm not sure if she's read this one yet."

I cleared my throat. "We could always sell you a gift card for her, and she could come in and pick out her own book."

"No." He shook his head. "My mother hates gift cards. She says they are a sign of a lazy shopper." He frowned. "A book itself would be best, and if she has already read it, I can return it and pick out something else for her." He smiled. "It will give me a reason to come back."

"Great!" I squeaked, and shoved Dickinson's poems

onto the science fiction shelf. "Is there anything else I can help you with?"

He opened his mouth, but I pretended that I didn't see it. I headed to the cash register. "Let me ring you up, then, and you can be on your way. I know, as the mayor of Cascade Springs, that you must be very busy, especially with the gala coming up this weekend."

Nathan followed me with the novel. "Are you coming to the gala?"

I stepped behind the counter and scanned the book's bar code. "I don't think so. I hope to be in back in Chicago by then."

"I hope you come if you're still here," he said.

My fingers froze over the cash register's buttons.

"I'd really like you to be there." His voice was low. "You're as much a part of the village bicentennial as anyone else who will be there."

Motor function returned to my fingers and punched in the buttons. The cash register *bing*ed and the drawer flew open. "That will be twenty-five ninety-nine."

Nathan sighed and swiped his credit card through the reader. He signed the screen with the light pen, and I slipped his book into a brown paper sack with the shop's logo on it. "Thanks for coming in today. I hope your mother enjoys the book."

"Vi," he said as he took the sack from my hand. He lowered his voice. "I'm sorry for letting you take the fall twelve years ago. I knew that you didn't do it, so I didn't think there was any harm in it. I didn't think the police would take it so far. My parents—"

I looked him in the eye for the first time. "Nathan, I

don't want to talk about it. I want to leave what happened all those years ago behind."

He squeezed the bag's brown paper, and it crinkled in his hand. "That's fair. I don't know if I could have forgiven you if our positions had been reversed."

He left the shop.

"That's the difference," I whispered when he was gone. "I wouldn't have put you in that position."

I propped my elbows on the counter, and a copy of Dickinson's poems appeared an arm's length from me. I bit my lip. "Fine," I whispered. "You win."

It may have been a trick of the light, but I thought I saw the book's pages flutter.

# TWENTY-FOUR

I tucked the book of Dickinson's poetry under my arm and waved to Grandma Daisy as I took my book up to the fairy children's room at the top of the stairs. Emerson followed me up the steps. I think it was the first time he'd ventured up the open staircase, because he walked low on his haunches with his white belly sliding along the steps.

Apparently, Faulkner wanted to join the party too, because I heard a flap of wings as he settled into the top branches of the birch tree, spinning to face us. Narrow branches and leaves from the birch tree snaked over the railing. Surprisingly, the crow didn't say a word. He only settled his feathers and looked at me expectantly.

The children's loft was as magical as I remembered it. Even though I didn't believe my grandmother's stories about the shop—or so I told myself—there was something magical about that space in Charming Books. My grand-mother had commissioned a local artist from the arts district to paint fairies that peeked out from around book-shelves and corners. She had commissioned a second artist, a carpenter, to make the bookshelves look like tree trunks. Overhead, the ceiling was painted like the summer sky. The effect was whimsical, and I could imagine the many children who came into the shop and were enchanted by this space. It was a wonderful spot to fall in love with reading. It's where it happened to me.

Beyond the children's room was a door that led to the rest of the house. Before Mom and I moved into Grandma Daisy's house when Mom got so ill, we had lived in that part of the bookshop. I tried the doorknob. It was locked. I'd have to ask Grandma Daisy for a key because I'd like to see those rooms again. I heard a sniffle behind me.

I turned to see a girl, who was maybe about eight, sit-ting on one of the low stools in the corner.

"Are you okay?"

She wiped a tear from her cheek and nodded. "There're so many good books here. I don't know which one to choose. Mama said I could have only one."

I hid a smile. I had the same difficulty every time I stepped into a bookshop or a library.

I knelt in front of her. "Have you let the book pick you?"

She squished her eyebrows together. "Pick me?"

"Sure. Walk over to the shelf and close your eyes. Let the book pick you."

She did as she was told and held out her hand. She peeked at me.

I laughed. "Keep them closed."

She gave me one final dubious look before closing her eyes again. She ran her small suntanned hand along the shelf of chapter books. She stopped suddenly and pulled a book from the shelf. Opening her eyes, she held it out to me.

*Anne of Green Gables.*

I glanced over my shoulder at the tree. I should have expected that one. I turned back to the girl. "See, the book picked you."

She grinned and hugged the novel. "It did. I know this is the perfect book in my bones."

I grinned back. "I have a feeling you and I are kindred spirits."

"What does that mean?" She searched my face.

I smiled. "Read the book, and you will find out."

"Lily!" a woman's voice called up the stairs. "Bring down the book you chose. It's time to go."

I peeked over the railing. The couple that my grandmother had been talking to stood under the tree.

Lily hugged her book one more time. "Thank you." She ran down the stairs.

I eyed the books. "Well played."

They remained silent.

After Lily's and her mother's voices faded away, I snuggled into one of the gray beanbag chairs painted to look like boulders. Emerson curled up on my feet, and I turned on my phone's browser. This time I typed in "Niagara Falls" and "Wolcott."

Immediately, I got a long list of news articles about Fletcher Wolcott. I sat up straight in the beanbag chair—which was no easy feat. Wolcott was a smuggler, and a decade ago, he was arrested for smuggling illegal goods into Canada via Niagara Falls' Rainbow Bridge. He was sent to federal prison. According to the article, he'd smuggled everything from fruit to guns.

Was Benedict mixed up in an international smuggling operation? I peered over the railing at my grandmother, talking to customers below. No wonder Benedict didn't want my grandmother to know about his past.

Emerson meowed and pawed at the book of poetry I had brought with me to the children's loft.

"Okay, fine," I said to the tree, and picked up the book.

I touched my head to test if it was hot from a fever. I couldn't believe I was talking to a tree. Animals were one thing. I used to speak to Jane Eyre all the time, but at least she had the ability to meow back.

The volume fell open to a new poem. I took a deep breath and let my eyes fall onto the page.

*Remembrance has a rear and front,—*
  *'T is something like a house;*
*It has a garret also*
  *For refuse and the mouse,*

*Besides, the deepest cellar*
  *That ever mason hewed;*
*Look to it, by its fathoms*
  *Ourselves be not pursued.*

I stared at the first stanza. The previous poem the tree had wanted me to read had been about remorse. This one was about remembrance, or at least that's what the first stanza was about on the surface. Remembrance and remorse were similar. A person could have remembrance without remorse, but he could not have remorse without remembrance.

Was the poem referring to Benedict or the person who killed him or both? I pinched the bridge of my nose. Some Caretaker I was. The bookshop had shown me three short poems, and I was stumped. Grandma Daisy had been completely wrong to think I would be the best Caretaker because of my education. In actuality, the opposite was true. My brain was trained to think critically. How could I apply critical thinking to this situation? If I didn't figure something out, I was doomed to fail.

I dropped the book when I realized for the first time that I thought of myself as the Caretaker. Did that mean I believed in the story Grandma Daisy had told me? I pinched the bridge of my nose harder.

"Remorse and remembrance. Emily Dickinson. Poet, recluse," I murmured. My head hurt and I couldn't think clearly. It was the same woozy feeling I had after a long exam. I was completely wrung out. Every thought in my brain had been used up. Maybe this was why I allowed myself to entertain the idea that Grandma Daisy's story about Rosalee, the tree, and my destiny might actually be real. But it wasn't. It couldn't be real.

I tossed the book to the next beanbag and closed my eyes.

Consulting the book to solve a murder was one of the most ridiculous ideas I had ever had. I had finally gone off the deep end. It was bound to happen. I hadn't cracked under the pressure of being taken into custody for Colleen's death or under the pressure of grad school. Nope, all it took was a story about a magical destiny to make my marbles scatter.

Emerson mewed.

"If we could figure out who murdered him, then life can go back to normal," I said to the cat.

"I couldn't agree more," a disembodied voice said from the stairs.

I screamed and rolled off the beanbag.

# TWENTY-FIVE

Chief Rainwater loomed over me as I flopped on the carpet like a beached flounder. He extended a hand. Grudgingly, I took it, and I shot Faulkner, who was preening his feathers in the birch tree, a deadly glare. Some watch crow he was. He could have warned me. I knew that he could talk when he wanted to.

"'Because I could not stop for Death,'" the crow cawed.

Rainwater's head snapped in the direction of the tree. "He seems chatty."

"When he wants to be." I removed my hand from Rainwater's grasp, trying to ignore the tingly feeling that remained on my fingertips. "For the record, I was talking to the cat."

Emerson swished his tail and jumped onto one of the bookcases in one leap.

"Okay." He flashed white teeth, which stood out against his tawny skin. He picked up the book I had tossed away. "Dickinson's poems. Interesting, considering Benedict Raisin was holding a copy of her poems when he died."

I lifted my chin. "I was reading it out of tribute to him."

"I see." He looked around the children's loft. "My five-year-old niece would love it up here. She's obsessed with fairies."

"You should bring her by sometime. She might like story time too. My grandmother dresses up like a fairy to read to the children. It's always a crowd-pleaser."

"I keep telling Daisy that I will bring her for a visit. No easy task. She's taking hip-hop dance, painting, and gymnastics. She's busier than I am, and I'm the chief of police."

"She sounds like a talented kid."

"You have no idea." After a moment, his smile faded, and the cop face was firmly back in its place. "We need to talk. I wasn't happy when I saw you at Falling Waters Livery earlier this afternoon."

"I'm not sure what there is to say about it, Chief Rainwater." I mimicked his businesslike tone.

"How about you tell me why you were there?"

I folded my arms. "I wanted to talk to someone about Benedict's past. I think it's related to his death."

The chief surprised me by what he said next. "I do too."

My eyes widened. "You do?"

"This might take a while. Mind if we sit?" he asked.

I gestured to one of the rock beanbags. "Be my guest."

"The floor will be fine." He sank to the floor and sat

cross-legged across from me. He patted the carpet. "Take a seat."

I stood there unsure what to do. The absurdity of being interviewed by the too-handsome-for-my-own-good police chief in the middle of Charming Books' fairy room with a cat, a crow, and a possibly magical tree and books looking on was just too much.

"Or if you prefer, we can take this conversation to the police station."

I plopped on the floor across from him. I sat cross-legged too. We were like two little kids all ready for circle time.

"How did you know to go to that livery?" he asked.

I thought the truth—or as much as I was willing to spare—was the best answer. "I found out where Benedict used to work before moving to Cascade Springs through Carly at the livery here in the village."

"What makes you think a job he had over ten years ago has any bearing on his murder, which occurred yesterday?" He asked this as if he already knew the answer. I suspected he did.

I had a friend in graduate school who was earning her master's in journalism. She told me once that a good journalist never asked a question that she didn't already know the answer to. I would think that a good cop followed the same rules, and for better or worse, I was beginning to realize that Chief David Rainwater was a very good cop.

I sighed. "Grandma Daisy told me that he moved to Cascade Springs to escape his past. She said there was something unsavory in it. He never told her what it exactly was, but it was the reason he left Niagara Falls."

He nodded as if this was a conclusion he had already come to and I was just confirming it for him.

"Did Les tell you about Fletcher Wolcott?" I asked.

"Yes," he said. "But I already knew about him. The moment that Benedict died, we ran a background check on him. Of course, it came up that he made a deal with the Feds so that they could catch Wolcott."

"Was Benedict involved in the actual smuggling?" I asked.

"How do you know about that?"

I held up my phone. "Google."

He smiled. "From his federal file, or at least the piece the FBI would let me see, it did show that Benedict was a small player in the smuggling operation. The important part was he knew all the big players, including Wolcott. Because of that, he was the perfect one to put pressure on to crack the case wide-open."

"How did the smuggling work?" I asked as I ran my fingers through my hair, brushing it away from my face.

The police chief blinked as if he momentarily lost his train of thought.

"Chief Rainwater?" I watched him expectantly.

"The smuggling, right," he said, shaking his head. Maybe I wasn't the only one whose brain was fried by this case. "Wolcott and his associates moved everything across the border from arms to even fresh fruits to avoid the international tariffs."

"Benedict was one of the men who did that?" I tried

to file the kind white-haired man I'd met on my first day back in the village under international smuggler. It didn't quite fit.

"He was a small cog in the wheel of smuggling. He was chosen to work for them because he had a license to be a carriage driver on both sides of the border. This was pre-9/11 days when he was working for them. Going back and forth at the Rainbow Bridge crossing was pretty loose. After 9/11, this changed. The federal government cracked down on the U.S.–Canadian border. Benedict was caught in the act. The Feds gave him two choices: go to jail or turn in his bosses and be free."

"He chose option number two." I held the volume of Dickinson to my chest.

Rainwater nodded. "That's right. All the key players were arrested in a matter of days."

"And Benedict?" I asked.

"The FBI kept their promise. They let him go. He didn't even have to testify in the case against Wolcott. There was so much evidence against him that Wolcott accepted a plea deal. It never went to trial."

"Then Grandma Daisy is off the hook. Benedict must have been killed by one of Wolcott's associates, or," I said, warming to the idea, "Wolcott ordered a hit from prison. People do that. I've seen the movies."

Rainwater bit his lower lip as if he was trying to hold back a chuckle. After a beat, he said, "Yes, that can happen, but it didn't in this case."

"How do you know? Go to the prison and find out."

"I can't."

I jumped to my feet. "I thought you were here to help Grandma Daisy."

He looked up at me. "Can you sit down for a second?"

I folded my arms.

He sighed. "I can't ask Wolcott because he's dead. He died seven years ago in prison."

"Did someone take him out in prison?" I asked.

The police chief did laugh then, so hard, in fact, it took him a solid thirty seconds to recover himself.

I stood over him with my hands on my hips, and that seemed only to make his giggles worse. He finally regained his composure. "I'm so sorry. I shouldn't laugh at you like that."

"No, you shouldn't."

He cleared his throat, but his amber eyes still sparkled. "No one killed Wolcott. He died of cancer."

"Oh," I said, and sat back on the floor. "What about someone who worked for him?"

The police chief shook his head. "Some of the smaller players got away, but they weren't dumb enough to stick around. The FBI believes they left the country and assumed new names."

"A dead end." My shoulders drooped forward. I'd thought that I actually had a good lead on what had happened to Benedict. Realizing that I had run into a wall almost broke my heart.

Keeping his voice even, he said, "I don't believe your grandmother is behind this. She is a very fit woman for her age, but it would have taken a great deal of strength to strangle a man like that even if he didn't fight back, and Benedict had defensive wounds on his knuckles. He tried to get away."

I shivered as the image of Benedict struggling with his attacker came to mind.

"Were you able to get any DNA, then? You know, skin under Benedict's fingernails? That sort of thing?"

He smiled. "Did you get that question from television too?"

"It's a fair question."

His face cleared, and his tone turned more serious. "We think the killer was wearing gloves. There was no skin under Benedict's fingernails, but there were traces of leather."

"Leather gloves?" I asked.

"It would be my guess." He paused. "I still have to follow the evidence where it leads me, and there is still too much pointed in Daisy Waverly's direction to rule her out completely."

I deflated. "Why are you telling me all this?"

He ran his hand through his hair. "I hoped that by telling you, you would realize how serious this situation is. Wolcott might not be behind Benedict's death, but it doesn't mean Benedict didn't return to his old ways and fall in with the wrong crowd."

"Grandma Daisy said he left that all behind when he came to Cascade Springs."

"He may have at first." He stood.

I scrambled to my feet too.

The police chief brushed cat fur from his pant leg. "I don't know who he may have become mixed up with now in Cascade Springs, but be sure I will find out. I don't want you getting in the way."

"I have to help my grandmother." I lifted my chin. "Excuse me if I don't trust the village police as much as most people do."

The hard lines of his face softened. "I know that, and you have every reason to be leery. If I had been on the case twelve years ago, you would have never been treated so poorly. The old chief was scared. A young, pretty, popular teenage girl was dead. Nothing like that had happened in the village before, and nothing like it has happened since. They couldn't believe that this perfect girl with the perfect life could die in a stupid accident like that. The town was up in arms. The chief had to do something to show that he was investigating the situation."

I opened my mouth.

"That doesn't mean that it was right, but it's what happened. I don't know if it will help much after all this time, but I want to apologize for how you were treated after Colleen died."

I felt tears gather in my eyes. I had blamed myself for Colleen's death all these years, and now the chief of police, someone in authority, believed me. "Thank you," I whispered. By hearing a village police officer say that I had been wrongly accused, I felt a little bit of the weight, not all of it, of Colleen's death lift from my shoulders. It was the lightest I had been in twelve years.

"I'm not one for a witch hunt, Violet." His voice was low. "I'm not out to get your grandmother, and I'm not out to get you."

"Les, the carriage driver, said the springwaters were magical," I said. I wasn't sure why I said that; it just popped out of my mouth. I wished that I could reach into the air and shove the words back into my mouth.

He smiled as if he knew that I needed to change the subject. Even talking about magic was more comfortable for me than talking about what happened to Colleen. "The waters are special and have been special to my people for thousands of years. I don't claim to understand what the water can do, but I don't believe its capabilities are impossible either."

It seemed like such an odd thing for a logical police officer to say, but maybe his culture had trained him to be more open-minded than my culture had me. I had spent a third of my life in academe; if anything would crush the dreamer out of you, it was that.

He brushed his hands against his legs. "I should go. I need to file a report about my trip to Niagara Falls before calling it a night."

I hadn't realized how much time had passed since I'd climbed up into the children's loft. Orange sunlight poured into the room through the oddly shaped windows. Rosalee had followed a plan in her own mind when building the house, choosing windows that were charming and unique. Of course, the birch tree was the best proof of that. "Is Officer Wheaton still on the case too?"

His jaw twitched. "The entire department is on the case." He paused. "You don't have to worry about Wheaton."

I wasn't so sure about that.

"Violet, please stay out of my investigation. I don't ask you this because it is a turf thing. I ask you for your own safety. A man was killed—a well-known and well-liked man was strangled in the middle of an upscale residential neighborhood. Whoever did this is very dangerous and, I fear, desperate." He headed to the spiral staircase. "Good night, Violet."

After he disappeared, I whispered, "Good night."

## TWENTY-SIX

Grandma Daisy was alone in the shop when I came down the stairs from the children's loft. I had the slim volume of Dickinson's poetry in the back pocket of my jeans. It was hidden under the hem of my long T-shirt. I didn't want Grandma Daisy to know I was consulting the book until I knew what I was doing. I carried Emerson in my arms. I seemed to need the cat's warmth ever since I'd talked to the police chief. I felt raw and vulnerable, more so than I had in a long time. I told myself that it was only because he had brought up Colleen, but I was afraid I might be lying to myself just like I was lying to myself about the book in my pocket. Because the more time I spent in Charming Books and the more times a book appeared in an unexpected place, the more I was starting to believe that it was all real. And that terrified me.

At the same time, I didn't want my grandmother to

know how much the conversation with Rainwater had shaken me, so I fell back onto my trusted friend humor to break through my awkwardness. "Do we need to put on our jewelry-thief uniforms to gather water from the springs again tonight?"

Grandma Daisy was carrying a large stack of new books to the mystery section. "No, the tree is only watered twice a week."

I arched my brow. "One little watering can of spring-water twice a week doesn't seem like enough to keep a huge tree alive." I held up a hand. "I forgot; it's magic water."

"No more jokes. I'd like to know about your trip to the Falls, and I want to know what the police chief said to you when he went upstairs looking for you."

"How did he know where to find me?" I asked.

"I might have pointed him in the right direction." There was a twinkle in her eye.

*Thought so.* I suppressed a groan, and I went on to tell her about Grant coming along with me to the Falls and the conversation we had had with the old carriage driver. I paused. "It seems Benedict was caught up with some type of smuggling ring in Niagara Falls." I waited for a moment and let that sink in. "Did you know about that?"

Grandma Daisy shelved the stack of mysteries with precision. "That was in his past. Benedict and I agreed to leave the past in the past. He didn't ask me about mine, and I didn't ask him about his."

My brow wrinkled. I didn't think that my grandmother had any past of significance, certainly not in the same way that Benedict did. But maybe she was referring to her life as the Caretaker of the tree and the books. Before

I could ask her what she meant by her comment, she asked, "What did David say?"

I started to pick up books that customers had left lying around the shop. I was relieved to see none of them were Emily Dickinson's poems. Maybe the books had decided to cut me a break. "Chief Rainwater doesn't think Benedict's death is related to Benedict's past. The head of the operation is dead, and the FBI reports all his cronies are either in prison or fled the country."

She looked up at me. "Then who can it be?"

I frowned. "Maybe it's someone right here in the village. Bad things can happen here, just like anywhere else."

She shivered. I knew my grandmother didn't like the idea of her friends and neighbors being capable of murder.

"There's always his daughter too," I added. "I need to learn more about her. Why was she always asking her father for money?"

"I think we both have had enough talk about murder for today. Why don't we grab a late dinner at La Crepe Jolie? I'd like to thank Adrien for those pastries." Grandma Daisy set a final book on the shelf.

I checked my watch. "Are they still open this late?"

"Oh yes," she said. "Most of the businesses stay open later in the summer months. I think there is a concert in the park tonight too—a string quartet, if I remember correctly. We could order our food and go listen to them."

"Are you sure you are up for that?" I didn't say it but I knew the village gossips' tongues would be wagging about Benedict's murder and the suspicions about Grandma Daisy.

My grandmother caught my meaning, and she dusted off her hands. "Yes, I can't hide in the shop all day. People are going to believe what they want to believe. I have to keep living my life." She smiled. "And I would much rather give them something to talk about than stay at home."

Faulkner swooped down from his perch on the birch tree and landed on the back of a couch. "Give them something to talk about!"

I grinned. "Sounds like a plan."

Before we went to the park, Grandma Daisy and I stopped at her house to drop off Emerson and to collect blankets to sit on during the concert.

As soon as Grandma Daisy and I walked into the café, Lacey ran forward and crushed my grandmother in a hug. "Daisy, are you all right? I've been worried sick about you. Are you staying to eat?"

My grandmother pulled away from the killer hug. "The beignets Adrien sent over this morning were delightful and delicious. Please thank him for me."

Lacey clasped her hands together. "He'll love to hear that."

Grandma Daisy smiled. "Violet and I were just here to pick up some food for the concert."

"Good for you. It's nice to see you out and about. If it gets slow, I might slip away for a moment to see part of it, but that might not happen. Everyone gets hungry at those concerts. Business has been brisk. I'm not complaining." She grinned. "I'll tell Adrien to put on a take-out order for you two."

Grandma Daisy smiled. "Thank you. Make it a double of my usual order for a picnic."

While Lacey ran off to the kitchen, I became acutely aware that all conversation in the coffee shop had ceased. I looked around the room and found everyone staring at my grandmother and me. My chest tightened. After Colleen's death, the sensation of being watched was one I had grown used to in this village. It was happening again, but this time it was directed at my grandmother, which was so much worse.

Grandma Daisy stood beside me holding on to her purse with her chin held high. She refused to look at any of the diners, who examined her as if she were a microbe under a microscope.

I wasn't above it all. I glared at the closest man, who was middle-aged. Finally, he looked away and spoke to his companion. Soon conversation and the clink of silverware against dishes resumed.

Lacey reappeared with a sack of food twice as heavy as the one I had taken to Grandma Daisy the afternoon before. If I kept eating this much French food, I was going to have to take up running to compensate, and I hated to run. Or I could keep riding my mother's bike about town. Maybe that would be enough to even it out.

We thanked Lacey for the food and left the coffee shop.

There was a white pavilion set up along Riverwalk Park, and the string quartet tuned their instruments and chatted among themselves on the stage. The sun setting behind the river was a perfect backdrop. Pink- and purple-bruised clouds floated in the light breeze, making me glad I'd grabbed my jacket before leaving Grandma Daisy's house.

"Oh, do you smell it?" Grandma Daisy asked as she

spread one of the blankets onto the grass. "They have popcorn."

I held up the overstuffed food bag from the French coffee shop. "Don't you think we have enough food already?"

She cocked her head. "There is always room for popcorn."

I laughed and set my blanket next to hers on the ground. "I'll buy a bag."

"For me? Great! If you want popcorn, you had better purchase a second." She winked.

I snorted and headed to the concessions. The line was about six deep. While I waited, I checked my e-mail messages on my cell phone. There were two from my academic adviser back in Chicago, asking to meet with me about my dissertation. I chewed on my lower lip. I should probably tell her where I was and that I might be in Cascade Springs for a little while yet.

I hit "reply" on my phone with the intent of telling my adviser I was out of state because of a family emergency, which was one way to describe the fact that your grandmother was a murder suspect.

A voice interrupted me before I could begin. "When I saw Daisy waiting for the concert, I thought you might be here too," Nathan said. He wasn't wearing a suit now, but khakis and a light blue polo shirt. The short sleeves of the polo shirt exposed his tan arms.

"Grandma Daisy thought coming to the concert would be a good distraction," I said.

"I'm glad. Have you decided about the gala yet?"

I studied him. "You only asked me a few hours ago, Nate."

"Fair enough." His brow cleared. "My mother loved that book you suggested for her."

"You already gave it to her?" I asked.

He nodded. "Her birthday was actually yesterday, but I couldn't get away to see her. Too much going on."

I knew "too much going on" was code for Benedict's murder.

"Anyway, my mother heard that you were in town and hopes to see you at the gala too."

I'd bet. Nathan's parents had never been fans of mine. I knew they would have much rather seen their son date a girl from another well-to-do family, preferably one from their many friends' families in the wine business. If Nathan was trying to talk me into going to the gala, knowing his parents would be there had the opposite effect. They were the ones who'd convinced him to abandon me to the police when Colleen died.

"I don't—"

"Popcorn?"

Suddenly, I was at the front of the line.

"Would you like some popcorn?" the bright-eyed teenager asked. I noticed that she directed her attention at Nathan, not me.

"Two, please," I said.

Her eyes flicked to me for a nanosecond before returning to Nathan. "That will be five dollars."

I reached into my tote bag for my wallet when Nathan said, "Don't worry. I've got it." He gave the teen a crisp five-dollar bill.

I accepted the two bags of popcorn. "You didn't have to do that."

"I wanted to. You don't have to answer now about the gala, but promise you will think about it."

Nathan looked so hopeful that I found myself saying, "I'll think about it. If Grandma Daisy feels up to it, we might both come."

He beamed, looking so much like the teenage boy that I remembered that it made my chest hurt. "Excellent."

I watched Nathan walk away, and just beyond him I saw Shane Pitman from the carriage house. He was looking around the park as if he was searching for someone. Suddenly, he flipped up the hood of his jacket and bolted down the Riverwalk.

I handed my popcorns back to the vendor. "Can you hold these for me? I'll be right back."

"We don't do that," she called after me, but I was already jogging down the Riverwalk after Shane.

# TWENTY-SEVEN

I thought that I had lost Shane completely until I spotted his black hoodie moving quickly past La Crepe Jolie across the street, heading in the direction of the carriage house. There wasn't anything suspicious about him going to the livery. He worked there, after all, but his movements were erratic as if he was afraid he was being followed.

I stayed on the river side of the road, walking parallel to Shane. Other than a few tourists heading to the concert, there was no one on the Riverwalk. Across the street, the businesses and buildings faded away the closer I got to the livery. I dropped back farther behind Shane to avoid being seen.

At the carriage house, I stood behind an empty carriage parked out front and watched as he entered the building through a side door. The main barn door was closed.

I stood there for a moment, debating if I should follow him. I gripped the side of the carriage so tightly that my fingers turned white. I forced myself to relax and acknowledge that I had no business being there. Grandma Daisy must be wondering what had happened to me. Although she might be more worried about her lack of popcorn than my safety.

Faintly behind me, I could hear the concert begin. I could have been mistaken, but I thought they started with the theme to *Star Wars*.

I was about to head back to the park when a terrible scream echoed from inside the barn. The scream was followed by silence. I hesitated for a second before I ran toward the barn.

I opened the same door Shane had disappeared through. The inside of the barn was dark except for the security lights along the floor. The sun had set now, and there were no streetlights this far beyond the Riverwalk to provide any discernible ambient light.

"Hello!" I called. "Is anyone here?"

"Back here!" a woman's voice called.

I ran toward the office, and as I got closer, I saw there was a soft yellow light coming from that small room. Through the window, I saw Carly in the middle of the floor, holding her left ankle.

I walked into the office. "Are you okay?"

She pushed her hair out of her face. "I'm fine, just clumsy and embarrassed for being so stupid."

"Did you hurt your ankle?"

"I don't think it's broken, only sprained." She winced.

"I heard your cry from outside."

"I'm glad you did. Can you help me to my feet?" She braced her hand on her leg as if she was trying to stand up.

I held up my hands. "Maybe you shouldn't get up. Do you want me to call an ambulance?"

"I'm fine. It's not my first sprain."

"Shouldn't you go to the hospital?"

"No, I have had worse injuries being thrown from a horse. You're bound to be hurt when you work with animals. In this case, though, I fell off a milk crate." She nodded at the two overturned milk crates in the middle of the office. "It's so embarrassing. Can it be our little secret if I tell everyone I was bucked by a Thoroughbred? I have to save face."

I smiled. "Sure," I said, and I helped her to her feet.

She hopped on one foot over to the desk. "Thanks."

"How did you fall?" I asked as I righted one of the milk crates.

"I was trying to reach that box on top of the shelf over there. Stupidly, I climbed on milk crates, thinking they could hold my weight." She laughed. "I'm small, but apparently I am not small enough."

When I picked up the second milk crate, it fell apart.

She leaned on her desk for support. "I guess I fared better than the milk crates. It's not easy being short. It worked to my advantage back when I was a jockey, but not so much in everyday life," she said with a self-mocking grin.

"You were a jockey?" I asked.

She nodded. "A pretty competitive one too. I always had dreams of riding in the Triple Crown." She laughed. "It wasn't meant to be, and so here I am."

I didn't know what to say to that.

"Don't look so sorry for me." She laughed. "I have my own business, and I'm still working with horses, which is most important to me." She hopped around the side of the desk and sat in her chair. "I'm really grateful that you came along. I was here all alone tonight. It might have taken me much longer to stand up by myself."

Where was Shane? I saw him come into the barn. Why hadn't he run to Carly's side when she'd fallen?

"Trey's not here?" I asked.

She shook her head. "He's out with his friends, doing heaven only knows. He goes to the community college in town." She sighed. "Before he left, I asked him to bring down that box for me. He forgot, as usual."

"Do you want me to grab the box for you?" I was a good foot taller than Carly.

"That would be great."

I reached for the box, but it was just out of my reach. Rather than risk my neck on the broken crate, I grabbed a step stool that was outside her office door.

She groaned. "That would have been a better idea over the crate. My old riding coach used to say that my impatience was what caused me to lose most races. I'm sure that comment can be applied to all aspects of my life."

I plucked the box from the top of the cabinet, walked it over to the desk, and handed it to her. "I hope it's worth a twisted ankle."

"Me too."

"What's in it?" I couldn't help but ask.

"Not sure, but the police chief wants to know if I have any more information about Benedict. He's been here longer than I've owned the carriage house. I thought there might be something in the box. My predecessor wasn't the best record keeper in the world." She sighed and dropped the box in the middle of her desk. "The problem is I hate paperwork."

"I don't mind paperwork," I said a little too quickly. "I could go through it for you in no time. Most of my life as a student is processing papers."

Her face brightened. "You'd do that?"

"Sure," I said nonchalantly, as if I weren't dying to crack open the file box and see what secrets it might reveal about Benedict.

"That would be a lifesaver. I really hate paper. Most of my files are electronic now, but I couldn't see the point of transferring over what the old owner had. I had always thought I would throw it out, but never got around to it. If it can help the police with Benedict's case, maybe it's a good thing that I didn't."

"Absolutely," I said. "I could come by tomorrow and look through it with you."

"Would you?" She smiled.

"Sure."

"If that's the case, I think I'll head home. My boot is already feeling tight from the swelling. I need to put some ice on my ankle."

"Do you want me to drive you home?"

"I'll be fine. I only live a couple of miles away. I'll let you help me to my car, though."

She hobbled to the door. After we both were out, she closed the door and locked it with her key.

Outside the music was louder than before. I could be mistaken, but I thought I heard the theme music to *Jurassic Park*. Must be a John Williams theme night.

My eyes flicked to the dark woods beside the carriage house. I could easily imagine a T. rex lying in wait somewhere in there.

"I'm not usually here this late, but with Benedict gone, we're short staffed. I used to let him close up and check on things every night. I have good guys on my team, but no one I trusted as much as I trusted Benedict. Until I find a worthy replacement, I'll have to keep doing it myself. This ankle injury is going to be a major inconvenience."

"Can you hire another carriage driver?" I asked.

"I can, and I'm already taking applications. I've gotten a lot of them, but so far none of them have carriage-driving experience. I need someone to step in Benedict's shoes right away. I don't have time to spend hours teaching someone to drive a horse in the middle of the summer season."

"What about Shane?" I asked. "He seems to have a lot of experience. Maybe he could train a new driver."

She snorted as she unlocked her pickup truck with her key fob. "Shane. I'm not that crazy. He would be the worst person to train someone to drive. He's great with horses, but he's so impatient with people. In fact, I had planned to fire him the day that Benedict died, but when I got the news, I changed my mind. I couldn't spare him. If I find a worthy replacement for Benedict, then I will let him go, but that is a real tall order." There were tears in her eyes.

Did Shane know that? Had he killed Benedict because he knew that Carly would be forced to keep him on because she was short staffed? It seemed like an extreme solution, but then again I had seen Shane sneaking into the carriage house. I was pretty sure he was still somewhere around when Carly fell. He couldn't have been that far away. He must have heard her cry out, but he did nothing.

I looked at the high step into the truck. "Are you sure you can get up there?"

"Sure. I've climbed onto a horse for a race with a bruised spine. A sprained ankle is nothing." She grinned.

I winced. Clearly, Carly was much tougher than I was. I gave her a boost up, feeling uncertain that I was doing the right thing by allowing her to go home alone. "If you give me your cell phone, I can punch in my number. Then you can call me if you get home and realize that you need help."

"That's kind of you." She handed me the phone. The phone's wallpaper was a picture of a young boy. I suspected that it was a younger Trey.

I punched in the number and handed it back to her. "Just give me a call if you need help."

Before she closed the door to the truck, she asked, "What are you doing here anyway? I mean when you heard me scream?"

I couldn't tell her the truth, that I was following her employee because I thought that he was up to no good. "My grandmother and I decided to go to the concert tonight down by the springs, and I went for a walk. I heard you scream and ran in to see if I could help."

That was mostly true.

"Oh, it was lucky, then," she said, and closed the door. I stepped back as she started the truck.

After she was gone, my eyes trailed back to the barn. Part of me wanted to go in there to see if I could find Shane, but I knew that was a stupid idea.

I sighed and headed back to the concert until someone grabbed me by the back of the neck and threw me against a tree.

# TWENTY-EIGHT

I struggled against the man's grasp, but it was too strong. He wrenched my right arm behind me, and I cried out in pain.

His hot breath was next to my cheek. "Stop poking your nose in where it doesn't belong. Leave it alone. You will ruin everything."

He let me go, and I crumbled to the foot of the tree. Rubbing my neck, I spun around with the hope of seeing my attacker. He was gone, melted into the woods. I struggled to my feet, and headed down the path toward the park at a run. I wasn't looking where I was going, because I ran straight into a man coming from the opposite direction along the Riverwalk.

I bounced off him, but he grabbed my upper arm before I fell to the ground.

I yelped in pain and wrenched my arm away.

"Violet?" Chief Rainwater studied me.

I held my arm, fighting back tears.

"What's wrong?" His amber gaze was sharp as it searched my face.

I took several gasping breaths.

"What's wrong with your arm?" His voice was commanding and demanding an answer.

"I hurt it," I finally managed to say.

"How?"

I licked my dry lips. "A man jumped me from the woods and twisted it behind my back."

"What?" he bellowed. He looked up the path as if he was going to bolt after whoever might have attacked me.

"There's no point going after him. He disappeared into the trees."

"Do you know who it was?"

"I know it was a man. That's all, and . . ." I trailed off.

"And what?"

"It could have been Shane Pitman."

He balled his fists at his sides. When he did that, I noticed the gun in his holster. "Why do you think it was Shane?"

I swallowed. "I sort of followed him here."

The police chief's eyes bugged out of his head. It was almost cartoonish and would have amused me if I hadn't been the one in the direct path of his fury. "You followed him? Why on earth would you do something so stupid?"

I ground my teeth, partly because of my throbbing arm and partly because I was annoyed at him. "I saw him at the outdoor concert, and he was acting strange. He kept looking around like he was trying to avoid someone—who that may have been I don't know. Then, he took off in the direction of the carriage house, and I sort of followed."

He ran his hand back and forth over his eyes as if trying to erase my face from his view. "You sort of followed?"

"I don't think he knew I was there."

He threw up his hands. "Until he nearly broke your arm."

"Yeah, I guess until then." I brushed bark from my T-shirt. "It was a good thing that I did follow him, because I was there to help Carly when she fell."

"I think you had better start at the beginning." His jaw twitched.

I told him the story from the moment that I found Carly until the man grabbed me next to the woods. He didn't ask any questions while I talked, only listened and watched me with his exotic-colored eyes.

"Where was Shane when you were helping Carly?" he asked.

I frowned. "That, I don't know. He couldn't have gone far, and Carly screamed pretty loudly when she fell. I heard her outside of the barn."

He pursed his lips. "Where's Carly now?"

"Home." I cradled my arm. "She insisted it was only a twisted ankle and a little ice was all she needed. I wanted to take her to the doctor, but she refused. She's going to call me if she needs any help when she gets home."

"So you were attacked after she left?"

I nodded and winced. My neck was a little sore, not as bad as my arm, but it would be in pain tomorrow, quite literally.

Rainwater noticed. "What's wrong with your neck?"

My good hand flew to my throat. "My neck?"

"It's red." He stepped closer to me, and my pulse quickened. "And those marks look like finger marks!"

"It's nothing." He was so close I could barely breathe. "He grabbed me by the neck and pushed me against the tree."

"Did he hurt you otherwise?" His eyes swept up and down my body, scanning me for other injuries.

"No. More than anything, he scared me."

"Which was the point. I told you to stay out of this investigation because it could be dangerous. I see that I've been proven right." He folded his arms. "You should see a doctor."

The last place I wanted to go was the hospital. Ever since my mother had died in one, I had avoided them at any cost. "I'll be fine. With a little ice and rest, I'll be as good as new."

"You know that's just what Carly said."

I shrugged.

"I can't let this go unreported." He removed a radio from his belt. "I need to call this in."

"But—"

He gave me a look that left no room for argument. I wrapped my arms around myself as Rainwater stepped away to speak on the radio. When he returned, he said, "I have officers on their way here. Are you really refusing to go to the hospital?" He studied me.

I nodded.

He sighed. "If you don't feel better in the morning, will you see a doctor?" He watched me as if to make sure I wouldn't lie to him.

I crossed my heart. "I promise, Chief."

He frowned. "I'll walk you back to the concert, and then come back and check out the area around the carriage house with my guys."

Silently, we walked back up the Riverwalk.

A police car rolled up alongside us and stopped. Rainwater turned to me. "Can you wait a moment, Violet? I need to speak to my officer."

I gave a small nod, being very careful with my neck as I did so.

Rainwater walked up to the cruiser, and Officer Wheaton rolled down his window. He glanced around Rainwater and glared at me. I had a feeling Wheaton and I wouldn't end up pals no matter how this case shook out. The police chief pointed up the Riverwalk toward the livery, speaking in hushed tones.

"Are you sure she's not lying?" I heard Wheaton ask Rainwater loudly enough so that I would hear it.

I clenched my teeth. He was really starting to get on my nerves.

"Go check it out." Rainwater's voice was sharp.

The cruiser drove away.

Now the quartet was playing the theme from *E.T.* I smiled and turned toward the music. It had been my mother's favorite movie. I think I watched it a million times growing up.

"What are you smiling about?" he asked as he joined me on the Riverwalk again.

"The music. *E.T.* was my mom's favorite movie. . . ." I trailed off.

The hard planes of his face softened. "Daisy has spoken of your mother many times. She sounds like an amazing person."

"She was." I concentrated on the path. I wasn't staying in Cascade Springs. I couldn't allow myself to become attached. Richard's suggestion to me to apply for the adjunct professor position at the community college flashed across my mind. I shook my head. I couldn't stay in the village. There were still too many memories of Colleen here.

"What's the deal with Wheaton?" I asked. "He seems pretty determined to dislike both Grandma Daisy and me."

Rainwater frowned but didn't answer. There was more to the story there; I knew it. I just hoped that Grandma Daisy wasn't caught in the middle of whatever was going on between Rainwater and Wheaton.

When he remained quiet for over a minute, I changed the subject. "Sadie told me that you write children's books."

His face brightened. "I do."

"I'd love to read some of your work sometime." My face turned beet red as I realized that sounded like some type of literary come-on. "I mean, Sadie gushed about what a great writer you were. She insisted you will hit the big time."

He smiled. "Sadie's a good cheerleader for the whole group. Every writing group needs a positive voice to keep everyone going."

"I think she was serious," I said.

"I'm sure she was, and I would be happy for you to read some of my stories." His white teeth flashed in the dark.

I blushed as if his answer meant something else too.

When I got back to the park, Grandma Daisy had the

dinner from the café spread out over both blankets. There was cheese, crackers, crepes, and even a small bottle of wine. Adrien had hooked us up. She must have been hungry because over two-thirds of the Brie was missing. I was happy about that. When my mother died, my grandmother had been strong for me, but she'd practically whittled away to nothing because she hadn't felt like eating. I was happy that wasn't happening with Benedict's death.

"Violet, there you are," she said in a low voice so that she wouldn't disturb the people listening to the music. "I was beginning to wonder what happened to you. Is everything okay?"

"Everything is fine," I said. "I got a little sidetracked, that's all."

She looked from the police chief to me and back again. "Oh!" she said, and her face broke into a grin. "Where's the popcorn?"

"The popcorn. I forgot. I'll go—"

"I'll go get you some," the police chief interrupted me, and went off to the concession stand.

"He seems very attentive." Grandma Daisy waggled her eyebrows.

I frowned. That's exactly what I didn't need. His attentiveness was a complication to my escape plan.

## TWENTY-NINE

I decided not to ruin my grandmother's night and tell her about my encounter with the man in the woods. The police chief knew about it, and he would take care of it if there was anything to be done. Thankfully, it was too dark for her to see the red marks on my neck, and I was careful not to move my arm too much and draw her attention to it by wincing.

The next morning, I jumped on my mother's bike and headed straight for Cascade Springs Livery. Carly had texted me in the middle of the concert that she had gotten home fine and her ankle was feeling much better. She also said she would be at the carriage house at eight the next morning, so I was welcome to drop by anytime the next day to help her go through the box.

When I arrived at the carriage house, I leaned my bike against a tree. Shane stood a few feet away, tethering his horses to his carriage for the day. I hesitated before walking the rest of the way to the livery. I wondered if Chief Rainwater had questioned him yet about last night.

He spat on the ground. "What are you staring at?"

I wrinkled my nose. "It's amazing that you are able to convince anyone to ride in your carriage."

He glared at me. "Who are you to know anything about it?"

"What were you doing in the livery last night?" I asked.

He scowled and took a step toward me. "Are you the one that sent the police after me?"

I swallowed but held my ground. "Why would I do that?"

"You tell me." He stepped back. "It didn't work. The police have nothing on me."

"Good to know."

"Because you know if they did, I would be in jail right now." He buttoned up his red riding jacket. "And as you can see, I'm right here."

I couldn't stop myself from asking, "What about Benedict?"

"What about that old man?" he asked as he collected his top hat from the back of his carriage.

"What do you know about his death?" I asked.

His thin lips curled into a smile. "I know he died. Nothing more, nothing less."

I didn't believe him, so I pressed on. "Did you know that Carly was planning to lay you off before Benedict died?"

He smirked. "Carly can't get rid of me that easily. Trust me on that." He climbed into his carriage. "You might want to step back." He adjusted the reins in his hands. "I would hate to run you over."

I jumped to the side. As I watched him drive away from the livery, I knew he would have no qualms about running me over.

I shook off the creepy feeling Shane had given me and marched into the livery's main barn. Inside, Trey mucked the horse stall closest to the door. The teenager didn't hear me come in because he had his earbuds in, and the volume was up high enough that I could hear all the rap lyrics. Java trotted over to greet me, though.

I gave the dog a pat.

"Violet." Carly came out of her office leaning on a sturdy old wooden cane.

"Nice cane," I said.

She looked down at it. "It was my grandfather's. It's served the family well over many years. It's amazing how an heirloom can be passed down from generation to generation and still be useful."

Her comment brought to mind the birch tree in Charming Books and my future as the next Caretaker if I accepted it. I adjusted my tote bag on my shoulder. The slim paperback copy of Emily Dickinson's poetry was in the bottom of it.

Carly lurched forward on her cane. "Are you all right? You look pale. Do you need to sit down?"

I forced myself to smile. "I'm fine. Tired, I suppose. These last few days have been more than I bargained for." I changed the subject. "How's your ankle?"

"I'll be fine in a couple of days. I still could kick myself for being so clumsy. In my business a twisted ankle is a liability. So much of my job requires use of all my limbs. The worst part is it was all for nothing."

"For nothing why?"

"Because that box I asked you to pull down last night—" She stared at me. "It's gone."

"What do you mean it's gone?" I asked.

"Come see for yourself." She spun around on her cane and hobbled to the back of the barn.

Before I followed her, I glanced back at Trey. I could still hear the rap music thumping, but the teenager no longer had the earbuds in. Instead he held them in his hand, and he stared at his sister's receding back. His brow furrowed in worry. He caught my gaze and resumed shoveling as if nothing had happened.

Inside of Carly's office, she pointed at the bare desk with her free hand. "It was right there."

"I know," I said, taking a step toward the desk. "I put it there."

She leaned on the desk. "It's gone. Poof. Disappeared into thin air."

"It didn't disappear into thin air," I said, thinking of Trey's worried expression just a few moments ago. "Someone took it."

She shook her head. "But why would anyone take an old box of junk?"

"Because it's related to Benedict's death, and something in there must reveal the killer, or the killer thought it might reveal who he or she was. We have to report this to the police," I said.

She groaned. "The police have visited so many times since Benedict died. I'm beginning to wonder if they should move their station here." She pulled her cell phone from the back pocket of her jeans and made the call.

I examined the office. Nothing else was disturbed. Only the box was gone. I wished that I had stayed the night before and searched the box.

Fifteen minutes later, when Police Chief Rainwater arrived, his eyebrows shot up when he spotted me next to Carly.

I tried to ignore the butterflies doing backflips in my stomach.

"Can you tell me what happened?" He directed his question to Carly.

Carly repeated the story that she'd told me a short while ago. "We left the box right there in the middle of my desk. Violet can vouch for me about it, and when I came into the carriage house this morning, it was gone. I've asked all of my employees, and none of them know a thing about it."

His amber eyes flicked in my direction. "And why are you here this morning, Violet?"

I straightened my shoulders. "Carly wanted to organize the documents in the box, and I offered to help."

His frown deepened, creating deep lines around his mouth. I knew he was thinking about my attack last night.

Carly looked from me to the police chief and back again. "Violet is going to be a college professor, so she's really good at making sense of papers. I have no use for them. You should see my files. They're a disaster. I make my accountant cry every year when tax time comes around."

Rainwater pursed his lips but kept any opinion about Carly's assessment of my paper-sorting skills to himself. "How do you think the person got in?"

Carly shrugged. "No idea. We were the last ones to leave the livery, and I locked everything up tight."

I wondered if that was true. Part of me still believed Shane had been inside the carriage house barn when I found Carly after her fall. My conversation with the disgruntled carriage driver less than an hour ago did nothing to dispel that suspicion.

The chief walked over to Carly's office and studied the doorjamb as if it were a bug under a microscope. "See those scrapes there?" He stepped back so that Carly and I could have a look.

Carly and I leaned in, and I noticed the small scrapes in the woodwork. They were tiny, barely the width of the lead of a mechanical pencil. I didn't even know how the police chief found them.

"My guess is whoever broke in used a flat screwdriver and another tool," Rainwater said. "He was a professional too. There is so little scratching, and then he locked the door when he left."

"What would someone want with a bunch of old files?" Carly repeated the question that she had asked me earlier.

"Depends what's in them," Rainwater said. "Did either of you look through the box before it disappeared?"

Carly shook her head. "After I fell, I wanted to go home and ice my ankle." Carly leaned on her cane. "I feel like such a fool with this silly cane."

Rainwater unclipped his cell phone from his belt. "I'm going to call some of my guys to fingerprint your office. It's a long shot but still worth a try."

Carly's shoulders slumped. "Is that necessary? I really don't care about whatever was inside that box. Whoever stole it was most likely disappointed because it was full of a bunch of old junk."

"It is necessary because someone cares enough about that box to break into your office and steal it." He put the phone to his ear.

She frowned. "Okay."

Rainwater stepped away to make his call. Trey, who had been mucking the horse stalls when I arrived, was nowhere to be seen, nor was his dog.

Had he finished his chores? Or had he left because he knew something about the missing box?

"They're on their way," Rainwater said, breaking into my thoughts.

"If you don't mind," Carly said, "I'll hobble around and make sure that my guys have everything that they need for the day."

"I'll need to talk to you again before I leave," the chief said.

"No problem." Carly nodded at her cane. "I can't go too far with this."

After she stumbled away to talk with her carriage drivers who hadn't left yet for the village, the police chief turned to me. He wasn't smiling. "Violet, can I speak to you for a moment?" He clipped his phone back onto his belt. "Let's go outside and talk."

Uh-oh. I was in trouble.

He walked to the edge of the trees where I had left my bike. "How is your arm?"

I lifted it. "It's fine. A little sore. I'm not going to be pitching a fastball anytime soon, but it doesn't bother me much."

"And your neck?" He peered at me more closely. "You're wearing a scarf. . . ."

I had a thin, light blue infinity scarf that I had taken from Grandma Daisy's massive collection that morning.

"May I see?" he asked.

I hesitated.

"Please?" he asked.

He looked so concerned that I relented and removed the scarf.

Rainwater winced when he saw the purplish bruise on the side of my neck. "Are you sure you're all right?"

I wrapped the scarf back around my neck. "I'm sure. The bruise will be gone in a day or two." After a beat, I said, "I saw Shane Pitman when I came to the carriage house this morning."

"And?"

"He accused me of sending the police after him."

The police chief sighed. "I spoke to him last night after I left you at the concert."

"And?" I asked, repeating the question he had asked me.

"He was in a pub on the edge of the village at the time of your attack. The bartender vouched for him."

"How did he get there so quickly?" I asked. "I saw him go into the barn right before Carly fell."

"Maybe he went straight there when he heard Carly cry out. I don't know, but I can't arrest him when he has so many witnesses backing up his story."

I frowned.

Rainwater's black eyebrows peaked together. "You didn't say anything about a box last night."

"I forgot," I squeaked.

"I'm not buying it." He folded his arms over his broad

chest. "You wanted a look at it before she turned it over to me."

I didn't say anything.

"And now it's gone." His unspoken accusation that the missing box was my fault hung in the air between us.

I rested my back against a tree. "How could Carly or I know someone would break into the carriage house after an old box?"

He rubbed the back of his head. "I told you that this case was dangerous, and you wouldn't listen. Even after being attacked last night, you're back here poking your nose where it doesn't belong. It's as if you are looking for trouble."

"I'm looking for ways to help my grandmother."

He sighed. "I know, and I can understand that. Daisy is my friend. If you would let me do my job, this would be over sooner."

I pushed off the tree. "Are you saying I'm making it worse for my grandmother?"

He rubbed his head some more. "I'm saying you're adding an unnecessary complication, and I don't quite know what I'm—"

Whatever else he was going to say was interrupted by the arrival of his other officers.

# THIRTY

Officer Wheaton dusted Carly's office door for fingerprints, while a second officer sprinkled powder on her desk and chair inside the room.

"Will that come off?" Carly asked nervously. She and I were watching the proceedings on the other side of the office window.

"Yes," Officer Wheaton said. "It would go more quickly if you two weren't hovering over my shoulder." He directed his last comment at me.

Carly chewed her thumbnail, turning to me. "This just goes from bad to worse. Do you think whoever did this will come back? I work here by myself late at night and more often early in the morning, especially now that Benedict is gone."

"I don't think they'll be back," I said, even though I had no way of knowing that. "They came for the box, and they got it. Even so, I don't think you should be at the carriage house alone until everything is cleared up."

"I suppose I could drag Trey to work with me every morning. My little brother will love that. He can barely force himself to roll out of bed for his nine a.m. classes."

"Does he go to Springside?" I asked.

She nodded.

That gave me an idea. If Trey was a student at the community college, perhaps Richard knew him. He'd said the school was small. He might have even had the teen in one of his classes.

"I think that's a good idea, and I'm sure that Trey would worry for you if you were in the carriage house alone," I said.

She laughed. "I'm not so sure about that. I may be the only family he has, but he's still a teenager."

"Your parents?" I asked.

"They're dead." She looked away, and then cleared her throat. "Besides, what I told the police chief was true. I don't care what was inside that box. As far as I'm concerned, they can keep it as long as they leave my livery and me alone."

I, on the other hand, did want to know what was in the box. If someone went to all the trouble to steal it, the box had to be important and related to Benedict's murder. Was it Shane? Was it the man who'd attacked me on the way back to the concert, who might also have been Shane? Or was it a complete unknown?

Everything about Benedict's death was a mystery to me. Grandma Daisy said that the books at Charming Books would show me the answer, but so far the poems the tree had shown me resembled riddles, not clues.

I touched Carly's arm. "If it is all right with you, I think I'll head back to Charming Books and check on my grandmother. Will you be all right here? Would you rather I stay?"

She smiled. "No, you go. You've been here far too long already. Thank you for being here. I'm glad you were, Violet. You've been so kind to me through this. I can already tell we're going to be great friends."

Her comment made me smile. It had been a long time since I had made a new friend. As a graduate student, I had allowed myself to become consumed by my research. I knew Henry David Thoreau and Ralph Waldo Emerson better than I knew many of my classmates. I wondered how much of my own life I had missed because I had been preoccupied with the lives of authors dead for over a century. "I do too," I said. "Give me a call if you need anything."

She nodded, and I slipped away unnoticed while the police chief was in the middle of a conversation with his two officers.

As I rode my bike to Charming Books along the Riverwalk, I kept a close eye on the woods. It was almost ten in the morning, but no one was going to jump out and catch me unaware this time.

When I made the turn in front of the spa toward my grandmother's bookshop, I gave a sigh of relief.

Sadie was hanging an OPEN flag outside her vintage clothing shop. She waved at me. "Violet, why don't you come in and see the shop?"

I parked my bike in front of the white picket fence that framed her front yard. I was curious about her shop and what Sadie could tell me about the police chief. She must know more about him, since they were in the Red Inkers together.

The moment I stepped inside, I was hit with a strong floral scent mixed with the faintest hint of old cloth. The shop was bright. Light poured in through the windows. Clothing hung from wood hangers on metal racks spray-painted white and separated by decade. All were evenly spaced. It was nothing like the crowded thrift shops that I had visited in Chicago.

I wandered over to the 1950s rack. There was an actual poodle skirt dangling from one of the hangers. "Your shop is beautiful. It didn't seem like it would be this large from the outside."

She beamed and her cheeks had a rosy glow. "Thank you. Like a lot of the old cottages on River Road, this one was made of many tiny rooms. I knocked down all the walls I could to make this large showroom. It works out well, because it increases the number of windows too."

"That must have been a big undertaking," I said, moving to the next rack, where there was a gorgeous flowered A-line dress that looked like it had belonged to a World War II–era housewife.

"My dad helped me. He's a contractor and did most of the work himself, which saved me a bundle." She ran her hands over her A-line cerulean skirt. It went perfectly with her black-cat-printed blouse.

"Does he live close by?" I fingered the silky fabric of the dress I was admiring. I loved all the clothes in Mid-century Vintage, but I would never be able to wear them. I wouldn't even know how to pull them off.

She shook her head. "My family lives out in Colorado.

Dad flew out to do the work. I'm the only one who lives east of the Mississippi."

"What brought you to Cascade Springs? It's a long way from Colorado."

"Grant," she said simply. "We went to college together in Lexington, Kentucky."

I dropped the skirt of the dress. "I didn't know that Grant went out of state for college." I don't know why that surprised me other than the fact Grant chose to come back. Considering the sibling rivalry between the Morton boys, I would have thought that he would have left Cascade Springs for good.

"I don't know how Grant settled on the college. He never said. I chose it because they had a great writing program. Even as a teenager, I wanted to be a writer." She sounded wistful, as if she wasn't sure anything would come of that dream.

I turned away from the beautiful clothes to face her. "You are a writer. You're only waiting to be a published one, and you will if you don't give up. I know plenty of published writers in my grad school program, and most of them tell me sheer stubbornness gets a book published more than anything else."

She smiled and her face lit up again. "Then I should be published with no problem. I can be pretty stubborn."

I raised my eyebrows at her. "What do you mean?"

"The moment I saw Grant across the campus, I was smitten. We became friends. We didn't start dating until I moved out here." Her face turned a beet red. "I followed him. I guess you can say that I finally wore him down into dating me with my stubbornness."

"I'm sure that wasn't it," I said. "He probably realized you were the right person for him." Even as I said that, I remembered how uncomfortable Grant had made me during the carriage ride in Niagara Falls the day before and Nathan's hints that Grant cheated on Sadie.

Sadie frowned. "He told me about your trip together to Niagara Falls yesterday."

"What did he tell you?" My voice was sharper than I had intended it to be.

She stepped onto the other side of a dress rack as if to put space in between us. "He said that you wanted to go there to see the Falls for old times' sake."

I didn't know what Grant's purpose was in telling Sadie about the trip to the Falls, but I suspected that it couldn't be good. However, since she brought up the subject of my trip, I saw it as an opportunity to talk about Benedict. "That's not really why we were there," I said.

"Oh?" she asked, looking faintly concerned. The corners of her bright red lips were pointed down in a frown.

"I was there to learn about Benedict. Grant and I visited the carriage house he used to work for before moving to the village."

Her face cleared again. "What did you find out?"

"We found the place he'd worked, Falling Waters Livery, and we spoke to a man who knew Benedict. In the end, I'm afraid it was a wasted trip and a dead end. To be honest, I was a little surprised when Grant offered to come along with me."

Sadie stepped out around the rack of patchwork skirts and dresses. "I'm not that surprised. Benedict and Grant were close friends."

I blinked at her. Grant had given me the idea they were merely friendly acquaintances. "They were?"

She nodded. "At least they seemed to be in the last several months. Many times, I would go to the water company and find Benedict's carriage parked out front. Benedict and Grant would be chatting together nine times out of ten."

"What about?" I tried my best to keep the urgency out of my voice.

She shrugged and straightened a pale yellow blouse with puffed sleeves on its hanger. "I don't really know."

"You never asked Grant?"

"I assumed it had to do with business. Most of Grant's conversations do." Her face darkened ever so softly. "I learned a long time ago not to talk with Grant about his work. He says he doesn't like to talk about work when we're together. He wants to concentrate on us. Isn't that sweet?"

"Very sweet," I murmured, but I wondered if Grant didn't want to talk about his business because there was something he didn't want her to know about it.

She sighed, clasping her hands together like the female lead in an old Hollywood movie. "Grant is such a dreamboat. I still pinch myself every day that we are getting married."

I smiled at her use of the old-fashioned word. Sadie even took her love of all things retro to her vocabulary. "He's a lucky guy," I said, meaning it.

She plucked a cherry-patterned dress from the rack and shook her head, putting it back. "I'm the lucky one. Were you out for a morning ride? I love your bicycle, by the way. Daisy told me all about her plans to repair it for you. I thought it was the sweetest thing I've ever heard."

I supposed Sadie heard the sweetest thing she had ever heard at least once a day. She was like a ray of sunshine and a lollipop all rolled up into one. Somehow on her it wasn't annoying, just adorable. I wondered if Grant Morton deserved Sadie.

"I went over to the carriage house."

She examined a royal blue pencil skirt with a ruffle at the bottom, then looked at me and back at the skirt again. "The carriage house? What were you doing there?"

"I met Carly the other day and dropped in for a visit. She's been pretty upset about Benedict's passing. The Riverwalk is a lovely ride that early in the morning."

She grabbed an ivory lacy dress with fringe on the skirt and grinned. "I love it when the morning sun sparkles on the river." She walked over to me and held it up. "This one, I think, and with your red-golden hair up and a red lipstick. You will be striking. Nathan will faint dead away."

I stepped back. "What are you doing?"

She frowned. "Finding you a dress for Friday night's gala."

I took another step back. "I'm not going to the gala."

"You have to go. It's the biggest event in the village. Cascade Springs can only turn two hundred years old once. Besides, Grant already told me that you'd be there." Her blue eyes twinkled. "And that Nathan asked you."

"I—I don't know for sure that I will still be in the village."

"You have to be." She held the dress to her chest like it was a security blanket. "You must be there. You have the perfect look for my clothes with your hair and pale skin.

I've been dying to dress you since the moment I met you."
She shook the dress at me.

"Umm . . ." I inched for the door.

Through the open door, there was the sound of hooves
and a carriage. I glanced out the window and saw Shane
in the driver's seat. He and his horse clomped up the
street. Both had their heads up, appraising everything
around them. Shane almost appeared respectable with
his top hat sitting squarely on the middle of his head and
the confidence with which he held the reins.

Sadie moved over to the shelves of shoes after taking
a close look at my feet. She shook her head. My sneakers
weren't up to snuff in her estimation. Sadie wore mint-
colored peep-toe heels.

"Do you know Shane Pitman?" I asked. I hoped the
subject would distract her from talk of the gala.

"Sure! He's a friend of Grant's too." She laughed.

The hairs on the back of my neck stood up. "He is?"
It seemed like Grant was friends with a good many people
related to Benedict's murder. Then again, I reminded
myself that the village was small, tiny even, and Grant
was a prominent member from an old family in Cascade
Springs. He would have reason to know everyone. "How
long have they been friends?"

"Shane moved here a couple of months ago looking
for work. Grant knew he was good with horses, so he sent
him Carly's way." She laughed. "I suppose everyone in
the village is a friend of Grant's. Everyone loves him."

Except his brother, I thought.

She picked up a pair of sparkling sandals, held them

against the dress I was supposedly wearing to the gala, and set the shoes back on the shelf.

"What do you think of Shane?" I asked.

"I like him. He can be grumpy, but he has a good heart under that. He's been a really good friend to Grant."

I frowned. Sadie was the type that would find something nice to say about Attila the Hun. She'd probably say, "He has trouble making friends, but he's really great with a sword."

"Does Carly know they were friends?"

"I guess so. I mean Grant put him up for the job." She picked up another pair of shoes. "Don't worry," she said when she saw me wrinkle my nose at a pair of penny loafers. "I'm not considering these to go with your dress."

"Sadie, it's so nice of you to want to dress me for the party," I began, "but—"

She turned and her skirt flared out when she moved. "You have to come. Nathan and Grant's parents will be there, and it will be nice to have someone else there by my side."

"Why do you say that?" I asked.

She frowned, looking truly sad for the first time. "I could use an ally, I suppose. Grant's parents have always been cordial to me, but I know they don't approve of Grant's and my engagement. They would much rather he marry someone—" She paused. "Well, someone not like me. They aren't sure what to make of me."

Seeing Nathan's parents was not a good argument for me to go anywhere. I blamed his parents the most for what had happened to me twelve years ago after Colleen died. However, I realized being back in Cascade Springs accomplished one thing. I was finally recovering from my guilt over Colleen's death. I would always miss her and losing her would be with me for my entire life, but I was letting go of the sick ache that had haunted me all these years. I feared that most of that had to do with a certain police chief saying that it wasn't my fault.

Sadie looked so worried about seeing Grant's parents—and I knew better than anyone what the elder Mortons could be like—that I said, "I guess it wouldn't hurt me to hang around the village until after the gala."

She clapped her hands and bounced. "Leave it all to me. I will make sure you are the belle of the gala." She bounced some more. "Nathan will faint dead away."

Nathan's wasn't the reaction I was curious about. I imagined whoever killed Benedict would have the greatest reaction to me being at the gala. And maybe there, I could figure out who that was.

# THIRTY-ONE

G randma Daisy was with a customer when I returned to the shop, so I quickly told her that I was headed to the community college to talk to Richard.

Her face brightened immediately, and I didn't have the heart to tell her that I wasn't visiting Richard about the adjunct job.

The college was on the edge of Cascade Springs, east of the actual spring. The quickest way there was to ride the paved path through the wooded park, right past the last place I had seen Colleen alive.

I straightened my shoulders and walked the bicycle behind the house and into the woods until I reached the paved path. Seeing the spot where I had left Colleen was something I had to do, no matter how much it turned my stomach. It was time I faced those old memories. I kicked off as soon as I reached the pavement.

I had pedaled into the woods and past the bubbling natural springs in silence. The only sound was the twittering of unseen birds and the spinning of my bicycle's wheels until Emerson's head popped up out of my bicycle basket. I screamed and the bike tipped over. Emerson landed on his feet, but I fell off the bike, landing on my hands and knees. I groaned. Between my encounter with the assailant the night before and my acrobatics falling from the bike, I was going to be black-and-blue when I headed west for Chicago. I scrambled to my feet. "Emerson?" I searched the path for the cat while I scraped out the gravel ingrained into my palms. Luckily, I had only minor scratches.

"Emerson?"

"Meow," he said as if to say yes, and he wiggled out from under the brush. Leaves and dirt clung to his fur.

I sighed. "What am I going to do with you?" I scooped him up and brushed the debris from his coat. "What on earth were you doing inside my basket? Where did you learn to be a stowaway?"

He purred, apparently determined to keep his stowaway secrets to himself.

I checked him over for any sign of injury, but he was fine, much better off than I was. I twisted my mouth and wondered if I should take him back to Charming Books before continuing on to Springside.

As if he could read my mind, he meowed loudly and pointed his nose down the path in the direction of the college.

"You shouldn't have snuck in there like that," I said. "You scared me half to death, and what am I supposed to do with you when I reach the campus?"

He washed his face with his paw as if he didn't have a care in the world.

I tucked Emerson back in his basket. It was then that I realized I was in the exact spot where I had last seen my best friend alive.

An enormous boulder twice my height loomed on the hillside. Colleen and I used to meet on the boulder. It was our secret rendezvous point in the middle of the woods and gave an excellent view of the springs. Beyond the boulder, evergreen shrubs and moss covered the rocky wall of the springs, where a tiny waterfall, no larger than the width of a man, wound its way down the hillside.

The night she died, Colleen had asked me to meet her at the boulder, but I hadn't wanted to go. I was studying for an AP English test and was determined to keep my perfect score in the course and earn the high school's humanities award. So I told her I couldn't meet her that evening.

In the end I went. It had been a cool April night. I remembered being cold because I had left my sweater back at Charming Books.

When I'd reached the boulder, my best friend had been unusually quiet. It was a detail that I remembered after the fact, but my self-consumed teenage self at the time had taken little notice of it. I had been too preoccupied with my studies and my obsession with winning the award to notice how upset she had been. She had just found out that she hadn't been accepted to her top-choice college and didn't know how to tell her perfectionist parents, who were almost as bad as Nathan's parents in what they expected from their children.

Growing up in the affluent village, all the students

were held to a high standard and expected to excel. Some, like Nathan and me, could handle those expectations. Others, like Colleen, could not, and when she wasn't accepted to the college of her choice, she'd been devastated. She had wanted me to go to Niagara Falls with her, to take the night off from her worries about college and exams, and just be kids.

I'd refused and told her that I had to study.

After I had went home, I felt guilty for blowing Colleen off. She hadn't answered her cell phone, so I went looking for her. I found her facedown in the Niagara River. She had fallen off one of the land bridges and cracked her head on a rock below. She was already dead by the time I found her. I should have called 911, but because I was young and scared, I called Nathan. He'd come to the river and found me standing over Colleen's dead body. His parents never forgave me for involving him, and they punished me for it by making their son imply I might have had something to do with Colleen's accidental death.

It was still difficult to come to terms with her death after all this time. On her way home from the springs, she'd died in a senseless accident. Tripped or fallen from the bridge over the river and swept away with the current. Her parents would not accept that their daughter, with so much promise, had died in such a senseless way. They pressed the police to investigate. They even hired a private investigator from Rochester because they thought the village police weren't doing enough to find out what really happened.

My senior year had ended in a series of questions and accusations and grief instead of excitement and celebration as it should have. I had been shocked when the police chief at the time came to Charming Books and dragged me to the police station, accusing me of murdering my best friend. The elderly chief of the village police had claimed I had pushed Colleen off the bridge in a fit of rage in my jealousy over her budding romance with Nathan. I had been the one who had been found standing over her dead body on the riverbank, after all. In the old chief's estimation, that meant I was guilty, and his suspicions were only made worse when Nathan agreed with them.

It was all lies. It had been the private investigator who had finally convinced the police and the Prestons that I'd had nothing to do with it. I'd spent less than twenty-four hours in the village police station, but I'd known when I got out that I had to leave the village and never come back, and I had stuck to that plan until I got that fake I'm-dying call from my grandmother.

I sighed and was about to climb back on the bike and leave the memories behind when a voice said from above, "I come here sometimes to think."

I gripped the bike handles for all I was worth and turned around. Nathan was wearing a suit and sitting on the moss-covered boulder. He stood and climbed down the side of the boulder with the same ease he'd had when he was a teenager.

When he joined me on the path, I asked, "How long have you been sitting there?"

He shrugged. "A little while."

I ground my teeth. He'd probably seen my graceful dismount from the bike as well. "See you around."

He jumped in front of my bike. "Wait. I want to talk to you."

"What could you have to say to me, Nathan? I think you've said everything that you needed to yesterday at Charming Books."

"It's about your grandmother."

Now he had my attention. "What about Grandma Daisy?"

"I don't believe she would ever hurt anyone. I told Chief Rainwater that." He paused, attempted to clear the tension in the air by giving me a wry smile. "Since I'm the mayor, he has to listen to me."

I doubted the police chief listened to anyone unless he had evidence to back up the person's statement. That made him a good cop, but it also made him dangerous where my grandmother was concerned.

Even so, I blushed when he said the police chief's name, and a fleeting expression crossed Nathan's face. He cleared his throat. "I come here a lot because it reminds me of my mistakes. It reminds me to do better."

My knuckles grew white as I held the handlebars a little bit tighter. "I'm impressed that you consider what happened after Colleen died a mistake."

"I do, and I never should have turned you over to the police like that. I never thought they would treat you so badly."

"They did."

"Chief Campbell didn't know what he was doing. He was scared of all the pressure he was under, and Colleen's parents were distraught. They needed someone to blame for what happened."

I didn't say so, but David Rainwater had basically said the same thing to me in the children's loft at Charming Books.

"I wanted to say I'm sorry. Truly, I am, and I want us to start over."

"Start what over?" I watched him, and tried to ignore the sound of the babbling water at my feet. "There's nothing to start over, Nate."

"A friendship, maybe. If you are going to stay in the vill—"

"I'm not going to stay," I cut him off, coming to a decision at that moment. I could not believe I'd even entertained the thought about moving to Cascade Springs permanently for even a moment.

"What does Grandma Daisy think of that?" he asked, frowning.

"She wants me to stay," I said. I didn't add that she thought it was my calling to stay as the next Caretaker of the shop. Nathan had already seen me riding a bicycle with a cat in the basket. There was no reason to look more eccentric.

"Then, why not stay? You are almost done with school."

My eyes narrowed. "How do you know that?"

It was his turn to blush. "Grandma Daisy told me."

Great, my grandmother was reporting back to my ex-boyfriend about me. If she thought that helped her cause for me to become the next Caretaker, she was sadly mistaken.

I shook my head. "My life is back in Chicago until I finish school. After that, who knows where I'll end up? I'll go wherever I can find a job. Likely, that will be very, very far away from here." Mentally I added, *I'll make sure of that.*

"It sounds to me that you already have a job here."

I wrinkled my brow. "How did you know about the teaching positing at Springside?" I asked.

"I was talking about Charming Books. Grandma Daisy has always planned for you to take over the shop. She's talked about it since we were kids. What's this about the community college?"

I stopped short of smacking myself on the forehead. Of course, he was talking about Charming Books.

"I was going to the college to do some research. I thought that's what you meant," I lied.

He gave a wry smile. "You always said that you would be a college professor someday, and you are about to make the dream come true."

"And your father always said that you would be a politician someday, and you've done that." My words had a bite in them, but I didn't apologize or take them back. I cleared my throat. "I'll stay here until everything is settled with Benedict's case and Grandma Daisy is in the clear. After that, I'm going home."

"You seem to forget this is your home, and always will be. No matter where you run, you'll always think of Cascade Springs as home."

He couldn't possibly know how true that was for me.

"I hope I will see you at the gala on Friday." He stepped aside.

I grimaced, but I knew it would be my best chance to see all the murder suspects in one place. The entire village would be there. "You will. I said that I would go for Sadie's sake."

He grinned. "See, you can agree to something. That wasn't so hard, was it?"

I scowled, and he turned and walked back toward the center of the village from where I'd come.

After he was gone, I leaned over the bike so that Emerson could hear me over the spin of the tires. "If I didn't know better, I would have said you planned to jump out of the basket at that moment because you knew Nathan was there."

"Meow," was his only reply.

~∞~

# THIRTY-TWO

~∞~

S pringside Community College was tiny and com-
prised five or six academic buildings around a single
green quad. It was much smaller than the sprawling universities that I was used to.

The college library was a large brick building in the
center of the campus. It was the most dominant with a
cupola and weather vane on the top. When we had been
teenagers, Nathan and I had climbed to the top of that
cupola once. I pushed that memory, along with our latest
encounter on the trail, to the back of my mind.

The library seemed like the right place to start for my
search, and there was a convenient bike rack right outside
the door under a large shade tree. I chained the bike to
the rack. Emerson leaned over the edge of the basket to
watch me work.

I frowned. "Now, what am I going to do with you while I'm inside the library?"

"Meow." He pawed at my tote bag.

I glanced at the cat and then at the library. I had been known to sneak food into a library—even a burrito once, which turned out to be a mistake. A cat was a whole different ball game, but then again, I couldn't leave him outside. What if something happened to him? At least Emerson was a small cat.

He pawed at my bag again. "All right. Get in." I held the bag open, and the tuxedo cat jumped from the bicycle basket to my tote.

I peered inside the tote. "Now, be quiet in there. Okay?"

"Meow," he replied.

This was such a bad idea.

As I walked up the building's stone steps, I couldn't help but think, *My life is just too weird.*

Inside the library, I walked to the circulation desk. A bored-looking undergraduate sat behind the counter, fiddling with his phone. When I approached, he smiled and appeared almost relieved to have someone to talk to. "Hi," he said.

I smiled. "Hi, I was wondering if you could tell me where I can find Dr. Bunting's office."

"I guess I could look it up," the student said.

"Kyle, why don't you go shelf-read the juvenile collection?" A woman a few years older than me, wearing jeans and a Springside polo shirt, approached the desk with a stack of books in hand.

His mouth fell open. "Renee, not the juvenile section. That's cruel and unusual punishment."

Her eyes twinkled behind her blue-framed glasses. "Sorry, kid. It must be done."

He groaned but dutifully got up and shuffled to the stairway that led to the upper floors.

I suppressed a smile. "The juvenile books is a tough section."

She grinned. "That's the idea. It'll keep him occupied for a few hours or at least until his eyes are crossed." She set her stack of books on the counter. "You were looking for Dr. Bunting?"

I nodded.

"I'm sorry to tell you that he's in a faculty meeting right now. All the faculty are actually."

My shoulders drooped. I should have called Richard before riding here. Grandma Daisy must have his phone number, since he was a member of the Red Inkers.

The librarian glanced at the watch on her wrist. "They should be out of the meeting in a half hour or so. You're welcome to hang out here."

"That's really kind of you. Actually, it'll give me a chance to do some research." I adjusted my tote bag, which was heavier than I expected it to be with Emerson inside of it.

Her brows shot up. "Did your bag just hiss?"

"No," I said a little too quickly.

"Meow," Emerson said from the depths of my bag.

She gave me an appraising librarian look and rested her elbows on the stack of books.

I sighed and opened the tote bag. Emerson popped his head out and scoped out the area; so much for him keeping a low profile.

"Hey there," Renee said with a chuckle.

"Sorry about the cat. He sort of tagged along with me. I can wait for Dr. Bunting outside."

She laughed. "Don't be silly. Kyle and I are the only ones here, and it's nice to have a feline visitor now and again." She tapped her fingers on the circulation desk, and Emerson hopped out of my bag onto the counter. He walked the length of it like he owned the place. I had a sneaking suspicion that Emerson thought the entirety of planet Earth was his private domain.

"Care if he stays here while I pull some books?" I asked.

She shook her head. As I walked to the stairs, I heard her say, "Kyle won't be happy to find out he missed seeing you to shelf-read the juvenile section."

With the precision of a scholar who has spent her life studying American literature and memorizing the Library of Congress call numbers for the authors in that category, I went to the stacks where Emily Dickinson was kept on the second floor of the library. My index finger slid lovingly across the spines of the books as I went. By the time I was done, I had a stack that was taller than the former jockey Carly Long.

Carefully, I carried them back down the stairs and found Renee teasing Emerson with the red beam from the bar code scanner. I set my stack of books and sorted them into piles on the closest table to the circulation desk.

Emerson jumped off the circulation desk and came running to me. I was gratified to know that even though he had made a new friend, he preferred my company.

Renee followed him with her eyebrows raised. "You look like you are ready to move in."

I flushed with embarrassment. "I'm doing a little bit of research."

She grinned. "It's nice to see. Things are slow in the summer, and I'm bored out of my skull. If there is any way I can help you, let me know."

I knew better than to scare away an eager librarian. "I'm actually trying to interpret a poem by Emily Dickinson." I removed the thin volume of Dickinson's poems from my tote bag. I knocked the cat hair off the cover and opened it to the page with the poem about remembrance before handing it to her.

She took the book from my hands. She was silent as she read the poem. "Beautiful and kind of haunting too." She handed the book back to me.

"I'm particularly interested in the second line," I said, reading it to her. "'Besides, the deepest cellar / That ever mason hewed; / Look to it, by its fathoms / Ourselves be not pursued.'" I paused. "Do you see the piece about the cellar? That's the line I'm most curious about." I took a breath. "In fact, I was wondering how that applies to Cascade Springs."

"Cascade Springs?" She studied me over her blue eyeglass frames. "Emily Dickinson never even came to New York State, as far as I know. She lived in Massachusetts and only left a few times. Philadelphia and Washington DC, if I remember correctly. Her father was a politician."

"I know that, but I'm doing a reader's response study," I lied. Goodness, I was doing that too frequently. "And seeing how the poem applies to my own life. I was born in the village and lived here until I was seventeen. I'm a graduate student at the University of Chicago. I'm visiting my grandmother for a few days."

The librarian seemed to be satisfied with that explanation. I supposed she'd heard stranger questions in her time. She tapped her cheek with her index finger. "I would interpret that saying quite literally, I'm afraid, especially in the case of the village. . . ." She trailed off.

"I would love to hear your opinion. I really am stuck on that line."

"It seems like that line is about someone hiding in a cellar or underground. If you think of the village, it could be referring to the Underground Railroad. That's only a guess."

My pulse quickened. "Cascade Springs was part of the Underground Railroad?"

"Oh yes," she said, warming to the subject. "We're a river away from Canada. This was a hot spot for crossing the border. Thousands of men, women, and children moved through the village before the Civil War."

How did I not know this? I searched my memory for any mention of this in my high school history classes, but I couldn't recall any.

"You know"—the librarian tapped her pencil to the side of her head—"I might have something that will help you if you are interested in learning more about the Underground Railroad in the village."

"I am," I said, feeling excited about the Dickinson poems for the first time. Maybe, just maybe, they would point me in the right direction. Finally.

"Wait here," she directed.

Emerson got up from the book he was lying on.

She laughed. "You wait here too. It might take me a few minutes to find what I'm looking for."

She was gone for nearly twenty minutes, and I started to worry that Richard would leave from his faculty meeting soon, and I would miss my chance to speak to him that day.

When she returned, she wore white cotton gloves and she spread an old map across the next empty table. She pointed at a second pair of white gloves sticking out of her jeans pocket. "You're going to want to put those on if you want to touch the map. This one dates back to 1851."

I removed the gloves from her pocket and slipped them on. I noticed two things right off about the map. First, it was of Cascade Springs. I could clearly see the springs, the river, and even the building that was now Charming Books on the map. Other landmarks were different, but those central to my life jumped out at me. The second thing that I noticed was little drawings of owls on the map, dotting a half dozen buildings.

"It's quite rare to have a map of the Underground Railroad." The librarian spoke in hushed tones. "And if the archivist knew I had taken this from his lair, he would have a coronary. He doesn't work during the summer months, so I'm not worried about him knowing about it." She smiled. "The archives are in the basement of the library, and it's too gloomy to be down there for any length of time."

"Thank you for bringing it up. It must be valuable."

"It's priceless. One of the few priceless items we have in our collection," she said reverently as she smoothed the curling corners of the yellowing map.

She pointed at one of the little owls. "Since the village is close to Canada, it was a major freeway, so to speak, and we're a much safer crossing than down the river by the Falls. That was far too dangerous." She tapped the owl again. "The owls indicate a safe house in the village. There's nothing on here that states that per se. The conductors would not have been so foolish as to write down what they were trying to communicate. The secrecy of the Railroad led to its success more than anything else. That and people willing to risk their lives for what they believed was right."

"That's amazing," I said. "But in that case," I asked, ever the critical scholar, "how do you know that that's what the owls indicate?"

"Thirty years ago, a historian visited the college to view the map and check its authenticity. He declared it authentic and, in his estimation, believed that the owls were in reference to the conductors who used owl calls to communicate during the night when most of the running took place. By the sound of the call, conductors knew if a place was safe to stop in for the night or not. With the Fugitive Slave Act of 1850, even this far north there was still a chance a slave could be sent back to the South. Until they were on Canadian soil, they lived in fear."

"Wow," I whispered in the same reverent tones she had used.

"When you asked if Dickinson's poem could be applied to the village, this was the only thing that came to my mind. I mean as far as cellars go." She laughed. "It's probably not at all what you were looking for."

My gloved index finger touched every tiny owl, and then I traced the river. I stopped when I came to the edge of the village and where the carriage house stood. I froze. It would have certainly been there in 1850. In fact, I remembered seeing the livery sign on my first visit. It had said EST. 1850.

That's when the building had been turned into a carriage house, but the barn would have been built even earlier than that. My mind raced, and I remembered Shane disappearing into the carriage house's barn, and never reappearing, not even when Carly fell and hurt her ankle. Was it because he was underground and didn't want anyone to know about it? But why? Why would he go underground?

Emerson jumped on the table and cocked his head as he stared at the map. He didn't come any closer to the map, as if he knew that it shouldn't be touched.

"That's the strangest cat I've ever seen," Renee said. "It's almost like he is studying the map right along with us."

I nodded absentmindedly. My head was still spinning with all this new information.

"Find something?" The librarian was watching me curiously.

"Oh, sorry," I stammered. "I was lost in thought. This is perfect actually, and exactly what I was looking for."

She beamed and blinked. "That's great!"

I tapped the old map where my finger had stopped on the carriage house. "That's the carriage house, right? Where the carriage drivers work out of today?"

She grinned. "It doesn't get much more Cascade Springs than the dapper carriage drivers," she said, nodding. "It was built about 1830. Actually, we have lots of information on that place being part of the Railroad. It was built by a wealthy logger and abolitionist. I suppose that's why it's so close to the edge of the woods. He couldn't stand to be away from the trees. It wasn't a working farm, but what is the carriage house today was his horse barn. In his prime, the logger had ten horses, I believe." She opened a manila folder that was on the table. I hadn't noticed before because all my concentration had been on the map. "I have something else." She handed me a flyer.

The flyer said, "Cascade Springs, one step from freedom. For a slave fleeing the oppression of the South before the Civil War, Canada would be the Promised Land, especially after the passing of the Fugitive Slave Act. Come to our program and see how Cascade Springs was a central player in the Underground Railroad."

"That's a flyer for a program the college hosted last year for Black History Month. It was well received. We had three Underground Railroad historians come in for a panel, and they showed off the map. Not the original, with that many people, but a projection on a screen."

I would have loved to have attended that talk, and the fact that the community college did such a wonderful program had me intrigued about what else they did for their students to enrich their college experience. Because of my field of study, I knew my fair share of Civil War and Reconstruction history. The Transcendentalist writers had been contemporary with the Civil War. A student of literature couldn't focus on writing without understanding the context of the time period of the writer. Where a writer lived and what was happening in the world was essential to understanding literature. Ralph Waldo Emerson had been in his fifties during the war, and he was at the height of his career when the South seceded from the Union.

"You can take that flyer," she said. "We have a ton of others in the archives. The archivist is trying to get rid of the duplicates of everything for lack of space, but it's a losing battle."

I thanked her and my thoughts turned to why I'd come to campus in the first place: to find Richard Bunting. "I should go see if I can track down Dr. Bunting." I started to gather up the books.

"Don't worry about those. I'll have Kyle put them away. It will give him a much needed break from shelf-reading." She laughed. "Dr. Bunting's office is in the humanities building." She walked to the closest window and pointed to a brick building directly across the quad. "It's right there. His office number is 103."

I thanked her, and added, "I can't tell you how helpful this has been."

"Don't mention it. Come back anytime, and bring your cat too. The library is open five days a week in the summer, closed on the weekends, and most of the time it's just me and a student or two working."

"Thanks again," I said, scooping up Emerson and gripping the flyer in my hand as I left.

## THIRTY-THREE

I smoothed the flyer in my hand as I ran down the library steps back to my bike. I couldn't wait to share what I'd learned with Chief Rainwater. I froze midstep, which caused me to stumble down the last two steps. I managed to keep myself from hitting the sidewalk with my face or dropping Emerson.

All my excitement flew out of me in a whoosh. Who was I kidding? What was I supposed to say to the police chief? *Oh, can you check if there are any secret rooms or tunnels under the carriage house because I think my grandmother's magical books are telling me to look there through Emily Dickinson's poetry?* Yeah, right. Not happening.

When I reached my bike, I placed Emerson in the basket. At the very least, I could walk over to the academic building to find out what Richard might know about Trey Long, if anything at all.

The tuxedo cat settled into the basket and gave an enormous yawn, showing off every last one of his impressively sharp teeth.

"Is it nap time?" I asked.

"Meow."

I could see a lot of our conversations going this way. The one positive thing to be said for Faulkner—I never knew what was going to come out of his mouth.

I was bent over the bike twisting the combination lock when a voice said, "Violet, it's nice to see you on campus."

I straightened up and found Richard Bunting, just the man I was looking for, standing across the sidewalk from me. Papers poked out every which way from the stack of books that he held.

"Richard, I was just about to walk across campus to see you," I said.

He smiled and wrinkled his nose as if to stop his glasses' downward descent. "I'm glad to hear it. Am I right to think you are here to apply for the adjunct position in the English department?"

There was so much hope in his voice I almost didn't want to tell him the truth.

"No." I pointed at the library. "I thought I would do a little research at the library."

His smile faded. "I know we can't pay much—few adjunct positions do—but it would give you plenty of experience as you looked for something more permanent."

"It's not about the money," I said. "I'm not sure I want to stay in the village."

"That's a shame. I hope it doesn't mean you have made your final decision not to apply."

"Not yet," I said. The words popped out of my mouth before I could stop them. Why had I said that? I had made my final decision, and I wasn't applying for the job. I was leaving Cascade Springs as soon as Grandma Daisy was in the clear.

He brightened. "Good, good. I'm glad you visited the library. We have a wonderful library, far superior to most community colleges'. You will see."

He knew the best way to an academic's heart was through a quality library.

I nodded. "The librarian was very nice and found just what I needed in no time at all."

"Renee is brilliant," he said enthusiastically. "She's helped me countless times with my own scholarship. I haven't been able to stump her with a research problem yet. We're lucky to have her on campus and in the village."

I suppressed a smile. Someone had a crush on the librarian, and that someone had elbow patches on his sport jacket.

He juggled the books in his arms. "If it wasn't the adjunct position, what is it that you wanted to talk to me about? About your research perhaps? I'm quite curious about your dissertation."

"No, but I might ask for your insight about that before I leave the village. I wanted to talk about a student you might have had in class."

He stood up a little bit straighter. "I'm sure you know

that we are not allowed to talk about our students with anyone outside of the college community. I'm not even allowed to discuss a student with his or her parents without the student's express permission."

"I understand that," I said. "And I respect that too, but telling me about this student might also help my grandmother."

He was thoughtful as if he was debating to break the rules just this once. I knew that Richard must be a rule follower and he would not break a rule without a very good reason and without a lot of internal debate.

"I suppose," he said slowly. "What is the student's name?"

"Trey Long. He's the younger brother of Carly Long, who owns Cascade Springs Livery along the river."

He relaxed. "I don't have much to tell. I know Trey is a student here, but I have never had him in class. I don't even know what his major or field of study might be."

"Oh," I said with shoulders drooping. With all that buildup I'd found nothing new.

"If you don't mind my asking, why are you so interested in Trey?"

"He worked at the livery with Benedict, and I thought he might know something about his death."

"Have you asked him directly?"

"Not exactly."

He adjusted the stack of his books again. "Then, I suggest that you go straight to the source and find out what the boy knows. That is always the best way to obtain the information you need. As I tell my students, go back to the text if they are being befuddled by what the critics have to say about a writer's work. No one can tell you more about a piece of work than the writer him- or herself."

He had a good point, but I didn't know how was I going to talk to Trey without Carly overhearing. I didn't want my new friend to think that I suspected her brother of anything until I knew more. I guessed that I could always tell Rainwater about my suspicions, but I was reluctant after my own experience when I'd been close to Trey's age. He could be completely innocent.

I could also apply Richard's comment to the Emily Dickinson poems that supposedly would help me unravel the mystery of Benedict's death.

I smiled at him. "That's a good idea. I should have thought of it myself. Thank you."

He straightened. "You are very welcome."

"Will I be seeing you at the gala on Friday night? I promised Sadie that I would stick around at least that long for the event."

He shot a look at the library. I wondered if he was thinking of the librarian inside.

"Oh no, I'm not really one for events like that. I have some of my own writing that I would like to get done. My story is starting to come together." His eyes sparkled as he spoke of his creative endeavor. "I must be some kind of silly cliché: English professor who is an aspiring novelist."

"I think it's great. You should do whatever makes you happy." And because I couldn't resist, I added, "And I bet Renee approves too. Do you know if she will be going to the gala?"

He swallowed and his Adam's apple bobbed up and down. "I—I don't know."

"Maybe you should ask her," I said, and then I nodded at the books in his arms. "You're going in there to return some books anyway, aren't you?"

"I am." He swallowed again as if the idea of asking the librarian if she was going to the village's bicentennial gala was too much to contemplate. "Yes, well," he said as if he had come to some sort of decision, "I had better return these to the library now." He held up the books. "It was nice to see you, and please give my suggestion about the teaching position some serious thought."

I nodded and watched as he tripped up the steps to see Renee.

## THIRTY-FOUR

As I rode back to Charming Books with Emerson peeking over the side of the bicycle basket, I couldn't help but believe that Richard might have been right. Instead of simply being suspicious of Trey, I should go right to the source and talk to him about Benedict. I should have done the same for Shane and Audrey too. After Colleen died, there were so many times that I wished the people in the village who suspected me would have asked me about it instead of assuming the worst. After my experiences, I had to give everyone, even prickly Shane, the chance to stand up for themselves.

Feeling like I finally had a good plan of action, I pedaled faster back to the bookshop. Emerson seemed to enjoy the increased speed, because he braced his forepaws on the front rim of the basket and let the wind whip through his whiskers.

As much as I wanted to go straight to the livery to track down Trey and Shane, I knew I needed to drop off Emerson first. Renee and Richard hadn't minded seeing him, but I doubted that Shane or Trey's dog, Java, would be as welcoming to my feline sidekick.

My bike bumped down the dirt path that led from the park into the back garden of Charming Books. I hopped off the bike right outside the fence and opened the gate. When I had closed the gate behind me, Emerson jumped out of the basket onto the grass and rolled in it.

I picked up the cat, who meowed in protest. "Sorry. I'm not leaving you out here with my bike so that you can stow away again. You can't come where I'm going next."

I walked through the back door of the old house and into the kitchen. Through the open kitchen door on the other side of the room, I could hear raised voices and one of them belonged to my grandmother.

"I demand that you arrest this woman. She killed my father for his money."

I set Emerson on the stool in the kitchen and went into the main part of the shop. Grandma Daisy had her back to me and the birch tree between us. She faced Benedict's daughter, Audrey Fussy, and a short bald man wearing a suit. His upper lip was sweating, and he kept giving furtive looks to the wide-open front door to the shop as if he was contemplating escape. Officer Wheaton stood on the other side of Audrey with handcuffs drawn as if he was just waiting for the right moment to slap them on my grandmother's wrists.

I was so focused on the scene in front of me I almost didn't see Chief Rainwater standing beside the sales counter on the left side of the large room until I felt someone watching me.

"What's going on?" I asked.

Grandma Daisy turned around, and her shoulders relaxed when she saw me. "Violet, did you have a nice visit to the college?"

My brows pinched together. "It was fine. I'm more worried about what's been happening here while I was gone."

"I'll tell you what's been happening." Audrey tossed back her head and one of her large hoop earrings bounced off her shoulder. "Your grandmother has committed murder, and no one in this backwater village will do anything about it."

The little man cleared his throat. "Now, Audrey, you shouldn't say such things when you aren't certain that they are true. Ms. Waverly could claim slander."

Audrey rounded on him, sending her hoop earrings flying. "It's not slander if it is true, and I know it is, Art."

So this was the Art Audrey she had been yelling at over the phone when she'd left the shop the day before. Poor guy. He was literally shaking with fear.

Audrey turned to the police chief. "Chief Rainwater, I demand that you arrest this woman, throw her in jail, and toss away the key."

Rainwater pushed off the sales counter. For the first time, I noticed that there were dark circles under his eyes.

I wondered how much sleep he had gotten since I had discovered Benedict's body. "I can't do that. There is not enough evidence to arrest anyone at this point in the investigation."

"But, Chief," Wheaton interjected.

Rainwater gave him a look. Officer Wheaton glared back and reattached his handcuffs to his duty belt.

I stepped around my grandmother, putting myself between her and Audrey. "If you think Grandma Daisy killed Benedict for his money, you have the same motive and it's just as strong."

Audrey's heavily made-up eyes narrowed into streaks of purple eye shadow. "You had better watch your mouth. You don't know what you are talking about."

"Don't I? Isn't it true that the only times you would come to the village to visit your father would be to ask him for money?"

"So what if it is?" She lifted her chin. "I'm his only child, and he owed me that much after the childhood that he had put me through."

"And you needed the money, right?"

"Yes, I need the mon—" She caught herself. "Just because I'm hard up at the moment doesn't mean I killed my father." She scowled. "The money is rightfully mine. I deserved all of it when he finally did the world a favor and died."

Grandma Daisy jabbed her fists into her narrow hips. "How dare you talk about your father like that? He was a kind and caring man. I think it's time for you to leave."

"He was a crook," Audrey snapped. "Ask anyone who knew him before he came to this village, and they will all tell you the same. I know the truth. I was the one who grew up with him. He was my father."

I winced, and for the first time, I felt a little bit sorry for Audrey—not a lot, just a tiny fraction of sorry. It couldn't have been easy for her to have a father who had earned his living by smuggling goods back and forth across the Canadian border. I wondered how old she had been when she realized what her father was doing.

"He changed when he moved here," Grandma Daisy said, defending her friend.

Audrey glared at my grandmother, and Grandma Daisy glared right back. I thought I might have to intervene before the glares turned into punches. Not that I thought my grandmother would lower herself to that, but Audrey seemed scrappy. I bet she'd been in a bar fight or two in her life.

"Ladies." Art cleared his throat. "Will you allow me to speak?"

Everyone stopped what he or she was doing and looked at him.

He relaxed when he had all our attention. "Thank you. What I have been trying to tell you for the last twenty minutes is it does not matter who inherited anything from Benedict." Now that he had our attention, he straightened his suit jacket. "After I have reviewed Benedict's estate, there is nothing left to be had. The house he lived in was rented. His few possessions are not worth much at all. He has little or no money in the bank, and his life insurance is just enough to cover the funeral and his remaining debts. From what I could tell, he lived hand to mouth much of his adult life."

"But that's not possible," Audrey protested.

"I am sorry to tell you that it is possible and true. There is no need for the two of you to argue when there is nothing to argue about."

Audrey shook her head, sending her earrings swaying like pendulums over her shoulders. She pointed at my grandmother. "But she didn't know my father was penniless. She killed him because she thought she could profit from his death."

"The same could be said for you, Ms. Fussy," Chief Rainwater said.

"I—I didn't do it. I have an airtight alibi."

The police chief folded his arms. "I know. I called your local police station in Rochester yesterday. You're well-known there, and you were in jail the night Benedict died, and didn't get out until the next morning." He arched a brow. "You were caught shoplifting again. Was this the fifth or sixth offense?"

She straightened her shoulders. "What did you expect? Did you think I would be a Goody Two-Shoes after the way I was brought up, exposed to one scam after another? I am my father's daughter, after all."

Grandma Daisy visibly deflated as she realized what Audrey was saying. Benedict's daughter had fallen into a life of crime just like her father. No wonder it broke Benedict's heart to talk about her. He must have felt responsible for the path she'd chosen in life.

My sympathy for Audrey was short-lived, by what she said next.

"There's the cat," Audrey said. "I should be allowed

to keep that animal. Maybe I could make a little bit of money by selling it."

I gasped. "Over my dead body," I said, and willed Emerson to find a hiding place somewhere in the house or garden where Audrey would never be able to find him.

Wheaton surveyed the room with narrowed eyes as if looking for the small tuxedo cat. I bet he'd hand Emerson over to Audrey without a moment's hesitation.

"Okay," the police chief said. "I think this conversation has gone on long enough. The cat will stay with the Waverly family."

"B-but—"

Rainwater shook his head. "Daisy was awarded Benedict's estate, so that includes his cat. You only want the cat out of spite. You can't possibly think you can sell the animal with thousands of stray cats in the world."

Audrey sputtered for a few seconds. When she finally regained her composure, she said, "I don't care about that cat anyway."

"Great, it's settled, then," I snapped.

She scowled at me before she flounced out the front door of the shop. Art and Officer Wheaton followed in her wake. If I never saw Benedict's daughter again, it would be too soon. Unfortunately after she left, I realized that I'd lost one of my best viable suspects. Now that Audrey was above suspicion—at least for her father's murder—that put even more pressure on me to find the killer. Even though Chief Rainwater didn't believe Grandma Daisy was guilty, Wheaton certainly did, and I still wanted to find out who the killer was before I left the village. Knowing the guilty party would give my grandmother at least a little bit of closure after losing the man she loved.

Shortly after Audrey left, I walked with the police chief outside. The early evening was cool as a breeze blew down from Canada over the river. I wrapped my arms tightly around my waist. "Thank you for what you did back there. I think you were the only one in the room who had any chance of shutting Audrey up. I'm especially grateful for Emerson. I would have hated to see her take him away. Who knows what would have become of him?"

"I wasn't going to let that happen. Especially now that I have seen you ride around the village with the cat peeking out of your basket." His amber eyes sparkled.

"Do you have any more leads?" I asked.

"I'm afraid not," he said finally.

"I might have one," I offered.

He raised one of his black eyebrows and waited.

I told him about my trip to the library and what I'd discovered about the livery being a main stop on the Underground Railroad. "The librarian, Renee, thinks it's possible that there is still a room or tunnel under the livery. It made me think about how Shane disappeared last night. Maybe that's where he had gone."

Rainwater was quiet as he considered my suggestion. He didn't criticize my idea, and I was happy for that. "It's a thought."

"I think we need to have another chat with Shane," I said. "And Trey too."

He shook his head. "*We* don't need to have another chat with Shane or Trey. I do. I need to talk to Carly too to see if she knows the history about her stables."

"I want to help," I protested.

"I know, and you have." He walked down the porch steps and turned. "Let me take it from here."

Fat chance of that happening, I thought as I watched him climb into his department SUV and drive away in the direction of the Riverwalk.

# THIRTY-FIVE

That night, I tossed and turned. I knew I was missing something important and simple related to Benedict's death. There must be something that I hadn't thought of that would point me in the right direction of the killer.

On top of those worries, I was concerned that I hadn't replied to my academic adviser back in Chicago yet. I wasn't sure what to say to her about why I'd suddenly up and left the Windy City for Cascade Springs.

Emerson, who had been trying to sleep at the foot of my bed, didn't appreciate my restless night. He finally curled up on the top of my head, flicking his tail back and forth over my nose as payback.

The next morning, I felt like I did whenever I had pulled an all-nighter studying for an exam. It was a loopy combination of vague and woozy, but I also felt so tired that I was past the point of being able to fall asleep even if I wanted to. My eyes were open just a little too wide and the left one twitched.

In the kitchen, Grandma Daisy sipped her coffee and closed her eyes for a moment to savor the taste of it. When she opened them again, she said, "Remember, Charming Books is closing at four today so that we can dress for the gala."

I made a face, which only made my eye twitch that much worse.

She waggled a finger at me. "You can't back out now. Sadie is over the moon about picking out outfits for the both of us."

I poured myself a mug of coffee to the brim. The warm mug was comforting in my hands. "She's dressing you too?"

Grandma Daisy smiled. "Why should you have all the fun?"

I watched her for a moment over the rim of the mug before I took my first tentative sip, wary of how hot it was. "You seem to be in a better mood this morning."

She set her mug on the granite counter. "That ugly scene in the shop yesterday with Benedict's daughter." She paused. "I thought about it all night. When I saw Audrey, it reminded me what bitterness could do to a person. I don't want to end up like that."

My mouth fell open. "Grandma, you would never be like Audrey."

She gave me a half smile. "Maybe not, but ever since Benedict died, I had felt myself start to wallow in self-pity. I've never been one to do that, not even after your mother died, and that was the greatest loss of my life."

My throat constricted.

She gave her head a little shake. "I'm not saying I'll forget Benedict, but I am going to take a page from his life and start again. He moved to Cascade Springs to start over, and I can start over too." She gave me a pointed look. "I would love it if you would stay in the village and help me with my new beginning."

I took a big gulp of my coffee, so that I wouldn't have to answer that right away. That was a mistake. The hot liquid scalded the roof of my mouth and my throat on the way down like I had taken a swig of battery acid. I coughed and sputtered. Grandma Daisy came at me with her hand raised like when I had choked before, and I backed away, shaking my head. The last thing I wanted was another thorough back pounding. I slid into a kitchen chair.

Emerson raced into the kitchen and slid across the laminate floor. His claws searched for traction as he tried to regain his footing. Emerson galloped across the floor and leaped onto my lap and meowed. His amber-colored eyes, the same shade as the police chief's, looked so concerned when he studied my face.

Grandma Daisy grinned. "I won't push you any longer. I want you to stay in the village and you know that, but it is your decision. I can't make you stay or take your place as the next Caretaker." She pointed at Emerson. "But wherever you go, you had best take that tuxie with you. He's become very attached to you, and I'm afraid I would be a poor substitute."

Coughing only a little now, I snuggled Emerson under my chin. "I've become attached too," I said, feeling a little bit guilty that I was so happy to have a cat who would be with his original owner now if that owner hadn't been murdered.

Grandma Daisy rinsed out her coffee mug and set it in the sink. "I'd best be off to the bookshop. What are you doing this morning?"

"I'm going to see what else I can find out about Benedict." I frowned. "Although I'm running short on leads."

She nodded. "But I don't like the idea of you traipsing all over the village hunting down a killer for me." She gave me an appraising look. "I know that David doesn't like it either."

I decided to ignore her comment about the police chief. "I'm not only doing it for you," I said. "I want to know what happened to Benedict too. No matter what he did in his past, Benedict was a good man, and someone needs to be held accountable for his death."

Grandma Daisy walked across the kitchen. Leaning over, she kissed me on the top of my head. "You have always been a driven and stubborn child. I'm afraid that you got that from Rosalee and me."

I smiled. "It would be nice to think I got something from the two of you other than the Caretaker gig."

Shortly after Grandma Daisy left for Charming Books, I headed for the door too. Emerson followed me. I looked down at the tuxedo cat. "You're not coming with me."

He sat in the entryway and his thin black tail swished back across the tiles. He meowed, showing off all his white, pointy teeth.

I shook my finger at him. "No complaining. I have a lot of places to go today, and I don't want to worry about you. Besides, this village talks about me as it is. I don't need to be seen with a cat riding around in my bicycle basket to add to their entertainment."

He cocked his head as if to say, "Tell it to someone who cares."

I took a step to the door, and so did he. I took another step, and so did he. This was never going to work.

There was a pen on the credenza by the front door. I picked it up and waved it at him. Like a dog ready for a game of fetch, Emerson stood up, and he stared at the pen. His head moved back and forth as I waggled it.

Finally, I tossed it across the room. Emerson was after it like a shot, and I slipped out of the front door, shutting it before Emerson knew I was gone. I wasn't proud of tricking Emerson, but it couldn't be helped. I was betting that he would have something to say about my trick when I returned home.

After jumping on my mother's bike, I turned in the direction of the river.

When I pedaled up the livery's long graveled driveway, shouts were coming from around the side of the barn. At the top of the hill, I jumped off my bike and let it fall onto the plush lawn. I was already running by the time it hit the grass.

I didn't know what I would see when I came around the side of the barn, but after the last few days anything was possible.

Around the corner of the barn, I pulled up short.

Trey was soaking wet and standing in the middle of a sudsy kiddie pool. Java was halfway in and halfway out of the pool. By the way the dog pulled Trey toward the edge, I guessed the chocolate Lab wanted to be all the way out.

"You need to finish your bath," Trey said through gritted teeth, completely oblivious that I stood a few feet away. "You have soap all over. I have to rinse you off, and then we'll be done."

It didn't look like rationalizing with the dog was working.

I took off my violet bike helmet and stepped forward. "Can I help?"

Trey and Java looked over at me as if I were an alien that had just been dropped from the mother ship.

At their blank expressions, I tried again and said, "I could rinse her off while you hold her."

"I'll get wet," he said finally.

I arched my eyebrows and looked him over.

"Oh, right. I'm already soaked," he said. "All right. There's the hose in the grass. The spigot is already on."

I dropped my helmet in the grass and picked up the nozzle. As soon as I turned on the water to test it, Java bounded forward, dragging Trey out of the kiddie pool with her. I jumped in front of her and grabbed her around the neck with my left arm.

My help was just enough for Trey to get a better hold on her. "Just rinse her off here," he said. "It will take too long to force her back into the pool."

I sprayed water on the dog as best I could while holding her with my other hand. By the time I had gotten most of the soap out, all three of us were soaked to the skin and smelled like flea soap and wet dog, which was not an appealing scent.

"Okay, you can let her go," Trey said.

Before we even had a chance to step back, Java shook out her coat, sending water flying onto Trey, me, and the side of the barn.

Gag. I could taste the soap on my mouth.

Java shook out her coat again, and we were subjected to another shower.

Trey picked up an old ratty towel from the small pile by the barn and walked toward the dog. Java saw him coming and took off around the side of the barn. Water and the last remnants of soap bubbles flew after her.

"Java!" Trey cried, and tore off after her.

By the time I ran after them, they were already around the side of the barn, but their trail of muddy paw and boot prints was easy to follow.

The prints led into the third stall of the barn, the same place I had seen Trey appear when I'd visited Benedict's horse.

Trey knelt next to the dog and started to dry her fur.

I leaned over the side of the stall. "You might want to consider taking her to a groomer next time."

Trey pushed his soapy bangs out of his eyes. "We tried that before, but she got loose at the groomer's and broke a bunch of expensive equipment. We were asked not to bring her back." He sighed. "She's needed a bath for a long time, and this is the first chance I've had to give her one. Usually, I do it at home in the bathroom. It's the first time I've given her a bath here and it'll probably be the last. Thanks for your help. I needed it," he added grudgingly.

"Maybe you can ask Carly to help you or another of the carriage drivers?"

His expression clouded. "Carly has too much to do to help."

"And she probably couldn't hold Java down with her hurt ankle," I said.

"Oh, right, her ankle." He said this as if it was an afterthought. "And we're too short staffed with carriage drivers as it is to ask any of them to help me give my dog a bath." He ran the drenched towel over Java's back.

I handed him the towel I had picked up from the grass. "Can I talk to you about Benedict?"

He took the gray towel from my hand and tossed the other into the corner of the stall. "I told you before that I have nothing to say about him. I don't know what happened. No one here knows what happened." He said it with so much conviction he either believed it with his whole heart or was trying to convince himself that it was true.

"It's the least you can do after I helped you with Java."

The dog shook the remaining water from her body, sending water droplets flying against the walls of the stall and onto the back of the door.

After she was finished, Trey attacked her with the towel again as if I had said nothing at all.

I decided to change my tactics. "Trey, did you know that the barn was part of the Underground Railroad?"

He looked up sharply. "What?"

Something in his expression told me what I had said hadn't come as a surprise to him.

"I was at the community college's library yesterday, talking to the librarian about the history of the village, and she showed me a map of places in Cascade Springs that were part of the Underground Railroad. The livery was one of them."

"Why did you do that?" he asked a little too sharply.

"She was helping me with research on another topic," I said. "And it came up. Why do I think you already know about this?"

"We both know about the livery's history," Carly said from behind me. "Trey learned about it at school last year, I think." She looked at her brother. "Isn't that right, Trey?"

He nodded dumbly.

"How did you learn about it?" I asked.

"A—a speaker visited the college and gave a talk about it," he said.

I nodded. "The librarian mentioned the program."

"It was very educational," Carly said. "I wished I could have gone too. It would have been fun to hear about the history of this barn." She shook her head. "I had too much to do around the carriage house. This business goes on rain, snow, or sunshine." She smiled.

Java whimpered and pawed at the wooden floor.

"What's she pawing at?" I asked.

"It's nothing," Carly said. "She does that when she's had a bath."

Trey resumed toweling the dog, and she stopped pawing the floor.

"Why are you interested in the Underground Railroad?" Carly asked.

"I just thought that it was an interesting fact when the librarian mentioned it and wondered how it could be related to the strange events over the last few days. Who else might know about the livery and Underground Railroad?" I asked.

Carly shrugged, looking confused. "Anyone who went to that program at the community college, I suppose. It was discussed at length in the village. I think the village council was even considering a tour of all the places. You know, to attract more historically inclined tourists." She paused. "I don't think anything ever came of it."

"Did Shane know?" I asked.

She frowned. "He might. I've never talked to him about it. Did you, Trey?" She looked to her younger brother.

Trey woodenly shook his head.

"The thing is," I said, "the day you fell off the stool, I saw Shane come into the barn. He came in just a few minutes before you cried out when you fell. When I got into the barn, it was like he disappeared. I had expected him to have run to see what happened to you, but he was gone." I paused. "There really wasn't enough time for him to run away from the livery—it was seconds—but he was gone. I wondered if maybe he found the Underground Railroad hiding place, and . . ."

She laughed. "There's no way. We haven't even found the hiding place yet. Trey and I both looked. Even if Shane somehow found it, there's no way that's where he would go."

I started to protest.

"Besides, it doesn't matter now. He's gone. He gave me his notice last night. He left me in a real bind. Now I'm two carriage drivers down."

I blinked. "Gone? What do you mean? He's a suspect in Benedict's murder—he can't just leave."

Her mouth fell open. "No one told me that." She paled. "Do you think he ran off because he's the one who killed Benedict?"

"It's a real possibility."

Carly shook her head. "I don't know what to say. He's not the best employee in the world, but I would never suspect him of murder."

"You have to call Chief Rainwater and tell him that he left."

"I'll do that right away," she promised. "You had better head back to the village if you want to be presentable for the gala tonight."

I looked at them. "Are you two coming?"

"We wouldn't miss it," she said with a smile.

"Hello?" a voice called.

Carly, Trey, and I turned to find Grant in the doorway.

"Grant Morton," Carly said, stepping around me. "This is a surprise. We have had so many guests today. Violet is here too."

He cleared his throat. "Th-that's why I'm here. I saw Vi's bicycle outside, and I thought I would drop in and see if she would like that factory tour now that I promised." He grinned at me over Carly's head. "What do you say, Violet? Want to see the factory?"

I looked down at my clothes. I was covered with water, dog hair, and who knew what else. "Umm." I wasn't really factory-tour appropriate.

# THIRTY-SIX

Grant laughed at my expression. "You look fine. This is the perfect time for the tour. We're closed a half day because of the gala. We're pulling out all the stops to impress the village council to earn those water rights. Most of my staff is at the main office on River Road."

I was curious about the water company. Maybe if I saw how they processed the water, I would have a better understanding as to why they thought they needed to restrict access to the natural springs to the rest of the village. "I would like to see it," I said, even though I wasn't completely comfortable around Grant after our trip to Niagara Falls.

His grin grew two sizes. "It's settled, then."

"Trey and I had better get back to work, or we won't be able attend the gala tonight." Carly took a step back toward her office. "There's much to do."

"We'll get out of your hair," Grant said, and led me out of the barn.

"What about my bike?" I asked.

"I can just put it in the back of my truck." He pointed at a red pickup parked in the grass by the barn.

After Grant loaded my bike into the bed of his truck and I climbed into the passenger seat, I spotted Carly watching us from the barn door as we drove away.

Grant kept up an easy chatter while we drove to the factory. "The factory is a mile from here. I was on my way there when I spotted your bike. I wanted to check on a few things before the big gala tonight."

The road widened and the trees became sparse. Soon the one-story sprawling building came into view. After he parked, Grant ran around the truck and opened the door for me. I frowned but accepted his help out of the truck. "I'm excited to show you what I do."

I stared at him. "Why? I mean I'm curious, but why are you so interested in showing me?"

He laughed. "I guess I want to impress you. I always had a little crush on you when we were growing up. You were another thing that my brother had that I wanted."

I mentally kicked myself over my poor judgment to come with him to the factory alone. Before I could make up an excuse about needing to get back to Charming Books, he opened the door leading into the factory. It opened into a long hallway. On the left side of the hallway there was a wall of windows overlooking the factory floor. I hadn't expected it to be right there.

Grant pointed to the window that looked onto the factory floor, which was a maze of stainless steel tubes and cylinders. "The water is brought to the factory by tanks. It's drinkable right from the source, but we run it through the factory and perform two forms of filtration to remove any particles and bacteria." He walked along the window. "And then we bottle it here." He pointed at the gallon jugs making their way down the assembly line. All the bottles are washed and sanitized before the water is added."

"Impressive. How—"

A short man in a lab coat ran out of the glass doors that separated the factory floor from the hallway and shook a piece of paper. "Grant, we have another complaint about the free samples we provide at the main office. The tourist is questioning the water's quality. This is the third time this month!" The man's voice rose an octave with his last statement.

"Andrew, I have a guest." He nodded to me.

The man turned beet red. "Oh, I'm so sorry." He swallowed, but then he added, "We have to talk about this. We've never heard complaints like this before, and now there are three!"

"I'll be with you just as soon as I take Miss Waverly home."

The man stopped just short of stamping his feet before he turned and went back inside to the factory floor.

"It looks like you have work to do," I said. "I can ride my bike home from here. It'll do me good."

"If you're sure," he said. "I should talk to Andrew. He can be a little uptight."

"I noticed, and it's not a problem." I headed for the door. I was eager to leave and more worried than ever about Sadie having her heart broken.

Outside, I waited as Grant lifted my bike out of the back of his pickup. He set the bike on the ground.

I jumped on. "Thanks again for the tour."

"Anytime," he said, holding on to the handlebars. "Will you be at the gala tonight?"

"I promised Grandma Daisy and Sadie that I would go."

"I'm glad." He let go of my bicycle. "Save me a dance."

There wasn't much chance of that, I thought as I pedaled away.

Instead of going straight to Charming Books, I went back to my grandmother's house to shower and change after my wrestling match with Java. When I walked into the house, I called Emerson, but he didn't appear. I frowned but shook off my worry. He was most likely hiding somewhere and pouting after I didn't take him with me that morning.

It was only when I rode my bike down River Road back in the direction of Charming Books that Carly's comment struck me as odd. She'd said that Java always pawed at the floor after her bath, but Trey had said earlier that it was the first time he had given Java a bath at the carriage house. I wasn't sure why that bothered me, but it did.

I turned into the driveway beside Charming Books with a sense of unease. Carly or Trey may have misspoken, but I thought there might be something else to their stories not matching. I parked my bike and hung the helmet on the handlebars before running up the steps to the bookshop.

I opened the door and pulled up short. Emerson stood on the other side of the door and scowled at me. His tail swished back and forth across the floor.

"What are you doing here?" I demanded.

A small smile curved his lips, and his whiskers pointed up.

Grandma Daisy peeked over one of the low shelves in the middle of the shop. "Violet, is something wrong?"

"Emerson," I said. "How did he get here?"

"He's been here for hours. I assumed you dropped him off while I was helping a customer."

"No," I said slowly. "I locked him in your house."

She chuckled. "I don't think he cared for that much."

I folded my arms and looked down at the cat. "Grandma, I think we have a serious escape artist on our hands. Emerson can't be out walking the streets. What if he got hurt?"

Her eyes twinkled. "You mean the mean streets of Cascade Springs?"

I frowned. I didn't like the idea of Emerson running loose in the village. What if something happened to him? I never let Jane Eyre out of my apartment in Chicago. I wouldn't even let her out onto my balcony. And sure, Cascade Springs wasn't the size of Chicago, but there were still cars, bikes, carriages, and potential cat snatchers like Audrey Fussy about.

"He could get hurt," I said. "And what will happen when I take him with me to Chicago? He can't leave my apartment."

Grandma Daisy arched her brow. "Maybe that means you should stay."

"For a cat?" I asked.

"And your grandmother and your inheritance." She gestured to the books.

I opened my mouth to argue, but a group of five ladies came twittering into the shop. All conversation about my destiny of being the Caretaker came to an abrupt halt as my grandmother went to see how she could help the newcomers.

"I'll be in the stockroom," I called to my grandmother.

She waved to acknowledge she heard me.

Emerson followed me through the kitchen and into the stockroom. I heard a flap of wings, which told me that Faulkner was coming too.

Inside the office, Faulkner landed on the table, walking across the books.

"Be careful," I warned him. "No one wants to buy a book with talon marks on it."

"Bah!" the crow said.

I turned to Grandma Daisy's desk. As usual, it was covered in receipts and sticky notes to herself. I cringed, tamping down the urge to organize it. A stack of books by the keyboard caught my eyes. A stack of books anywhere in Charming Books wasn't that noteworthy, but this one was. It was a stack eight high of Emily Dickinson collections.

I didn't even think to ask my grandmother if she'd left the volumes of poetry there. She would say the shop was trying to tell me something. What that was, I wasn't sure.

I sat in the computer chair, and Emerson, after hissing at the crow on the table, jumped onto my lap. When I looked up again, there was another volume of Dickinson's poetry on the stack, or at least, I thought there was. I could have sworn that there had been eight there when I sat at the desk. Now there were nine. I rubbed my eyes.

"Fine," I said. "Fine." I wasn't entirely sure whom I was speaking to. It could have been Emerson, the tree, the books, the universe.

Emerson placed a paw on the keyboard.

I frowned. "You're getting into the cryptic message business too?" I asked him.

I turned on the computer. It was time I solved the problem of Benedict's murder, and the best way I knew how was through research. The first place to start was learning everything that I could about Benedict's former employer Fletcher Wolcott.

In a matter of seconds, I had pulled Wolcott's obituary up on the screen. It didn't say anything about his criminal activity, his having died in prison, or his sketchy past. I looked closely at the other names in the obituary. They belonged to his closest family members. If anyone wanted to avenge his death, it would have been one of those people. Potentially, they were the ones that lost the most from his arrest.

The obituary said his wife had died two years before he did. I frowned. She must have passed away right after he had gone to prison.

There were three children—Brian, Karen, and Adam—listed. There were no ages and no indication if they were children or adults by the time that Wolcott died.

"Violet?"

I tore my eyes away from the computer screen and found Sadie standing in the stockroom's doorway with a dress bag over her arm.

"Violet, I have your dress for tonight." She hopped in place, barely able to contain her excitement. "I can't wait for you to see it."

I looked from her to the computer and back. "I'm kind of in the middle of something."

"Oh." Her pretty face crumbled.

Suppressing a sigh, I pushed the chair back. "But I can take a quick break to try on the dress."

Her face lit up again. "You won't be disappointed. You will love it."

I stood up, and as I did, Emerson jumped onto the floor. "I already do. I saw it yesterday in your shop, remember? It was the ivory dress with fringe. Very *Great Gatsby*."

She shook her head, beaming from ear to ear. "That's not the dress. I realized last night that I had an even better look for you." She patted the garment bag. "I have it right here. It's even more spectacular than the last dress."

Since the last dress had been made almost entirely out of fringe and sequins, I was a little frightened to see a dress that Sadie thought was even more spectacular. Part of me was afraid of going to the gala dressed as a disco ball. "I thought that last dress was just fine."

She shook her head. "It wasn't even close to your look. I have it now." She beamed. "I'm almost jealous. You will be the belle of the gala."

"I'm not going to the gala to attract a guy," I yelped. Far from it, I was going to catch a killer, or at least I hoped that would be the end result.

She clasped her hands in front of her chest. "You're going, whether you want to or not, in this dress."

I winced. "I guess I had better see it."

She grabbed my arm. "Come to Midcentury Vintage now, and I will get you glammed up."

"Already?" I frowned, giving the computer a forlorn look. I wasn't done with my research. "Can't I see it now and get dressed later? You have it right there." I pointed at the garment bag.

"I know. The only reason I have it is because I just picked it up from the dry cleaner's. I took it to them first thing this morning and insisted that they clean it right away, so that you could wear it tonight. I want you to look perfect." She smiled. "You can't try it on here. We need mirrors. You're going to want to see yourself from every angle. Trust me."

"But I really want to get back to what I'm working on," I said.

Her face fell, and she hugged the garment bag to her chest. "Oh." She took a step back. "I don't want to keep you from work. You can come over to the shop whenever you are done." Her voice trailed off.

My heart was constricted. It was Colleen all over again. I was putting my quest for information before my friend.

She turned to go, and her black ponytail hung limply down her back.

"Sadie, wait!" I called.

She turned.

"I'll come with you now." I gestured at the computer. "This can wait."

Her face broke into a smile, and I knew I'd made the right decision.

# THIRTY-SEVEN

Sadie and I walked arm in arm across the street to her cottage store. When we reached the porch, she stopped. "You stay here. I want it to be a surprise." She slipped into the store. After five minutes, she poked her head out of the shop door. "I'm ready!" She stepped back and opened the door wide.

When I entered the shop, Sadie clapped her hands with barely contained excitement. In the middle of the shop there was a dress on a dress form. It had an A-line skirt, cap sleeves, and a lace overlay. And it was violet.

She jumped up and down. "What do you think?"

"It's beautiful," I said, and I meant it.

She grinned. "I knew you'd love it." She ran around the back of the dress form and unbuttoned the dress, removing it from the dress form. "Now, you must put it on, and I'll style your makeup and hair."

I hesitated. "Don't you have to get ready?"

She waved away my concern. "I have everything I need here. Grant is going to walk over and pick me up after he leaves the office."

I bit my lip at her mention of Grant. The more I got to know Sadie, the more I knew flirty Grant didn't deserve her. Would she believe that? She had followed Grant all the way from Kentucky to Cascade Springs. She'd fought a long battle to win him. Could she accept that he hadn't been worth it?

Sadie held out the dress to me, shaking those thoughts from my head. "Now, go and put it on. I can't wait to see it with your hair."

I took the dress from her hand and went into one of the two fitting rooms in the back of the shop, separate from the rest of the room by only a damask curtain.

There was no mirror in the fitting room, so I wouldn't be able to see myself before stepping out.

"Violet, come on," Sadie called.

I sighed and smoothed my skirt before throwing back the curtain.

I found bouncing Sadie just on the other side of the curtain. She looked adorable in a 1950s bubble dress that matched her personality exactly. I was certain that no one else in Cascade Springs or even in all of New York State could pull off that look.

"How did you change so fast?"

She laughed. "You took forever in there, so I threw on my dress." She twirled. "What do you think?"

"You're adorable."

"But you're beautiful. I knew that was the right dress." She clasped her hands. "What a transformation."

I chuckled. "Did I look that bad before?"

"You know I don't mean it that way."

I glanced around for a mirror. There was a full-length one in the corner of the room, but it was covered by a sheet. "Can't I see how I look?"

She shook her finger at me. "Not until I complete the look. Let me pin up your hair and you will be perfect. You might be my best makeover ever." She rolled a black stool across the room. "Sit," she said in a very uncharacteristically commanding voice.

She pulled a rolling tray over, laden with hair baubles and makeup.

"I don't mind doing my own hair and makeup so that you can get ready." My voice wavered.

"Don't be silly. Now, hush while I work. I need to concentrate." She stuck three bobby pins in her mouth.

I felt her twist my hair and poke pins in the back of my head, and I was silent until she walked around to the front of me with a bright red lipstick in hand.

I held up my hand. "Whoa, what is that? I am not a red lipstick kind of girl."

"You are today. You agreed to let me style you, and that includes the lipstick."

"But—"

"No buts, and it's an orange-red anyway. It will look perfect with your pale skin and hair."

How could orange lipstick be an improvement on red lipstick?

I closed my eyes and let her do her worst.

I heard Sadie take a step back. "You are a vision."

I opened my eyes. *A vision of what?* I wanted to ask, but I held my tongue. "Can I see myself now?"

She nodded and walked over to the floor-length mirror. She pointed in front of it. "Stand right there." With a flourish, she removed the sheet.

She had been right. The orangey red lips did go well with my strawberry blond hair and blue eyes. My hair was pinned on the top of my head in an elaborate bun. Had I done it myself, it would look like a pom-pom, but somehow, Sadie made it appear elegant.

I smoothed the skirt over my thighs. I had never looked like this before. I couldn't remember the last time I had worn a dress like this. I guessed most girls would have worn such a dress to prom, but I hadn't gone to my senior prom because of Colleen's death. Nathan and I were broken up by then, and I refused to go when everyone thought I had something to do with my best friend's death.

"Well?" she asked.

I swallowed. "It's beautiful. I mean, I'm beautiful."

She grinned. "That's all I need to hear. Oh!" She held up a hand signaling me to wait. She ran behind the sales counter and came back with a pair of nude open-toed heels. The heels had to be five inches.

I took a step back, waving my hands. "No way. I'll break my neck."

She shook them at me. "You have to wear them. They complete the look."

"I'm already tall," I whimpered.

She put her free hand on her hip. "You should be glad you're tall. Look at me. I have to wear heels to make it up to your shoulder."

Reluctantly, I took the shoes and put them on.

After that, Sadie shooed me from her store, so that she could prepare herself for the gala.

I teetered across the street in the heels. They were more comfortable than I expected them to be, but I knew that wouldn't last. I would be lucky to wear them more than a half hour before crying uncle.

Slowly, I climbed the steps to the Charming Books front porch. I heard the faint sounds of a jazz band practicing. They must be in the tent beside the town hall. It was after four, and Grandma Daisy already had the CLOSED sign in the window, but she had left the door unlocked for me. "Grandma," I called. Emerson sat on the end table. "Well, you're dressed, you tuxedo," I teased.

He meowed.

"But you aren't going to the gala."

His whiskers pointed down.

Grandma Daisy gasped from the top of the stairs. "You look just like your mother."

There was no bigger compliment that she could have given me. I laughed and blinked away the tears in my eyes. I wondered what my mom would have thought if she could see me. I hoped that she could.

Grandma Daisy came down the steps wearing a sparkly flapper dress that fit her personality perfectly. An extra-long string of pearls hung from her neck.

"Grandma." My mouth fell open. "You look amazing, like an old Hollywood siren."

She patted her silver bob. "I do, don't I? Courtesy of Sadie." The redness was gone around her eyes. Maybe she had Sadie and her face cream to thank for that too. She paused. "You really are beautiful."

I found myself blushing. "Well, looking nice won't do me any good if I break my neck in these shoes Sadie says I must wear."

Grandma Daisy winced when she saw the shoes. "You can take them off after you're at the gala for a little while."

My brow wrinkled. "Did you get dressed in the children's room?"

"No, I changed in one of the spare bedrooms down the hall."

I moved toward the stairs. "Oh, I meant to ask you about that area. I tried to go in there the other day to see Mom's and my old rooms, but it was locked. Can I see them now?"

Her brows pinched together. "Not right now. We don't want to be late."

"Grandma, the gala is a block away," I protested. "It won't take but a minute for me to peek through the door."

She pointed at my feet. "It's going to take you some time to walk there in those shoes."

That was true, but I didn't think that was why she didn't want me to see the upstairs bedrooms. "Are you hiding something?" I studied her. "How many secrets do you have, Grandma?"

She chuckled. "I have nothing to hide."

I snorted.

She pretended not to hear me. Instead she said, "You look lovely. I wouldn't be surprised if the mayor and the police chief trip over each other to see who wins the first dance."

"Dance!" I yelped.

She grinned. "Oh, yes, what do you think a gala is?"

My stomach sank to my too-high heels.

"I hope one of them can convince you to stay in the village." She twirled the end of her necklace.

"Grandma, I can't stay here. I only stayed through the gala because it seemed to be so important to you. I need to go home."

Her face fell. "This could be your home. This is your home."

I picked up the impossibly small clutch that Sadie had also lent me and wedged the paperback edition of Dickinson's poetry inside. It barely fit. "Now is not a good time to discuss it. We have a gala to attend."

# THIRTY-EIGHT

Villagers and tourists strolled down the Riverwalk in their finery. Most were wearing black or another subdued color. I was the only one in violet and the only woman over six feet tall, thanks to my heels.

Grandma Daisy poked me as we approached the town hall. "Stop fidgeting."

"It's these shoes," I complained.

Sadie stood at the bottom of the town hall's steps and waved to us. She'd pulled her black hair into a sleek ponytail, which went perfectly with her bubble dress and the vintage choker around her neck.

I stumbled over to her. "Where's Grant?"

"He's inside already," she said. "I told him I would wait out here for you. I didn't want to go in without you. I need your support before I face the Mortons."

"Or my distracting presence," I said with a laugh. "I haven't seen Nathan's parents in twelve years."

She grinned. "That helps too."

Grandma Daisy ushered us to the door. "Let's head inside now. If we don't hurry, we'll miss all the good food, and I'm starving." She marched into the gala without waiting for us.

Sadie laughed and looped her arm through mine. In a low voice, she said, "Nathan is going to faint dead away when he sees you. I did that good of a job. I can't wait."

If Sadie thought that I was dressed like this to please Nathan, she was sadly mistaken.

She led me into the gala. A large banner hung from the observation deck: "Two Hundred Years of Cascade Springs." Strings of white lights hung from the domed ceiling and climbed up the pillars. At least a hundred people were gathered around the town hall's main atrium. Women wore cocktail dresses, and men wore tuxedos or suits and ties.

"I'm so nervous." Sadie's manicure dug into my arm.

I found myself smiling. Sadie had known me for only a few days, and she had already come to depend on me. I hadn't had a girlfriend like that in my life since Colleen. Of course, I'd had friends in college, in grad school, and at my various jobs, but no one I could call a kindred spirit. Colleen had been that. I realized that I'd not made any close friendships after she died as a way of punishing myself for her death.

The village police and Colleen's parents had thought I might have had something to do with Colleen dying. I didn't push her off that bridge like they thought, but I had pushed her away. I'd made my studies more important than she was. When I left, my subconscious had forbidden me from growing close to anyone else. Entering the gala with bright and shiny Sadie clinging onto my arm made me realize all that I had missed out on.

"Don't worry," I said. "And loosen your grip. You're cutting off my circulation." I scanned the room for Carly or Trey. I didn't see either of them. They had said they were coming.

"Oh, sorry," she whispered. "There's Grant." Sadie waved frantically to Grant, standing on the stage next to the jazz band and, unfortunately, his brother.

Nathan's eyes bugged out of his head when he saw me. Despite the thin dress, I felt like it was a hundred degrees inside the town hall.

Sadie yanked on my arm. "Look, you're taking Nathan's breath away. He can't stop staring at you."

The band began to play, and the Morton brothers left the stage. I gave a sigh of relief when someone stopped Nathan as he made a beeline for me. He was the mayor, after all. There was a good chance I would be able to avoid him for the entire night because he would be busy talking to constituents. I would take that on as my mission.

Several couples moved onto the dance floor. Grant wove through the dancing pairs to join Sadie and me. Sadie stood on her tiptoes and kissed him.

"You are breathtaking," Grant said.

Sadie preened, but Grant was looking at me. I scowled in return and shuffled back, bumping into someone. I turned to find Nathan's parents standing behind me. I felt

Sadie step closer to me. I didn't know whether she did this to protect me or for me to protect her.

Mrs. Morton looked exactly as she had when I left Cascade Springs over a decade ago. Her perfect hair was styled short and her delicate figure was that of a woman half her age. Nathan's father, on the other hand, had put on a few extra pounds and the hair at his temples had begun to turn white.

Mrs. Morton nodded at Sadie. "Sadie, dear, you always have the most interesting clothing. It's a wonder where you find your outfits. They are so *unique*."

Sadie's face fell, and I wanted to kick Nathan's mother in the shin.

"It's nice to see you again, Violet," Mrs. Morton said to me. "Nathan told me that you were the one who suggested the novel he gave me for my birthday. Thank you. I'm enjoying it immensely."

I forced a smile. "I'm glad. It's nice to see both of you too," I said, including her husband in the greeting.

Mrs. Morton balanced her wineglass in her hand. "It's something that you remembered I enjoy science fiction after all this time, but then again, you always did have your nose stuck in a book. Nathan tells us you're a college professor."

"Almost," I said. "After I complete my dissertation."

Mr. Morton sipped from his own wineglass. I was certain it was Morton Winery vintage or he would not be drinking it. "Nathan is very pleased that you are back in the village. He's spoken of little else."

I smiled, unsure of what to say to that.

"It's too bad this sad business of the murder has to spoil your visit," Mr. Morton added. "Brings back some unpleasant memories for all of us."

My body tensed.

He cleared his throat. "I hope there aren't any hard feelings for what happened all those years ago. You must understand that we were trying to do right by our son. I'm sure if you ever have a child, you'll understand."

The band picked up, and more couples joined the dance.

Then, I saw my grandmother. "There's Grandma Daisy." I pointed to the other side of the atrium where she had cornered the waiter carrying a tray of shrimp. "If you'll excuse me, I think I'll go check if she needs anything. Sadie, do you want to come with me?"

"Yes," she said a little too quickly.

We said good-bye to the Mortons and made our way across the atrium and around the dancing couples. Keeping my eyes on my too-high shoes, I moved across the atrium, trying my best to be invisible, which was not an easy task as the tallest woman in the room. It certainly didn't help that Sadie was bopping beside me and waving at everyone she saw like she was Miss America on a float.

"Ma'am," the young waiter said, "I have to circulate among the other guests."

My grandmother grabbed one last shrimp from the tray. "Oh, all right, off with you, then, but swing by later." She winked at him.

He hurried away without a backward glance.

"You really shouldn't harass the waitstaff," I said.

"Bah." Grandma Daisy handed me a huge cocktail shrimp. She had several on tiny plates lined up on the windowsill behind her. Leave it to my grandmother to stock provisions.

My stomach rumbled. I had been so invested in Emily Dickinson and the Wolcotts that I wasn't sure when the last time I had eaten was or if I even had that day. I took the small dish from her.

"Would you like one, Sadie?" Grandma Daisy asked.

She wrinkled her button nose, and it possibly looked even more adorable. "I don't eat anything with antennae."

I bit down on my shrimp.

"There's David." Grandma Daisy waved over my shoulder.

I turned around to see the police chief in a tuxedo, weaving through the crowd to reach us. A white grin flashed across his tawny face, and I think I must have blacked out for a second, because the next thing I knew, he was standing directly in front of me. He smiled at me. "I'm glad you all came."

"We missed you at writers' group," Daisy said.

Sadie beamed. "We sure did. It was Anastasia's turn to read. It was a real snore-fest. Her character was contemplating the meaning of life for six pages. Six. I mean, who cares? I want action."

A smile quirked at the corner of his mouth. "And what was her conclusion about the meaning of life?"

Sadie placed a hand to her heart. "That life has no meaning, that we are just specks of dust moving through time." She paused. "At least I think that was it. I zoned out around page four. Life could have had a different meaning on pages five through six."

I stood there holding the half-eaten shrimp in the air like some sort of prize.

He turned to me. "I'm glad you're here too, Violet. You look—"

Without thinking, I tossed the half-eaten crustacean, tail and all, into my mouth. Immediately I started to cough.

Chief Rainwater's smile vanished. "Are you all right?"

I waved my hands, unable to speak.

Sadie linked her arm with mine. "She's fine. We'll be back in a minute." She yanked me across the atrium's marble floor down a hallway. As she pulled me along, I saw Carly, wearing a simple blue dress, and Trey in a sport coat and tie walk into the atrium. I was relieved to see them despite my near-death experience.

Sadie pushed open the door to the ladies' room and shoved me inside. A woman powdering her nose took one look at my hunched-over, hacking form and bolted.

I spat the uneaten shrimp into the trash can.

"Gross!" Sadie squealed. "Why did you put the whole thing in your mouth like that? It was a very cavewoman move."

My cheeks felt hot. I knew it was more from humiliation than nearly choking. "I—" I couldn't think of a reason that would make any sense to her. Sadie was adorable and bubbly. She wasn't a complete social failure like I was. She probably didn't even know what it was like to lose all motor function in the presence of a beautiful man like the police chief. "I don't know," I finally said because she seemed to expect some sort of answer.

She went to the mirror to make sure that her hair was in place. It was, of course. "For the record, I think the chief was going to ask you to dance before you started choking."

How was that supposed to make me feel better? I grabbed a paper towel from the dispenser, ran it under the sink.

"Are you okay?" Her expression turned to one of concern. "Seriously. I thought David was about to give you the Heimlich right there in the middle of the atrium."

I groaned.

"We should go out." She gave her hairdo one final pat. "They will be worried about you. If we wait too long, they might send one of the off-duty EMTs in here to check on you."

As if shrimpgate couldn't be any more embarrassing.

"I'll be fine," I said, realizing that my voice was a tad bit hoarse. "Go back to the party and tell them I'm okay. I'll be out as soon as I regain my dignity."

She laughed as if I were joking. She didn't know me well.

"Go on," I insisted. "You should be celebrating the night with your fiancé, not standing in the bathroom with me."

"If you are sure." She paused.

"I'll be out as soon as I can."

"I'm glad you're okay," she said, and went out the door.

I waited in the empty restroom for a few minutes more, listening to every sound on the other side of the door like a fugitive on the run. There was no way I was going back into the gala after making such a fool of myself.

I crept to the restroom door and opened it a crack. I looked both ways down the hall. In the opposite direction from the atrium, there was an open side exit. I could see the traffic moving by. It must be River Road. I snuck one last look at the atrium and made a dash for the door.

## THIRTY-NINE

Thankfully, no alarms sounded when I went through the exit. I found myself between the town hall and La Crepe Jolie.

Guests from the gala strolled around the lawn, in and out of the big tent on the green, and along the Riverwalk across the street. I paused on the sidewalk as a carriage crossed my path, and then I hurried across the street. I walked down toward the closed spa, where I knew it would be quieter, and sat on one of the wrought iron benches facing the river.

I thought about what the librarian Renee had told me about Cascade Springs having been a major player in the Underground Railroad. What had a former slave thought in the mid-eighteenth century when he or she had reached this very spot at the edge of freedom? I knew that had to be an important piece of what the poems were telling me, but then self-doubt began to seep in. Emily Dickinson herself was alive during the Civil War, but made little mention of it in her poetry or letters, other than to mention young men who left for the front.

The streetlamps along the Riverwalk reflected off the surface of the water. I took the volume of Dickinson from my small purse. It took some effort to remove it. The satchel wasn't made to carry a book. Clearly, it was an inferior accessory for that reason. Why would I ever carry a bag that couldn't hold a book? There was a reason I used a tote bag as my purse.

The corners of the paperback were a little bent from being cramped in the evening bag, but otherwise it was intact.

I stared at the words of the three poems the bookshop seemed to have wanted me to read. What was I missing? I reread the poem about remembrance. My head hurt. Why was I consulting Dickinson's poems at all?

Someone touched my shoulder, and I screamed. The book went flying out of my hands onto the riverbank.

Nathan stepped around the bench and retrieved the paperback. He wiped dirt off the back cover. The book was still open to the page I had been reading. Nathan scanned it, and it took all my strength not to snatch the book from his hands. Something about him reading the book seemed like an intrusion.

"What are you doing out here?" I asked. "Shouldn't you be at the gala?"

He handed the book to me and stuck his hands in the pockets of his tuxedo pants, and the yellow light from the streetlamp a few feet away reflected on his blond hair. "It's really Grant's night. He should enjoy it and everything he's accomplished in the last year. The water company is footing the bill for the whole thing."

"That was generous."

He gave a wry smile. "They want to convince the village council to grant them exclusive rights to the springs."

"And how do you feel about that?" I asked, standing up. I wasn't comfortable with Nathan looming over me.

"It will never pass. Ninety percent of the village is against it. It would be political suicide to give the water company permission. No one on the village council will be reelected if they allow the water company to have its way."

I gripped my clutch and paperback. "Then why let them host this grand gala?"

"That was the village council's idea, not mine. The council saw a way to have the bicentennial party paid for and they took it."

I frowned.

"I know what you're thinking, and I tried to talk them out of it." He paused. "I was overruled." He gave me a small smile. "I didn't come over here to talk to you about my brother or about the gala."

I waited.

When I didn't say anything, he said, "I saw you sneak out of the atrium and wanted to make sure you were okay after your close encounter with that shrimp cocktail."

I covered my eyes with my hand. "I'm so humiliated."

He laughed. "I don't think many people saw it. You

were too far across the atrium, and the police chief stood between you and the rest of the room."

"You saw it." I dropped my hand.

He rocked back on his heels. "Because I couldn't take my eyes off you," he said quietly. "You're beautiful."

I blushed and was grateful for the darkness. "Nate—"

"It's an observation, and I'll leave it at that for tonight." He changed the subject. "I can't say that I'm surprised that you walked off by yourself to read. You used to do that all the time when you were upset."

I didn't say anything.

After a full minute, he said, "I'm glad you're okay, and you're right, I should probably get back in there." He turned to go.

"Nate," I said.

He turned around and waited.

"About Colleen," I began.

He stiffened.

"I forgive you for that."

His hands fell limply to his sides and he slumped forward as if he had just set down a two-ton elephant onto the ground. "Thank you, Vi. Thank you for saying that. You don't know what it means to me."

"I wanted to tell you before I left the village."

"You don't have to leave. This is your home," he said, unknowingly repeating what Grandma Daisy had said earlier that evening.

Before I could respond, he walked across River Road back to the music, the hall, and his village of constituents.

After he was gone, I smoothed the rumpled page with the poem on my lap. I reread the verse about remembrance.

*Remembrance has a rear and front,—*
   *'T is something like a house;*
*It has a garret also*
   *For refuse and the mouse,*

Wolcott's family would be the ones that would remember him the best, and that thought reminded me of my abandoned Internet search, the one I had given up so Sadie could show me my gala dress. I opened my tiny clutch and removed my phone and found Wolcott's obituary again through the browser. I stared at his children's names: Brian, Karen, and Adam. How old had they been when their father died? That was easy enough to find out.

I had spent a good part of my life tracking down obscure relatives of long-dead authors. For someone living in the digital age, it wasn't even a challenge. My university had a genealogy Web site for just the barest of facts. You could plug in a person's name, place of birth, and parent's name, and come up with his birth certificate, marriage license, death certificate, and other documents, depending how much information was in the public record about him. It was a tad bit scary. I typed in "Brian Wolcott, father, Fletcher Wolcott."

There was only one result that listed a sister named Karen and a brother named Adam and a birthplace of Niagara Falls, New York. I skimmed the records about Wolcott's children. Brian would be in his midforties today, and from the record appeared to have a different mother. There was no record of Wolcott being married more than once. Brian must have been a child from a previous relationship. However, Karen, who would be thirty-one today, and Adam, who would be eighteen, were the children of Wolcott and his wife.

I felt sick to my stomach, and I didn't think it had anything to do with the shrimp I'd eaten. This was what the shop had wanted me to discover all this time. The Dickinson poems about remorse and remembrance had been about this, Wolcott's children. I knew it.

With shaky fingers, I typed "Karen Wolcott" in the browser.

The search results came up immediately, and Karen Wolcott, wearing purple and white jockey silks, stared back at me through the computer screen. It wasn't her outfit that caught my attention. It was her face. Although she was at least ten years younger in the racetrack publicity photograph, Carly Long stared me squarely in the eye.

I dropped my phone into the grass. I scrambled to pick it up and clutched it and Dickinson's poems in my hand. Hadn't Carly told me that she hadn't known Benedict before moving to Cascade Springs? Could it be possible that she didn't know the men who were part of her father's smuggling business? I supposed that was possible. It was such an odd coincidence. It seemed a little too convenient to be a coincidence to me.

I could understand why she might want to keep her name and her father's name hidden. The Wolcott name would make it hard to run a business in the area, or at least it would have ten or so years ago.

Another thought struck me. Could Carly be the killer? A chill ran down my back. It could be Carly, but it could just as easily be Trey.

The second part of Dickinson's remembrance poem came to mind.

*Besides, the deepest cellar*
  *That ever mason hewed;*
*Look to it, by its fathoms*
  *Ourselves be not pursued.*

Had Carly and Trey also been lying to me about not knowing where the Underground Railroad compartment was in their carriage house?

I shoved the volume of poetry into my impossibly small bag. The time for reading was over. It was time to act. There was only one way to know whether my theory was right about the carriage house being involved, and that was to find the underground hiding place for myself. This was as good a time as any to check, since the entire village would be at the gala.

I headed for Charming Books. Before I began my mission, I needed to change my shoes.

# FORTY

Because I had taken the time to run back to Charming Books to change my shoes, I decided to ride my mother's bike to the carriage house. I pedaled down River Road in my violet dress and sneakers. I doubted it was the look Sadie was going for, but I didn't want to waste any more time changing back into my jeans. I didn't know how long Carly and Trey would remain at the gala, and I wanted to get in and out of the livery before they returned.

The carriage house was dark when I arrived, and I leaned my bike against the side of the barn. I placed my hand on the doorknob, and it turned easily.

A horse in one of the stalls neighed. I tried to tamp down the unease I felt over the door being unlocked.

"Hello?" I called as I went in. "Carly? Trey?"

There was no answer. Good.

I scanned the barn. The overhead lights were still on,

so it was very possible that there was still someone there. But I knew this was my only chance to satisfy my curiosity about the Underground Railroad room underneath the barn. I knew the first place to start was the empty stall where Java had been scraping at the floor.

In that section of the barn, the beams above my head were darker than the others. The dark beams were older, aged over time, which confirmed my suspicion that this was the original part of the barn, and the most likely spot for a hidden room that dated back to before the Civil War.

Inside the stall, I scraped the bottom of my sneaker across the wooden floor, searching for any sign of a door or an opening. The bottom of my sneaker caught on a piece of wood. I squatted in place and ran my finger along the cut in the boards. It didn't follow the grain of the wood. I couldn't get my finger around the edge, so I stood up and searched the stall for a tool to lift the door. I didn't see anything, but there was the small crowbar I had seen Trey with a few days ago outside the next stall. I ran out of the stall and grabbed the tool and a large flashlight.

I slid the flat edge of the tool under the lip of the door and lifted it up enough to peer inside. There was a dark hole in the dirt. I couldn't see the walls. The space was large. It might have run the whole length of the barn. I shone the flashlight's beam inside the hole. A long metal table caught the light. There were a number of glass vials, measuring cups, and droppers on the table. At the far end there were several bottles of Cascade Springs Water. Some of the water bottles were full of water. Others were empty and looked like they'd never been used.

I blinked. It was almost like I was looking at some bizarre laboratory from a Frankenstein movie. Why in the world would someone hide a lab under the livery's barn? Then, I remembered that just a few hours ago, Andrew from the water company had told Grant that they were receiving complaints about the water's quality from tourists, and another memory came to mind of the tourist complaining that the water tasted like tap water. I stood up. I didn't know how this all fit together exactly, but I knew that water somehow was the motive for Benedict's murder. I needed to return to the gala and tell Rainwater everything I'd learned. I shivered, realizing now how stupid it was for me to come to the barn alone.

Leaving the hatch open, I ran out of the stall door and into the main part of the barn.

"Where are you running off to so fast?" Carly asked as she came into the barn. She was wearing the same blue dress I had seen her in during the gala.

"Carly, there you are! Why didn't—" The rest of what I was going to say to her was cut off because she stood across from me with a gun pointed at my chest, and it wasn't just any gun. It was a big one. Although I suppose the size didn't matter when the bullet hit its mark.

"Carly, what are you doing? Put the gun down." My voice shook ever so slightly.

"I can't do that." She shook her head as if she really regretted saying it.

"I saw the water and know Grant must be behind this somehow. If Grant put you up to this, you can turn him in and get out of it," I said.

She snorted, still pointing the gun at my chest. "Do you really think Grant could have come up with this plan?"

"You're tampering with springwater from the water company right here in the Underground Railroad hideaway underneath the barn." It was the only purpose the lab below my feet could possibly serve.

She smiled. "Very good, Violet. But Grant didn't put *me* up to anything. I gave him the idea to dilute the springwater with tap water."

I blinked. "Why?"

She adjusted her grip on the gun. "I see you have as much vision as Grant does. It's so we could sell it in bulk. When the water company secured the only license to use the springwater, no one would know the difference."

Again, the memory of the man complaining about how the bottled water tasted came to mind. "And you've been testing your diluted springwater on the tourists visiting the water company. When the water company had exclusive rights to the springs, there would be no other Cascade Springs water to compare the taste to."

She smiled. "Now you are getting it. I saw there was a potential profit there. By diluting the springwater with tap, we could increase production tenfold and increase our distribution without ever incurring costs. Of course I had to explain all of this to Grant. He was too stupid to see it himself," she scoffed. "It's been a challenge to get the right balance of springwater to tap. You wouldn't believe the number of fussy springwater drinkers there are out there."

"Why hide the lab in your barn?" I couldn't help but ask.

"Until we had the perfect ratio of tap water to spring-water, we had to keep it separate from the actual product the water company distributes, and we couldn't do it at the factory. We couldn't have anyone asking questions about it," she said. "When Trey came home all excited about our barn being part of the Underground Railroad, I knew that would be the perfect place to create and test different dilutions of the springwater. So you see, this was all me." She paused. "Grant went along and played his part. He's a complete dolt and has spent his entire life trying to play catch-up with his older brother, the mayor. I knew he would be the perfect candidate to help me out. He was in the right position, and he was eager to show Mommy and Daddy what a big success he could be." Her eyes narrowed. "He will never live up to his brother, but you knew that already, since you go way back with the family."

I swallowed.

"I was oh so interested when Grant told me about Colleen Preston. It must have been nearly impossible to live with the guilt of causing the death of your best friend for the last decade."

I balled my fists at my sides. "I know your real name is Karen Wolcott."

"Very good again, Violet. I was wondering when you would work that out. I thought you might have known sooner than this. I guess book learning isn't everything. Everything I learned I earned."

"Just like your father?"

She moved the barrel of the gun to point at my head. I imagined the bullet hitting me right between the eyes.

She circled around me, stepping between me and the

stall where the cellar filled with stolen springwater was. I glanced at the door.

She laughed as she followed my gaze. "If you run, I will shoot you in the back before you even reach the doorknob."

I knew it was a threat she would carry out. "Did you kill Benedict because he recognized you?"

"No. I killed him because he found out about our operation and wanted me to become one of the good guys like him. As if I could do that. Swindling is the only life I know. I am my father's daughter," she said, sounding just like Audrey had when she'd made excuses for her own petty crimes.

"Benedict didn't leave me any choice," Carly went on. "Do you think I wanted to kill him? I didn't. He was one of my best carriage drivers. The rest of them are worthless. When I first came to Cascade Springs, I recognized Benedict right away, but it took him much longer to realize who I was. He looked the same, but I had changed in the intervening years. I wasn't a child anymore. I was a woman, and I knew what I wanted from the world.

"He was kind enough not to reveal who I was. He even said he was sorry to hear about my father passing. That was a lie. I was the only one sorry to hear about my father passing. Not even Adam cared. He was a little boy when our father went to prison."

"What about your brother Brian?"

She smiled. "I *am* impressed. Brian ran off to Mexico with the rest of the cowards who abandoned my father. I've only spoken to him a handful of times since. A month ago, I called him and told him that he should come back home and that I had a new plan that would put our family back together, but he refused to come. He's still a coward. Always will be."

"I still don't understand why you had to kill Benedict."

"Benedict promised not to tell anyone who I really was, and we left it at that. I thought we were fine, but then he started poking his nose in my business." She tightened her grip on the gun's hilt.

"The deal you had with Grant."

"He begged me to give it up and said if I didn't, he would be forced to go to the police. As if I could let that happen."

"How did Shane fit in all of this?"

"Shane?" she scoffed. "Nothing. He just worked for me."

I frowned. That didn't seem right. I knew Shane had to be somehow involved, but Carly appeared honestly surprised by my question. Then again, she could be lying. She was a murderer, after all.

"Did you kill Shane too?" I started to shake.

"Of course not," she said as if she found the very idea offensive. "He quit just like I told you he had."

"I see your leg is better," I said.

She looked down and laughed. "It was never hurt. That was an attempt to distract you. I saw you snooping around the barn that night. Even when I threw that worthless box away to make it look like someone robbed me, you wouldn't give up." She almost looked disappointed in me.

"Did you break in and search Benedict's house too?"

"I had to make sure that the old man didn't keep any proof."

"But why did you kill Benedict?" I asked.

"I had no choice. I offered him money and he wouldn't take it. He said he left his life of crime behind in Niagara Falls." She waved the gun around. "I killed him right here in the carriage house while he was napping in his carriage. The stupid man didn't even know what hit him. I saw the book from Charming Books in his hand, and that gave me an idea. I waited for night and drove him over to your grandmother's house and left him like a present in the middle of Daisy's driveway. I think my father would have enjoyed my creative touch."

"He would have enjoyed you murdering a defenseless man?"

"My father died in prison because cowards like Benedict chickened out when the Feds came knocking. If they had kept their word, my father would still be alive, and I would still be riding and have the life I deserve."

"What about Trey?" I asked. "Does Trey know?"

"Leave my brother out of this. Adam knows to trust me. I was the one who raised him. Do you think any of my father's associates offered to help?"

"No," I guessed.

"That's right. They scattered as soon as my father was sentenced to life in prison, and then he died from cancer. I knew he wasn't getting the treatment in prison that he would on the outside. They killed him. I know they killed him." She shook so hard the tip of the gun wavered back and forth. "And now, I'm going to have to kill you. I'm sorry. I really did like you, and I wasn't lying about what I said the day I met you. I really did want to be friends. I could use a friend in my life, but you had to keep digging and searching, even after Shane ran off." She glared at me. "Why did you do that? You could have let it go, and we could have been fine, just fine, and now, because you wouldn't let it go, you are forcing me to kill you."

I took a step back. "You don't have to kill me. You can leave and create a new identity and life like you did before."

"No, I'm tired of running. It will be you who has to go."

"I'm leaving," I said. "I have no plans to stay in Cascade Springs. I only stayed for the gala."

"You should have stuck to that plan instead of coming here tonight. Do you think any of them at the gala have even noticed that you're gone?"

I took another step back. "My grandmother has." I was certain this was true.

"Then where is she? Where is the police chief to rescue you?"

I swallowed.

"I thought so. I'll make this quick, I promise." She raised the gun.

"Carly, what are you doing?" Trey—or should I say Adam?—stood at the edge of the barn, staring at the gun in his sister's hand.

The gun dropped a fraction. "Trey? What are you doing here? You should be at the gala."

He looked from his sister to me and back again. "What is going on?"

She took a step back into the stall and fell through the open hatch in the floor, and I heard the gun go off.

Trey ran to the edge of the opening. "Carly! Carly!"

There was no answer.

"Police!" Chief Rainwater and Officer Wheaton, both

still dressed for the gala, raced into the barn. Within a second, they assessed the scene. I remained frozen where I stood, and Trey stood over the hole in the floor. Tears ran down his cheeks. Wheaton went over to him.

"Where's Carly?" the chief wanted to know.

Before I could answer, Wheaton said, "She's down there."

"And?" Rainwater asked.

Wheaton gave the slightest shake of his head, and I knew Carly was dead. Before I could process this, Grant and Shane Pitman ran into the barn. I blinked. What was Shane doing there with the police? What was Grant doing with them for that matter?

"Violet," Grant exclaimed. "Thank goodness you are all right. When Sadie realized that you had left the gala and I saw Carly was gone too, I knew it was bad. I told Sadie everything, and she said I had to go to the police."

"You were in on this with Carly," I accused.

He dropped his head. "I was, but I didn't kill Benedict. All I did was give Carly access to the water, I swear. Then when you showed up, I tried to distract you away from the livery."

Grant's flirting, it made sense now. Knowing the reason for that made me feel a little bit better, but I was still furious with him. I glared at him.

He held up his hands. "I saved you—or I would have if we had gotten here sooner."

"Where's Sadie now?"

He swallowed. "Back at the gala. She said she'd never speak to me again if you were hurt." He looked like he might cry.

Maybe he really did love her.

"I just couldn't have a repeat of twelve years ago," he said mournfully.

I shivered. "What do you mean, Grant?" My voice was hoarse.

He paled. "I saw Colleen fall from the bridge that night. She was already dead when I reached her, or at least I assumed so."

I stared at him and felt a hand under my elbow as if it was trying to hold me up. It took me a moment to realize it was Rainwater. "You *saw* her fall? And you never said *anything*?"

"I was afraid. I saw how my parents freaked out about Nathan's involvement, and he was the perfect son. I'm sorry, Vi." He took a step toward me.

I held up my hand. "Not now, Grant."

He nodded and walked to the edge of the barn. I watched him go, seeing a man I didn't recognize fill the door. While it was a relief to finally know the cause of Colleen's death, I knew that it would be a while before I could process all this new information. And with the timely details of Benedict's case becoming exposed, I had to keep my focus in the moment.

"What's he doing here?" I asked, pointing at Shane Pitman, who was speaking with Wheaton at the edge of the hole.

Shane walked over to us. Instead of his riding boots and tails, which had been his carriage driver uniform, he wore a wrinkled gray suit.

He flashed me a badge. "FBI."

I blinked.

"Special Agent John Marks," he said. "I've been following Karen and Adam's movements for weeks after her older brother, Brian, tipped us off that she might be following in her father's smuggling footsteps."

"She told Brian that she had an idea about how to put their family back together, but she never told him the particulars about Cascade Springs or the springwater dilution plan."

He nodded. "That's right. He, after the childhood that they all had had, naturally assumed she was smuggling goods into Canada. In this day and age, the federal government can't ignore a tip like that and had to check it out." He frowned. "I knew about the water lab but didn't move on it because that wasn't my concern. I was waiting for her to smuggle goods across the border, since we suspected that's what she was up to. I was just about to abandon the case for lack of evidence when the carriage driver was killed. I decided to hang on a bit longer after that to investigate what part he played in the operation."

"And Trey?" I glanced at the boy. "Was he involved?"

He shook his head. "He may have suspected his sister was up to something, but he wasn't involved."

"Why did you let the other crime go?" I demanded. "Benedict might still be alive if you told the local authorities here."

His jaw twitched. "That wasn't my case, and I would have had a lot less trouble investigating my own case if you hadn't kept getting in the way."

I took a step toward him. "It was you! You were the one trying to scare me off!"

Rainwater pulled me back by the elbow. Maybe he

thought I was going to hit Special Agent Marks. Maybe I was thinking about it.

I turned to him. "Did you know about this?"

"No." His voice was tight. "The FBI will be receiving a complaint from my department. Not sure how much good it will do."

Marks gave Rainwater a smile before sauntering back to Wheaton.

"Violet," Rainwater began, "I—"

"Violet!" Nathan ran into the barn.

The police chief stepped back from me as Nathan wrapped me in a hug. "Violet, are you all right? Sadie said you were in danger, and she thought you would be here." He was panting hard as if he'd run the entire way from the gala to the carriage house.

I struggled out of his embrace. "Nate, I'm fine."

"What's going on?" Nathan asked.

I watched Rainwater over Nathan's shoulder. "I'll let the police explain."

Nathan wrapped his arms around me. "I'm so glad you are all right. I've never been so scared in my life."

Over Nathan's shoulder, Chief Rainwater glanced from Nathan to me, and regret clouded his amber eyes. I wanted to tell him he had it all wrong, terribly wrong.

# EPILOGUE

"This is crazy. Books can't predict the future. They can't solve a murder," I told my grandmother two days later. I was still grappling with the events of the night of the gala.

She fed Faulkner a cracker from her lunch.

The crow took it and flew to the top of the birch tree to enjoy his snack away from Emerson, who was curled up on my lap.

"They aren't predicting it," Grandma Daisy said. "They only provide hints to what is already known."

*Oh, well, that clears it up.*

I stared at the tree, realizing I was on the brink of making a decision, one that would change the course of my life. "Staying here to be the Caretaker is a terrible idea," I said more to myself than to my grandmother.

"Is it? You can be the Caretaker, and I know Richard

will give you that job at the college if you only apply. You can write your dissertation anywhere and travel back to Chicago when you need to. All the pieces are in place if you would just look at the puzzle board."

"But my life is there." My argument was waning. Everything she said was true.

"What life?"

"Grandma, that's a little harsh." I dropped the cracker I was holding on my plate.

"It's true, Violet. You haven't lived a real life since you left Cascade Springs twelve years ago. You've had your nose stuck in a book. The only time you seem to have anything resembling fun is when I force you to go on vacation. What twentysomething goes on vacation with her grandmother?"

I crushed the cracker with my fork. "I like spending time with you."

"I know you do, and I love spending time with you. I hope we have many more adventures, but I also want you to have adventures of your own."

"Living with my grandmother will make that possible?"

She smiled. "Who said you're living with me?"

I frowned. "Are you going to kick me out of your house?"

Her eyes twinkled. "Follow me, and bring the cat with you."

I put Emerson on my shoulder. "Where are we going?"

She didn't answer and instead led me up the stairs to the children's room. When I climbed the stair to the loft, she removed a skeleton key from her pocket and slipped it into the locked door that led to the rest of the house. After a little bit of effort, the door swung inward. "I think you and Emerson will be very happy here," she said.

I stared into a newly renovated one-bedroom apartment. The walls between the first two rooms had been knocked out to make a larger living room.

She pointed. "Your bedroom and bathroom are at the end of the hallway in the tower."

"This wasn't like this when I was a child." It was all I could think to say.

She smiled. "It wasn't. It's a project I have been working on the last couple of years. The books have been telling me the time was near for you to take over. You are the Caretaker now. They will talk to you, not to me. They need you." Her eyes twinkled. "I thought I might need a bribe to convince you to stay, so I had this done."

Emerson wiggled in my arms, and I let him go. He leaped onto the extra-long royal blue sofa, turned three times, and settled in. Sighing contentedly, he placed his paws on the arm of the couch and looked at me expectantly.

"Did you put him up to that?" I asked Grandma Daisy.

"Nope, but at least his mind is made up about staying. What about you?"

"The books . . ." I couldn't even say it. The books in Charming Books were actually charming, magical even. But then again, I couldn't deny that they'd led me to Benedict's murderer. "I'll give it a try until I finish my dissertation at least," I said, ever cautious of commitment.

She smiled. "Good. Emerson and I won't be the only ones happy to hear this."

I snorted. "I'm sure Faulkner is delighted."

"Oh, I wasn't thinking about Faulkner," she said with a chuckle. "Only two very handsome young men."

Read on for a sneak peek of

# MURDER, HANDCRAFTED

*an Amish Quilt Shop Mystery*
*written by Amanda Flower*
*writing as Isabella Alan.*

**Available now!**

The phrase "It looked so easy on YouTube" would go down in infamy in the annals of Braddock family history. It was what my father had said twice after he attempted to demo my mother's kitchen in their new home in Holmes County.

The second phrase would be "You have no idea what your father's been up to."

I held my cell phone away from my ear as my mother screeched that last statement at me.

Mattie Miller, my twenty-two-year-old shop assistant, stocked the needle display in the front corner of the shop and raised her eyebrows at me, and I rolled my eyes in return. It was still morning and Running Stitch, my Amish quilt shop nestled in the center of Sugartree Street in Rolling Brook, Ohio, had just opened for the day. Through the large front window, I saw business on the street was beginning to pick up as early May tourists strolled from shop to shop. As usual, the first stop on any tourist's itinerary was Miller's Amish Bakery, across the road from Running Stitch. I could see my best friend and Mattie's sister-in-law, Rachel, doing brisk business. A line of customers extended out of the bakery and curved along the sidewalk.

Oliver, my black-and-white French bulldog, lifted his head from his dog pillow, watching us with his big brown eyes. Dodger, my gray-and-white cat, jumped up onto the cutting table in the middle of the room and pranced back and forth.

"Get down," Mattie hissed at the cat.

Dodger sat in the middle of the cutting table and began giving himself a thorough bath. It was a normal day at Running Stitch, except for my mother's hysterical phone call. Then again, that wasn't that unusual either.

When Mom took a breath, I moved the phone closer to my ear. "What did he do?"

"He threw his back out while removing the kitchen cabinets. I told him over and over to let me call a professional, but no, he insisted he could do it himself. I knew this would be a disaster," she groaned.

"Is he all right?" Worry crept into my voice. Like my mother, I had wanted to discourage my father when he announced that he would be doing the demolition portion of my parents' massive kitchen renovation. As a former corporate executive, Dad was a wiz with numbers, spreadsheets, and board meetings; DIY stuff, not so much. In the end, I said nothing because he had looked so pleased with himself to be taking on this home improvement project. I hadn't had the heart to tell him it was a *really* bad idea. Ever since my father had retired, he had been floundering in search of a purpose. He finally thought he had found it in my mother's kitchen remodel. Who was I to squash that ambition?

"He's in X-ray right now." My mother sounded close to tears, and my mother never cried.

"Oh no," I groaned. "Do you want me to come to the hospital? Is that where you are?"

"No, we're at an X-ray clinic. That's where our doctor sent us when I called and explained what happened. Then we have an appointment with the doctor. He wanted the X-rays first."

"Is Dad okay?"

"He will be. I'm sure." She paused as if trying to collect herself. "If only that man wasn't so stubborn."

"What do you need me to do?" I asked.

"Go to the house. When your father knocked down the cabinet, he broke the French doors leading into the backyard. I need you to wait there until I can get home and figure out what to do about the doors."

Outside the shop, I saw Jonah, my best childhood friend, riding by in his market wagon. The bed of the wagon was filled with crates of berries, and another Amish man with dark brown hair, whom I didn't know, sat on one of the crates. Jonah tipped his black Amish hat at some tourists, who snapped a picture of him.

Jonah would know what to do. I had to catch him.

"Mom, I'll be there as soon as I can." I said a quick good-bye and headed for the door. "Mattie, I'll be right back."

"What happened?" Her gray eyes filled with concern as she smoothed her hands over her plain lavender dress and black apron. There wasn't the tiniest wrinkle in the fabric, nor was there a loose piece of chestnut hair from her impeccable bun.

I didn't stop to reply, because I was hoping to catch Jonah before he disappeared from sight. I ran out of the shop. On the sidewalk, I called Jonah's name.

He pulled back on the reins of his horse and turned in his bench seat to look at me.

I waved. As I ran up the sidewalk toward him, he maneuvered his horse to the side of the road so that the sedan behind him could pass.

"Angie?" Jonah asked with the usual sparkle of humor in his dark eyes. "What's got you all worked up this morning?"

The man in the bed of the wagon shifted his seat on the crate of berries. Now that I was closer to him, I saw that he was much younger than I'd first thought. He couldn't be more than twenty and was clean-shaven. In the Amish world, a beardless face meant that he was unmarried.

I rested my hand on the side of the wagon. "It's my dad. He hurt his back while demolishing their kitchen."

Jonah grimaced and touched his sandy blond beard, which stopped at the second button of his plain navy-colored shirt. "What is your father doing a thing like that for?"

My fingers dug into the side of the wagon. "He thought he could manage it."

Jonah shook his head. He had tried to teach my dad

woodworking after Mom and Dad moved back to Ohio. It had not gone well. It could have been worse, I suppose. Both Dad and Jonah came out of the experience with all their limbs intact.

"Mom said there is a broken window," I said. "I need to go over to their house to see what needs to be done."

"And you want me to come?" He smiled.

"Well, yeah." I smiled.

He laughed. "Not a problem. Let me drop off these berries at the pie factory, and I'll head straight there." He nodded to the young man in the back of the wagon. "Do you mind if Eban comes with me?"

"That's fine as long as you beat my mother there." I nodded to the young man. "I'm Angie Braddock."

"Eban Hoch," he said with smiling light blue eyes. "It is *gut* to meet you. I am new to the county and Jonah is showing me around."

"Oh, where are you from?" I asked.

"A little ways up north in Wayne County."

Jonah held up the reins. "We had better go if we want to beat your mother to the house."

I stepped back from the wagon. "Thanks, Jonah."

He winked and flicked the reins. The wagon and horse clattered down the street. I hurried back to Running Stitch. When I stepped in the shop, I was happy to see Mattie with a customer, who was closely examining my aunt Eleanor's stitches on a Goosefoot quilt.

I grabbed my hobo bag from the drawer under the sales counter and slipped it over my arm.

Mattie said something to the customer and stepped over to me. "Are you going out?"

I nodded and gave her a brief description of what was going on with my parents.

She covered her mouth. "Is your father okay?"

"I hope so. I don't really know for sure. He was getting X-rays when Mom called." I clicked my tongue. "Come, Oliver," I said to my Frenchie, who was snoozing in his dog bed in the window. "We're going to Grandma and Grandpa's."

The dog jumped to his feet. He loved going to my parents' house. He mostly enjoyed this because my father constantly fed the little black-and-white dog beef jerky while we were there.

"You're leaving Dodger here?" Mattie didn't even bother to hide her distaste. She and my gray-and-white cat had a strained relationship.

"I can't take him to my parents' house," I said. "Remember the last time he was there? He shredded my mom's curtains, and she talked about it for weeks."

Mattie pursed her lips. The cat, still sitting on the cutting table, cocked his head to one side as if in challenge. Mattie's frown deepened.

Those two would be at each other's throats the moment I stepped out of the shop.

"Dodger will be fine, and you won't even have time to know what he's up to. The street is filling up. I think it's going to be a busy day."

"That's what I'm afraid of. That's when he gets into the most trouble." She eyed the cat with suspicion.

Oliver waited for me by the door.

"I'll be back as soon as I can," I told my assistant. "Just call my cell if you need anything."

"You'll be back by one, won't you?" Mattie asked nervously. "I'm filling in at the pie factory later today, remember?"

"Yes, don't worry. I'll do my best to be back at one. I'll call you if I can't get away."

Mattie chewed on her lip.

I didn't have time to ask her what was wrong. Sometimes I wonder whether things would have gone much differently if I had.